MW00577834

DARK ARE THE STEPS OF TIME

Lance S. Barron

*Thank you for visiting
Mammoth Cave
Lance S. Barron*

DEDICATION:

To the greatest caving partner ever.

ACKNOWLEDGEMENTS

This is a work of fiction. The characters are fictional except for the people in the distant past. Some readers may recognize more modern character names, but these names are applied to fictional characters who have only a passing resemblance to any persons now living. Several friends have graciously permitted me to use their names in this work. For that consideration, I am grateful.

Over the last thirty-nine years, I have experienced some of my best times in Mammoth Cave. Among the best of those was time spent with Bob Cetera, trailing and later guiding with him on the 10:30 Scenic Tour and the 5:00 Frozen Niagara. Bob was kind and patient enough to let me tag along on after-hours photography trips, which included Zona, his wife now for over 50 years. Over this span of time, Bob and Zona have included Barbara and me in their photography trips in the Cave and out on the surface. Through Bob and Zona, I have maintained my connection to and interest in The Mammoth Cave. For that I am eternally grateful. They, and Mary Bowers, Zona's sister, have been patient and understanding readers of the manuscript.

Keven Neff had been a seasonal cave guide at Mammoth Cave National Park for a number of years when I reported for my first summer. He was on an earlier shift than I, but his sense of humor and enthusiasm for Mammoth Cave were very apparent in the guide lounge, on the information desk, and at pot-luck dinners at seasonal housing. Keven is appreciated not just by me, but by thousands of visitors to the Cave and by his many co-workers. Thank you, Keven, for sharing your dream. Keven and Myrna have kindly read several versions of this manuscript.

Daran Neff, John and Pam Yakel, Deborah Ross, and Charles Burton were kind enough to read the manuscript and offer helpful suggestions.

My loving, wonderful wife, partner, and editor-extraordinaire, Barbara, has labored as a full-fledged co-author, editor, and first reader. In addition, she has put up with me during less than pleasant times. She has been supporting in every way imaginable. Without her, there would be no story.

Of the remaining mistakes and errors, I hold full responsibility.

TABLE OF CONTENTS

Prologue

The intergalactic, Andromeda-class, attack cargo ship *Do It There* materialized out of nothing two thousand meters above a shallow, sub-equatorial sea that extended thousands of kilometers in every direction. That is, it would have appeared to materialize to any creature present to observe the scene. Any eyes in the vicinity belonged to sharks. And in this storm, they were hugging the bottom. The largest cyclonic storm, ever to disturb this watery planet, tossed the sea into a roiling mess and disrupted the otherwise placid lives of its inhabitants. Marine life dominated this planet, and the rebel branches that had made recent forays onto land were over a thousand kilometers to the east.

Super-hurricane-force winds lashed the view ports, rendering them gray-green, swirling abstracts. The pilot glanced across at the co-pilot who plotted and controlled their arrival. In a language no life form of this planet would ever understand, he said, "Nice." The tone of sarcasm, however, remained recognizable across the universe.

The *Do It There* belonged to the Galactic Fleet. The larger battle group stayed in deep space where they could maneuver in fleet formation. Where they didn't have to muck about with orbital mechanics of planets and moons and things like that.

This attack cargo ship was seconded to the Astrodetic Survey, which explained its presence in the super cyclonic storm over this *developing* planet. Instead of troopers and weapons, the cargo bay held survey stations, small, rugged structures that contained navigation beacons, cultural development alert systems, transporters, and comfort stations for travelers.

"How do you think Ensign *Jumpy* is doing?" asked the pilot, referring to the junior officer in charge of the cargo bay. "I wonder how he's going to screw this up." What the pilot wondered to himself was how could he get an assignment with a battleship when his crew kept screwing up milk-run assignments.

Before the co-pilot could answer, a large-amplitude shudder ran through the structure of the ship. Little red lights blinked all over the console.

"Panic! Panic! Panic!" came the voice over the ship's public address system. Computerized warning messages all across the Universe and from time immemorial had used this same female voice.

"I guess he's living up to his nickname," said the pilot.

The ensign, fresh from the academy, ran the cargo bay, and thus the deployment of the survey stations, in a frenzy. He hated his assignment to a survey ship, which he thought was the joke of the Galactic Fleet. He wanted to see action! He was tuned to perfect pitch to react to the danger of battle with alien life forms. He didn't worry a lot with planning. *What could happen on this bucket of bolts?* The moment the Full Materialization light illuminated on his console, he started the cargo bay door opening sequence and released the cargo latches on the survey station. He should have checked the weather first. He should have followed standard operating procedures.

"DAMN!" He and his exclamation were sucked into the tropical cyclone that engulfed the cargo bay.

Galactic Engineering and Exploration (GEE) promoted the survey station as one of its finest achievements. The rugged construction and perpetual internal power required no footnote in the operating manual defining how long perpetuity lasted. When installed per GEE's instructions, these stations offered clean drinking water, twenty-four-volt D.C. power, and a wide range of interfaces for electronic devices — including a socket for a quarter-inch phono plug and *What You Feel, Is* (WYFI) connection. After millennia of superseded and obsolete products, the disgusted and abused universe of consumers stood up and screamed, "No more! You will standardize this connection and quit jacking us around."

In rooms on one side of the long, narrow station were waste transfer facilities that came as close as science and engineering could come to another "universal" standard. A hallway three meters wide and ten meters long ran down the longitudinal axis. On the other side of the corridor were three doors with signs that read, "Employees Only." The middle room contained pumps, processors, and power circuits. The far end room contained monitoring equipment for the Galactic Security Agency – the listeners. Marking these doors for employees only kept up the mystique of the engineering staff. But the room on the near end contained a very nice break room for the engineers. At the time the station left the *Do It There*, that door was ajar.

The hallway served as a four-dimension transporter. Galactic travelers with remote controls and the proper codes could maneuver in either three-dimensional space on the occupied planet or in four-dimensional space to on- or off-planet coordinates, which, adjusting for the incomprehensible, yet still calculable distances, required movement through the fourth dimension: time.

As the ensign entered the maelstrom, lightning hit both the forward and aft ends of the ship at the same time. With the cargo bay door open, the aft lightning bolt penetrated inside the heavy armor and electromagnetic shield of the cruiser. That strike, combined with the movement of the survey station out the door, caused all the little lights to blink red on the console of the ship's bridge.

"Son of a ..." began the pilot, as he reached for the emergency extraction button. A plastic guard protected the big red button in the middle of the console from accidental contact. Flipping it open delayed the pilot by a few milliseconds. From the point where the survey station left the ship's cargo bay, the ship traveled 100 kilometers where it pitched toward the roiling sea.

The ship dived nose down because the emergency extraction protocol switched off all power and used that power to transport the ship to its pre-programmed place and time. Those milliseconds delayed the transfer of the ship until the tip of the nose entered the ocean floor of calcareous ooze and slime. After that moment's delay, the extraction system pulled the ship out of this benighted solar system to safety, leaving nothing more than a cone of disrupted sediment on the seafloor – and an ensign and a survey station.

When the GEE factory shipped the survey station, they programmed the default settings to transport whatever occupied the central corridor through time equal to a period of one hundred seventy-five orbits of the local star at the same three-dimensional coordinates (guaranteed within one meter) in space. It happened that GEE started its business with the production of a xenon laser, which has a wavelength of 175 nanometers. In this one case, engineering over-rode marketing, and the number 175 became a sacred concept for the company. During installation and commissioning of the station, the full programming would be activated for use by the knowledgeable, well-equipped, galactic traveler. With the factory default settings, a series of electromagnetic pulses in the 2,500-megaHertz radio spectrum would activate it.

They designed the survey station to survive; and that, in terms of the civilization that deployed it, meant *last forever*. They designed equipment to endure.

As soon as the inertial guidance and intergalactic positioning system of the station detected its free-falling position outside the ship, the station's programming triggered the deployment of huge, biodegradable parachutes to control its descent. The survey station splashed through five-meter waves that churned the gray-green sea and settled twenty meters into the sand formed from the calcium carbonate shells of tiny, invertebrate life forms and came to rest with its base one-half meter below a silica-enriched layer of sediment formed by mass concentrations of sponges. When the storm ended, an enormous submarine dune of calcareous sand covered the station for all time. Well, a lot of it anyway.

The ensign survived the fall to the sea and held on through the end of the storm, whereupon a couple of sharks ate him.

One
Boone's Avenue – Mammoth Cave, Kentucky
(323 Million Years Later)

"Fire!" The strobes send bursts of high-energy photons flaring through the darkness, burning enduring images onto our retinas when they bounce back. The total darkness of the cave returns and is relieved by little red lights on strobes and by the screen on the back of the high-end digital SLR camera.

"Close." Bob Cetera signals that the shutter is closed, and that people can switch on their flashlights and relax until the next shot.

"I think that worked just fine," I say. "I didn't see any direct flash."

"Good," says Bob. "Everyone hold your position."

Bob makes more adjustments to positions for strobes and for the models clinging to the canyon wall. His voice booms up to the top of the underground canyon where Myrna and Barbara hold strobes for back lighting. With everything set, he begins his cadence of, "Ready! Open! Fire! Close."

"Ready!" It's not a question, but a command.

We anticipate the next command of *open*, but the sound of boots on the trail behind us interrupts.

"Bob! Bob, we've seen a ghost! Keven needs you to come up the trail. You and Walt." It's Craig, the first Wild Caver out of the Snake Pit earlier this morning. His headlight slings wild arcs of light around the limestone passage.

"What the hell?" says Bob, with cable release in hand. "You're Craig, right?"

"Yes. Keven said to tell you that no one's hurt, but he wants you and Walt to come right away." Craig has run all the way, and he bends at the waist with his hands holding his sides, catching his breath. When he straightens up, his face shines with sweat and excitement. Not fifteen minutes before, Keven Neff had led his fourteen wild cavers including his tag-along federal agent past our position down into lower Boone's

Avenue on the second leg of their Wild Cave tour in Mammoth Cave.

I hurry down from my perch above the camera, hoping for a real ghost. I join Bob, Craig, and Bob's wife Zona.

"Okay," says Bob. "Calm down. Tell us what happened."

"We saw a ghost! Oh, and he wants you to bring the lantern."

"You're sure no one's hurt," says Zona.

"Yes, ma'am. We're all okay. I don't know why he needs you. Maybe this is a new ghost?" says Craig, his breathing closer to normal.

"A ghost?" says Bob. "If there's a ghost, it's definitely a new one."

"Well, a ghost lantern, like. You know?"

"No, I don't know. Did you see the lantern and the ghost?"

"Just the lantern. We all saw it. Freaked some of them out, but not me," says Craig. He has had the benefit of the time it took to get back to us to settle his nerves. Yet, he did it alone. But, being alone may explain why he ran.

"Please hurry."

To Keven's adult son, Bob says, "Daran, why don't you come with us? Zona, I don't know how long this will take. Will you get everything packed up? We'll meet you back at Snowball as soon as we can. John, will you take an extra pack and escort the group back?"

"Sure. No problem," says John, still up on the ledge where he and his wife Pam have been standing in for intrepid cavers climbing in this canyon passage. I can tell in his voice the disappointment at not being included, but a national park employee has to escort the other members of our photography trip.

Pam climbs down, undaunted by the canyon height, with a smile on her face. "So much for my legacy as a Wild Caver."

"We'll be back," says Bob. Pam smiles and nods at John.

"Bob, should I go, too?" says Myrna, Keven's wife, still up at the top of the canyon.

"Could you go with Zona? You and Barbara?"

"No problem. Thanks."

"Don't be long, okay?" says my wife Barbara.

"We may be escorting someone back to the surface for Keven." I run through the roster of the tour and wonder who it could be.

"Walt, grab the Coleman lantern. Craig, you lead. Walt, do we have everything?"

"I have the lantern and my flashlight." I wave up to the top of the canyon where Barbara stands. She waves back.

"Ready, Daran?" Daran swings his flashlight. "Let's go," says Bob.

Craig strides off down Boone's Avenue.

"Bob, what do you think Dad's up to?" says Daran.

"Since Craig says no one is hurt, he must want us to take someone off the tour back to the elevator at Snowball."

"What about the ghost though?"

"There's always a first time. Walt has always thought that there was an unnatural lack of ghost stories here in the cave, right, Walt?"

"It was surprising, yes. Was anyone giving Keven any trouble?" I say.

"No. Even that guy in the red hard hat has been quiet." Craig refers to the agent from the Department of Homeland Security who is along on Keven's trip to evaluate breaches in cave security that terrorists could exploit on cave tours. My earlier impression during our first photo session had been that Agent Rod had earned this assignment with something less than valor and critical thinking. I wonder if Craig would have picked up on any continuing conflict between Keven and Red-Hat Rod.

"We'll see what's going on when we get there," says Bob, the solid, unflappable cave guide, even in retirement. Boone's Avenue continues its narrow winding way through a deep canyon of irregular ledges of limestone. The walls are close, but dark, and soak up quite a bit of the lantern light.

We come to a set of steep, steel steps — more of a ship's ladder.

Craig, with his headlight, leads us down. I get in the middle with the lantern. Looping back under the stairs, we scoot through Pinson's Pass and scramble down a rocky slope into the larger passage of Martel Avenue. We strike out along this passage near the lowest level in this area of the cave, where water dropping through vertical shafts often accumulates in puddles on the rock floor.

As a geologist, and former cave guide, I point out the nodules and beds of the Lost River Chert projecting black from the walls of the gray and more soluble limestone. I'm sure Keven pointed these out to the tour, but I can't resist.

Keven is standing with his back to us, and he's *filling their buckets* with more cave lore. Having guided at Mammoth Cave since the late 1960s, he has more stories about Mammoth Cave than he could ever tell on one tour.

"... so, for a very short time, visitors entered Mammoth Cave down a very tall and quite possibly shaky, wooden staircase from the Cathedral Domes entrance in the side of Houchins Valley. Although it was never clear, we think that the climb back up all those steps caused the cave entrance to be closed soon after it opened. Now ... Hey! Craig's back. Remember Bob? He photographed you this morning crawling out of the Snake Pit into Cleaveland Avenue? And Walt here guided tours in the seventies. Somehow Bob has convinced Walt to help him with cave photography. And, Daran, whom you saw crouched with a strobe in that last bend in the Snake Pit, has decades of cave experience, and also happens to be my son.

"Bob, we're making a brief stop here because we saw a lantern flying across the passage as we came into Martel. Right back there." He points to where we had climbed down. Before we head on out to Cathedral Domes, I wanted to chat with you." Keven steps away from his group and motions Craig to join his companions. At Keven's direction, I leave the lantern with the group. I wave at Dan Ross and his wife Sophy, whom I had met at the morning photo shoot. He's an FBI agent on his first cave tour. He's amused by the Homeland Security Agent.

With the yellow light from Keven's carbide flame the only illumination for us, I switch on my flashlight. Bob does the same.

"Fine," says Bob. The four of us stop about fifty feet away from the group. "You called us back here to chat?"

"I think we've seen a ghost. A ghost carrying a lantern," says Keven in an urgent whisper. He looks all around. The angle of the light exaggerates his serious expression. "I'm pretty sure we've seen an apparition. What I don't know is, whether or not it's some sort of special effect, or ... or something else."

"Dad! What did you see?"

Two
The Lantern

"When I came down into Martel Avenue, a lighted, lard-oil lantern was floating, more than flying, slowly in front of us. It sailed off to the left," says Keven, still whispering and gesturing. The lard oil lanterns of the past were simple lanterns with a fuel container — they burned bacon grease or lard as the fuel — a tiny cotton wick, and a wire bail for the handle. They were a useful light in the total darkness of the cave. But, bright, they were not.

"Who was carrying it?" asks Bob. "You said a ghost."

"No one carried it. That's the point. Or if a ghost carried it, I couldn't see it. Him. Or her."

"You don't seem all that upset," I say. Keven could be a prankster, but I didn't think this was one of his classic stunts. His stunts were usually for other guides, not for visitors. And not with an overzealous agent from Homeland Security on the tour. "Did anyone else see it?"

"They all said they saw it. I was a little ahead of the group and got very excited at first. It disappeared around that bend over there. I couldn't chase it with the group here."

"Are they okay now" I ask.

"I'm not sure. A couple of them almost hyperventilated. If you don't mind, I would like to offer to let anyone who wants to, to go back with you. You can take them up the elevator. I sent Craig back for you guys to give us some calibration time before proceeding. Once we leave here, you know how hard it will be to get anyone out in a hurry. I've been telling cave stories to make it seem that we stopped here on every tour." Keven's breath was normal, and the cadence and inflection of his speech appeared to be normal. He was a confident guide, calm under fire.

I would have been in with the hyper-ventilators.

"Describe it again," says Bob.

"It just floated through the air about two feet off the ground."

"Was it swinging like someone was carrying it?" says Bob.

"Not much, but the flame flickered. Like it does when you walk with a lantern."

"Did it glow ghostly green? Did you hear eerie soundtrack music?" asks Daran.

"No, silly. It was just a lighted, lard-oil lantern moving along. It was silent."

"Dad, are you feeling all right?" asks Daran.

"I'm fine. No, I'm not feverish." He waves away Daran's hand. "It was real."

"What do you want us to do?" asks Bob.

"I'm going to take the tour on to Cathedral Domes. I need you to get anyone that wants to leave moving out. I know Zona and Myrna are back there waiting — and Barbara and the others — but can one of you go back up the passage while someone waits here in the dark? See if you can tell where the lantern appears when you come back into Martel? And then take a quick look around in here for a projector or something. I have to get a move on, or I'll be late. It looks like someone – an unauthorized someone – has been messing around in the cave."

"Sure. We can do that? Right, Walt? Daran?"

"Are you kidding? Of course, we can," I say. At last a ghost in Mammoth Cave. Forty years ago when I trailed cave tours for the summer, I had expected ghost stories to be around every bend in the passage. Precious few stories, and no apparitions.

"Cool, a ghost hunt," says Daran.

"Great! I'll call you after I get off work. And, hey! Not a word of this for now? Okay?"

"Sure, Keven. We won't let people know you're this kind of crazy. Not yet anyway," Bob says, chuckling. Daran laughs.

Keven walks back to his tour.

"Listen up, now. You are fortunate to have been present during this apparition or a nice hoax, whichever way it turns out. This is not a normal occurrence. Some of you may not feel fortunate and find yourselves unhappy to be in the cave right now. Any of you that want to leave, Bob has offered to take you out by the elevator behind the dining room. However, we will not be able to refund your ticket purchase. Any takers?"

From the outside edge of the group, a hand shoots up. "Will there be any more ghosts?"

"That's a hard question," says Keven. "I have been guiding here since the late sixties, and this is my first apparition. I think it would be against all the odds for us to have another unusual experience. I can't make any guarantees."

Another voice from the group, "It wasn't threatening. We've seen scarier stuff at amusement parks, right?"

The general chatter that followed appears to be in agreement.

"Anyone?" says Keven. "No? Then follow me." And off they go. Fifteen lights bob along until they disappear one by one around a bend.

"How do we do this?" I ask Bob, happy that I don't have to lead someone out and miss the ghost hunt. We stand in an irregular patch of light formed from two flashlights pointed to the ground. The lantern is over where Keven had stopped his tour. Daran waves his light around on the ceiling looking for something. But what? A projector?

"Walt, why don't you take the lantern and go back up to Pinson's and leave it there? That should be far enough back to not block this ghost lantern. Come back down slowly and carefully. Use your light like normal."

"Right." I grab the Coleman lantern securing my flashlight in the leather holster on my belt. Clambering back up to Pinson's Pass, I hear Bob send Daran off in the direction the lantern came from, then heads across to the left where Keven lost sight of it.

I reach the top of the slope and go a bit farther into Pinson's Pass and set the still-lit, double-globe lantern along the right side of the passage on a flat rock. I pause for a moment in the darkness at the top of the pitch. I see no light from below, so I switch on my flashlight and descend. Down-climbing emphasizes why headlamps are such a good idea for caving. It's hard to climb down and light the footholds with a hand-held light, so I move with caution from one foothold to the next.

At the bottom, I follow the tour route to Hovey's Cathedral Domes, the way Keven would have gone. I see no lard-oil lantern. No other light. I stop, flashlight pointed straight down.

Within seconds, a lard-oil lantern appears out of invisibility ahead of me, near where Daran must be waiting. It moves at an oblique angle across and in front of me. The light from the lantern does not illuminate the cave. I can see the lantern in full detail, but the wall and floor around it are dark. There is no green glow. No sound track.

The lantern floats down the passage toward the bend where Bob is waiting. It appears to be three-dimensional and solid. The air in the passage seems still, but the flame flickers as if moving through the air. Not from a wind. I take slow, careful steps to follow it. It disappears round a bend. As I follow it, a bright light assaults my wide-open pupils.

"Ah!"

"Oh, it's you," says Bob. He moves the flashlight out of my face. "Sorry."

"Where'd it go?" I ask.

"What, Keven's lantern?"

"It came this way right ahead of me."

"I didn't see anything. I just heard your footsteps. What did it look like?"

"It looked solid. Real. The flame flickered, but it didn't cast a light." I paused to replay the sequence in my head. "The flame made no sound."

"No sound?"

"No. You know, the crackling of the flame. And it didn't smell. Certainly not bacon grease." When it burned, the lard fuel smelled like bacon cooking.

"Interesting," says Bob. "Where's Daran?"

"Here," calls Daran from down the passage. "Did you see anything?" He jogs toward us.

"Yes, just like Keven described. You saw it, right?" I say.

"No. Nothing. What a bummer. But you saw it?" says Daran.

"Sure did. It floated along from over there to the bend right here. What now?"

"Let's scout around for a projector," says Bob.

The passage is filled with too many small cracks and ledges to search with any degree of thoroughness, and the others are waiting. We look in the obvious places, but find nothing.

"They're making some very small projectors. Small enough to fit in a smart phone," says Daran.

"If this is a hoax, whoever set this up owns a really nice lard oil lantern. I don't know much about these things, but it seems like it would have to be a sophisticated projector to achieve the sort of reality you describe, wouldn't it?" says Bob.

"Some sort of very advanced holographic device, I guess. But, how? And why down here? And most important, who?" I say and make a note of the time and sketch the passage and the path of the lantern in my notebook.

"Why not a ghost?" says Daran. "Why does it have to be technology?" This question from the techie.

We pick our way through the rocks up the slope.

The Coleman lantern I left behind sits in the dark on the cave floor at the entrance to Pinson's Pass. I pick it up and check the valve.

"It's been turned off and moved."

"And you didn't turn it off when you left it there?" asks Bob.

"No. It would be too hard to re-light. And I didn't leave it here. It was on that flat rock on the right."

We look all around. I aim my flashlight up to the ceiling, but there are no obvious hiding places for a prankster.

"You don't think John came back this far to check on us and decided to play a trick, do you?" I say.

"Could be, but he's not much of a practical joker. Not with things like lighting in the cave."

"Sounds like Dad's ghost to me," says Daran.

We hurry along to re-join our five companions at Snowball.

Three
Lunch Underground

"Oh, Bob. What's going on? Is Keven alright?" says Myrna.

"Myrna, Keven's fine. He saw ... something, and he wanted to tell someone about it," says Bob.

"What? What did he see?" she asks.

"A ghost lantern," says Daran.

"Yes," I say. "A lard oil lantern floating along by itself." I look at Barbara and signal to her that there is more to tell in private.

"Mom, he hasn't lost it. The whole tour saw it. And Walt saw it, too."

"Daran, didn't you see it?"

"No. I'm not crazy." We all laugh with Daran. Well, most of us.

"Keven says he saw a lantern," says Bob. "A lantern drifting down the passage. Walt saw it, but not us." Bob looks at the others. "I'm sorry to make you folks wait so long. Zona, these people must be freezing. Let's eat."

"*We're* all ready, Bob. We've just been waiting on you to finish your ghost hunt." She points to a picnic table covered with a checkered tablecloth and an inviting picnic spread.

Empty, with the lights out, Snowball Dining Room is a little eerie. It's similar to going into your high school during the summer with the hall lights off. We get by with just the security light over the serving line. The person in the group who has seen the ghost lantern thinks we could use a little more light.

Working in the cave makes us hungry. After we wash our hands, we dig into ham and cheese sandwiches, homemade potato salad, coleslaw, and hot, white-bean soup carried in a wide-mouth, vacuum bottle. There's coffee, soft drinks, and water. We would be eating simpler lunches if we had had to carry the food down the one hundred sixty-seven steps at the Carmichael Entrance and lug it a mile to our lunch spot instead of riding down on the elevator that is up the passage behind the serving line. Over lunch, the conversation moves on to historic and recent ghosts in the cave. And the lack of ghost stories.

"They called Gothic Avenue the haunted chambers, but that was because of the aboriginal remains on display there, not because of any ghosts, right?" I say.

"That's true," says John. "And there was Martha Washington's statue. The tour on their return through Main Cave thought that was a ghost, didn't they?"

We're trying to find parallels to the ghost lantern, but no one comes up with anything.

Once we take the edge off our hunger and our need for warm liquids, Bob sits back and expands on what Keven told us, and what we did trying to solve the mystery of the ghost lantern.

"Walt, tell them what you saw."

"Well, I saw what Keven described. A lard-oil lantern floating about two feet above the cave floor with no visible means of support. It seemed real. Solid, you know. Not an old, rusty one, but new looking. The flame flickered. The strangest thing though, it didn't light anything. The cave around it stayed dark, if you know what I mean.

"I followed it down the passage, and when it went around the corner where Bob was waiting, it disappeared." I show John the sketch in my notebook. He passes it around to the others.

"Didn't you see it, Bob?" says Zona.

"I heard Walt's footsteps, but saw nothing. No light. Nothing," says Bob.

"I didn't see it either," says Daran. "And Walt said it started right where I was standing."

"Was it some sort of special effect? You know, a projector?" asks John.

"Keven asked about a projector, and we looked for one, anything to explain it. But we didn't have time for a thorough search."

"Interesting," says John, who has decades of experience in the technical side of theater productions and special effects. "I don't have much experience with holographic projections, but it must be an effect, or else, it's a ghost."

"Say, John, speaking of special effects," says Bob. "You didn't, by chance, come down to Pinson's Pass, did you?" John swivels his gaze away from the dark passage leading to the elevator.

"No, I didn't. Why?"

"John stayed with us," says Zona. "The whole time." She's packing up, so I grab another sandwich before they disappear.

"He led us back here," says Pam. "Why?"

"Well, we left the Coleman lantern in Pinson's, and when we came back, someone had turned it off and moved it," I say.

"You mean it blew out," says John.

"No," says Bob. "The valve was off."

"The valve was closed?" says John.

"Right. Closed tight," I say.

"Maybe it *was* a ghost," says Zona, packing up the remains of the feast. Barbara helps her pack. "It sure sounds like one to me." She shivers.

"Me, too," says Pam. From her smile, I think she likes the idea of a ghost.

"A ghost would be neat," says John, appearing intrigued by the possibilities. "I'm going to check that out the next time I'm in that part of the cave."

"What did Keven do?" asks Myrna. She seemed concerned that her husband may be seeing things — even if they were things I had seen, too.

"He seemed more curious than worried. He said he would check with us tonight. And, he asked us to keep it to ourselves. Keven seemed more concerned about making the schedule on the way out," says Bob. "He offered anyone on the tour a chance to go out with us. They seemed to think it was no big deal."

I see a lack of understanding in Barbara's face, "The Wild Cave guide has to mesh schedules with the guides on the Grand Avenue and the Frozen Niagara – or the New Entrance tour. All three tours go out through Frozen Niagara."

"It can be quite a line waiting to leave if the guide on the Frozen Niagara stays on the rock too long or the guide on the Grand Avenue arrives ahead of schedule," says Zona.

"Does it work out most of the time?" asks Barbara, folding the tablecloth.

"Most of the time. Yes," says Zona.

Pam looks all around as though she's taking inventory.

"Bob, what happens if the elevator doesn't work when we go to leave?" says Pam. The original freight elevator served the Cave for decades – since 1956. The new, slick, commercial-office-building elevator that replaced it in the 1990s failed after only a few years. After years and funding from the corporate sponsor, they replaced it with the current, open-cage elevator designed for deep mines. I like it a lot better. With an open cage similar to the original elevator, I can see the strata of limestone and sandstone during the 267-foot trip. With the temperamental, office-building elevator, but for the lack of elevator music, you could have been in an office building in downtown Louisville.

"Oh, that's no problem at all, Pam. We can amble along in that direction for a mile and climb one hundred sixty-seven steps." Bob points back along the length of the dining room toward Cleaveland Avenue, the way we had gone to shoot our first photograph of the Wild Cave tour. "We hike back to the elevator building to get our cars. Or, we can zip back that way," he points to the way we had come from Boone's Avenue, "and cover three miles, three major hills, and go out through Frozen Niagara. Either way beats spending the night in the cave."

"And carry all this stuff?" asks Barbara.

"We leave the lunch things back by the elevator with a note, and take the cameras with us," says Bob. Leaving the picnic gear would lighten our load, I think, but we're carrying a lot of camera gear.

"I hope the elevator works all the way up," says Pam. She smiles. None of us relish climbing the steps at the Carmichael Entrance. I notice that Bob assumed that any elevator malfunction would be with us outside the cab. He doesn't mention that the elevator still isn't used all that much, and we could get stuck on the way up, so I don't say anything either.

"I would really like to go back and take another look around where that lantern appeared. We're not set up for that, but if it ever comes up, I think that Denise would understand our scouting for other cave pictures. Nothing else need be mentioned," says Bob.

"Dad really should be in on that trip," says Daran.

"I'm sure he would like to, Daran," says Myrna. "But he would like it a lot better if the mystery were solved, don't you think?"

Bob nods his agreement and looks around at our little group. "You're right, Daran, but so is your mother. If we don't figure it out, Keven can have a shot at it another day. I planned to shoot one more picture after lunch anyway. John, you said that you and Pam have plans for this evening, right?"

John nods his head. "Lorrie has a new evening program she's trying out tonight at the amphitheater. We told her we'd give her some feedback."

"And, we have to check on the dogs and clean up before that," says Pam.

"If we all go back to Martel and spread out across the passage, we should be able to find anything obvious," says John.

"Great. I was going to shoot that little tri-color bat hanging under that ledge at the restrooms. You can never have too many pictures of bats," Bob says, glancing around at us. "But, we'll save that for another day."

"Sounds good to me," I say. Shooting the bat could take a while, even if it cooperates.

"Bob, let's move all this food and equipment up to the elevator before we go gallivanting off to Martel."

"Great idea, Zona," says Barbara. "I'm not sure how we'll feel after ghost hunting and climbing through the cave." Barbara's in great shape, but I can tell she's a bit worried about Zona, and maybe more so about Myrna who has less experience in the cave.

Four
Boone's Avenue en Masse

After making quick stops behind what the guides describe as piles of rocks, but which are modern restroom facilities, we troop out through Washington Hall toward the glistening cave grapes at Mary's Vineyard and Boone's Avenue. Barbara walks at the rear with me. We pause at the grapes, and I peer down the narrow steps that lead to the Pass of El Ghor and the route to Echo River.

"There's some nice cave back that way," I say. "It leads to Echo River, where we took your parents on the boat ride." I refer to a trip back in the nineties when the Echo River tour was back on the schedule for a short time, and we had taken my in-laws on the trip. It had been my first and last time on the river. The annual flooding of the passages made the tour too expensive to maintain. A lot of mud had to be moved off the walkways after each flood.

"That was a good trip."

"I'm glad we caught it while the park had it open," I say. We scurry a bit to catch up with the group.

Down the steps and right into Boone's Avenue. I catch the light switch and switch off the lights behind us. Up ahead I look for shadow formations on the ceiling forty feet overhead.

"Do you remember where the switches are from all that time ago?" says Barbara, referring to my time as a seasonal cave guide.

"Most of them. Usually they're pretty obvious. When they took out the old incandescent fixtures in here, they lost several shadow formations. These new lights have a cold, brave-new-world feel to them."

"What were your favorites?" says Barbara.

"The laughing man, I think."

"Do you remember where it was?"

"I think so, we'll check."

We get through Boone's with good speed. No laughing man. Once again at the junction with Rose's Pass, I leave the group to go to the switch to kill this section of lights. Earlier this morning when I had been up Rose's Pass to the light switch, I had been loaded down with a pack full of camera gear and a large tripod. This time, the short trip is pleasant. When I push the button that opens the relay for the lights, I pause for a second in the darkness. The total darkness of the cave. I savor it and the silence before switching on my flashlight and rejoining the group.

When I had returned from the light switch earlier this morning, I had heard the scuffle of the boots from Keven's Wild Cavers and had to hustle to stay ahead and warn Bob that they were right behind me. Now, I can stroll along and catch up with the group where they'll bunch up at the ship's ladder down to Pinson's Pass. I enjoy being in the cave, and I have been in Mammoth Cave all alone on several occasions. Today, I find comfort in knowing there is a group of friends just ahead.

In the 1912 revision to his definitive book on Mammoth Cave, *Mammoth Cave of Kentucky*, the Reverend Doctor Horace C. Hovey wrote that this trail had shown evidence of plenty of traffic in 1908. Except for Wild Cavers, few visitors have traveled this way since 1954 when the original, incandescent lights were installed in the passages from the Snowball Dining Room to Mt. McKinley over the route followed by today's Grand Avenue tour. Electric lights never illuminated this section of lower Boone's.

I catch up with Barbara before she descends the ship's ladder.

"This is interesting," she says.

"Yes," I say. "There are some on the Grand Avenue tour where you go up through Big Break from Grand Central, but you climb those, not descend them. I think that's easier."

"Are there a lot of these?"

"No, not back here. These steps haven't been used that much compared to those in the rest of the cave. Once they put in electric lights, the tour by-passed lower Boone's following the lights. It's just the Wild Cave back here now."

"It's interesting being in the cave without the electric lights. Your sense of size and distance really changes," says Barbara.

"Yes, it does."

At the bottom of the steps, we loop under through Pinson's Pass and stop at the top of the slope down into Martel Avenue. Pinson's is one of those little passages that make moving from one level to the other easy in some cases and possible in others.

"Okay, everyone here?" says Bob, eyeing me as I step into the passage.

"All present and accounted for, sir." I snap him a proper salute."

"At ease, airman. All right, John, how do you think we should proceed?"

"Let's try to reproduce Keven's movements. He must have been a little ahead of his tour, but not too much. Bob, why don't you go down, and we'll follow six or eight feet behind?"

"Sounds good. Walt, since you've already seen the damn thing, why don't you trail?" says Bob. I nod in agreement. The others file in behind John who waits until Bob gets a little ways down the slope.

Barbara signals that she is going to stay close to Zona and Myrna. I think she's anticipating a rougher slope than it has become with the traffic of Wild Cave tours over the years.

The little group going down the slope bunches up because it seems that everyone has the same idea about being close to help someone else. I follow about ten feet behind Daran.

The lantern does not show itself.

John walks over to where Bob was standing. "Walt's sketch showed him standing right about here." Bob nods in agreement. "So a regular projector would have to be above or behind him, right?"

"That's right, but wouldn't he have cast a shadow if it had been behind him?" says Daran.

"You're right, so a regular projector would be up near the ceiling."

"What if it was not a regular projector though?" says Daran.

"You mean a holographic projector?" says John.

"Yes, where would that have to be?"

"I'm not sure," says John. "Bob, what do you think?"

"I don't know much about these things, but doesn't a hologram require more than one projector?"

"Well, since we're not sure, look for anything that's not limestone. Everyone line up where Daran was standing. Then sweep back up the passage to where Bob was standing. Concentrate on the ceiling," says John.

We troop down the passage and line up abreast. There's enough of us that we aren't even an arm's length apart. We work in silence. After thirty minutes of bouncing spots of light across the ceiling, we find nothing.

"John, what else can we do?" says Bob.

"Look carefully on our way back up to Pinson's. A box, a length of cord, a scratch, anything."

More silent spots of light bob across the ceiling, up and down the walls, and across the rocky floor. More nothing.

"Maybe Daran was right," I say at the top of the slope. "Maybe it's not technology."

"Isn't this where Watson says, 'But Holmes, we are men of science,'" says Barbara.

"It is, and this seems to be an unlikely spot for the supernatural to delve into the world of Mammoth Cave," I say.

"I, for one, would like some daylight and bird song," says Barbara with yet another reference to *The Hound of the Baskervilles*.

"I'm with you, Barbara," says Myrna.

"John, will you lead us out?" says Bob. "Walt, if you will, bring up the rear with an eye on our back trail?" With that, we string out through Pinson's Pass and spring back together going up the ship's ladder. I sidle along crab-wise looking back into the dark for who knows what. No lights glow green or any other color.

The elevator works, and soon we emerge on the surface. It's about four o'clock, and the September sun shines through the canopy of oak and hickory that covers the sandstone on top of Mammoth Cave Ridge.

I like limestone and caves, but the contrast of the brilliant blue and green when I come out of a cave always delights me. Pam and Barbara appear to agree. Barbara takes a deep breath and stares at the blue sky.

Daran and I help Bob load the camera gear into the Suburban. John and Barbara finish loading the picnic supplies into our station wagon.

"Zona, why don't you ride with Barbara back to our house? Walt and I will go check out with Denise," says Bob, looking around. Denise supervises the shifts of guides for the National Park Service, and Bob coordinates with her before and after his photography trips.

"Myrna, would you like to go with us to report to Keven about the lantern?" asks Bob.

"Yes, that would be great. Thanks. Then he can bring me back to my car."

"Daran?" says Bob.

"I'm going to check in at work. Thanks." To his mother, Daran says, "I'll call you later." Daran is sort of a trouble-shooter for the pharmaceutical giant that is the sponsor for the park and conducts research programs in the cave.

"John and Pam? Thank you folks for helping us out today. I'll let you know when the pictures are ready. Enjoy the evening program," says Bob.

"See you," says John.

I join Barbara on her way to our station wagon.

"Thank you for going with Zona. We shouldn't be very long." I give her a kiss.

"Be careful, and don't let Bob get you in trouble," says Barbara, smiling. "I want to hear more about the lantern. A lot more."

"We'll cover it in detail. I promise."

Five
The Wait

Bob steers the Suburban to the right out of the small parking lot at the top of the freight elevator. At the four-way stop with the wider Mammoth Cave Parkway, Bob turns the truck toward the visitor center and away from the main entrance at Park City.

"Bob, do you think Keven's okay?" says Myrna.

"He knows that part of the cave as well as anyone. From Cathedral Domes, it's walking with a little scrambling. He's fine."

"You know, I'm thinking less about his physical safety than other things."

"I see," says Bob. "You mean, 'Is he seeing things?'"

"Yes, but I've never known him to hallucinate."

"I don't think he was hallucinating today either," I say. "Remember, I saw the lantern that he described. And the tour saw it, too. Keven is like he always has been. He showed that spark when he guides a trip. But he didn't hyperventilate about the lantern. He's a scientist. He's interested."

"Oh, good. That makes me feel better," she says. Bob and I glance at one another. Is it sarcasm or genuine relief?

"Whatever else is going on," says Bob, "The oddity is not with Keven. He's fine."

We pull into a parking space near the temporary trailers housing offices for the interpretive staff while the second phase of the new visitor center is completed. Bob double-checks the doors of the truck to make sure they're locked. Too much camera gear to risk.

"Walt, why don't you wait with Myrna over at the bus circle? I'll check out with Denise."

"Sure thing. Tell Denise I said 'Hi.'"

We amble across the lot to the circular drive at the south end of the new visitor center. For decades, the buses that took the tours to the Carmichael, New Entrance, and Frozen Niagara entrances parked along the east side of the visitor center. With the new building, they re-routed traffic and provided a pickup/discharge point along a circular drive designed to reduce traffic congestion.

"He gets back between four-thirty and five, doesn't he?" she says.

"That sounds about right. Based on my memory of the old schedule, they leave between the last Grand Avenue on its way out and the last Frozen Niagara going in." I say.

We sit on a bench and enjoy the sunshine. Myrna tells me about her other children, grown now; and we talk about the potluck suppers the guides used to throw on a regular basis over in the seasonal housing area. Keven worked the seasonal guide schedule for decades, working each summer until he retired from teaching. He and Myrna sold their house and moved to Cave Country.

The first of two green school buses pulls into the circle and stops. A young female guide who had stood in the front of the bus exits ahead of the visitors. Before the first bus empties, the second one pulls in behind. The second guide gets off the other bus. I approach him.

"Hi. I'm wondering if you saw anything of the Wild Cave tour before you left."

"No, we didn't. Do you have someone on the tour?"

"No, I'm a friend of Keven's. Walt Breedon. Used to trail tours here in the seventies," I say, holding my hand out.

He shakes. "Nice to meet you. I'm Chad Stewert. This is the New Entrance tour. Keven'll be out after the Grand Avenue. Do you know Alan, the guide on the Grand Avenue tour?" I nod. "He was right behind us. Some guides let the Wild Cavers mix in with the Grand, but Keven's pretty good about holding them back. Maybe another forty-five minutes or an hour. You do know that they take the Wild Cave over to the dorms to change clothes?"

"No, I didn't know that. Thanks for your help."

I rejoin Myrna and fill her in on what I've learned.

"I never worry when Keven is in the cave, but I'll be happy when he's above ground today. You don't need to wait with me, you know."

"I don't mind at all. What do you think of the changes? The new visitor center?"

And so we talk about the park and the guides and life in Mammoth Cave Country. Forty-five minutes pass before I'm aware of it. The first green bus for the Grand Avenue tour pulls up and begins to disgorge visitors who have gone two and a half hours since their last restroom stop. Before everyone gets off the first bus, the second bus pulls in behind it; the third follows. Alan Arkwright and the guide who trailed the tour ride in on the last bus. I intercept them after they leave the last group of visitors.

When I rejoin Myrna, I say, "Alan said they didn't see Keven after Snowball. No blink of the lights at Grand Central or at Flat Ceiling." The protocol says that when the guide leading a tour comes to a section of lights that are already on, the guide should blink the lights to let the tour up ahead know that there's a tour behind them so they won't cut off that section of lights. "Alan thinks Keven is leading a rowdy bunch."

"They didn't seem rowdy to me when we were taking their pictures this morning at the Snake Pit," says Myrna.

"No, but sometimes the tour will change after Snowball. I don't know if it's the chili, the extra calories, or maybe some of the scary has worn off. Even Half Day tours will do that to you. Grand Avenue, I mean. And, remember the guy from Homeland Security in the red hat?" Myrna nods. "That guy could have slowed the tour down with his questions and complaints." She laughs.

Bob joins us. He shrugs his shoulders.

"I talked to Alan and Chad. They didn't see Keven or any light blinks after they left Snowball."

"I talked with them both out here. The floating lantern did throw him about ten or fifteen minutes behind. Myrna and I were just talking about Red Hat Rod," I say.

"I told Denise about our trip, minus the lantern apparition, and that Myrna was here with us. The Wild Cave bus will wait for them, but they have to go change over at the dorms. I told her that we wanted to hear about how the tour went with the Homeland Security guy. Denise said it was okay for us to wait for Keven at Frozen Niagara."

The three of us climb back into Bob's vehicle and drive out to the Frozen Niagara entrance. In the 1920s, George Morrison bought and leased land outside the bounds of the Mammoth Cave estate. Using cave surveys obtained in secret during trespasses into the cave, he blasted in the New Entrance to Mammoth Cave, built some long, elaborate wooden steps, and offered tours through the *New Entrance to Mammoth Cave*, the only entrance other than the natural entrance that was used for thousands of years. In 1925, guides working for Morrison made their way through Big Break, an enormous pile of breakdown at Grand Central Station, and discovered the Frozen Niagara section of the cave. Since Morrison came from New York, they named the huge flow stone formation that resembles a waterfall after the oldest tourist attraction in the United States. Mammoth Cave, of course, was the country's second oldest tourist attraction. From there, Morrison opened a third entrance into Mammoth Cave: *The Frozen Niagara Entrance.*

We sit in the Suburban with the doors open. Bob opens the outer door of the concrete block airlock and goes inside. He's back in less than ten minutes.

"The lights are off. I think we should wait for Keven out here."

"When he's been this late before, it's been because someone on his tour became ill. I hope no one's hurt," says Myrna.

"Me, too," says Bob.
We wait.

Six
The Buzzing

Keven stopped and faced the tour. He held his hand in front of his eyes.

"I know it's a natural impulse to look at me when I'm talking, but please remember that when you do that, you're shining your light in my eyes. Everyone but Rod looks away. "Thank you." Keven shifted so that Rod's four LED lights no longer blinded him.

"History indicates that Stephen Bishop discovered this area, and the Cathedral Domes area where we're heading, a few years after he crossed Bottomless Pit. However the Domes were not visited by many tours, and the Right Reverend Hovey reported that cave guides had *re-discovered* the domes in 1907.

"He wrote about his trip into the 'newly discovered passages' at that time. However, the men in the *discovery* party included a guide, so we think the reverend used the term *newly discovered* to add dramatic tension to his narrative. Reverend Hovey reported a set of footprints near where a Mr. Creighton carved his name in the limestone. The name appears in several documents with dates around 1848, but we know very little about Mr. Creighton beyond his name and shoe size. The location of the footprints is shown on Hovey's map in the 1912 edition of his book.

"Reverend Hovey acknowledged that he added Creighton's name and footprints to his map, along with some other changes, after he managed a glance at Max Kaemper's Map. Max Kaemper mapped the known reaches of the cave and some new areas he and the guide Ed Bishop pushed into. Hovey describes the series of re-discoveries, who made them, and how they culminated in his seeing one of the most dramatic areas of the cave. Hovey's Cathedral Domes. Any questions?"

Keven led them along a narrow, damp passage with shallow puddles of water near, but not quite at, the base level of cave development. The water enters through sinkholes at the surface and falls through vertical shafts to this level of the cave. From the bottom of a vertical shaft, it's called a dome. From the top, it's a pit. However, the amount of water at this level seldom amounts to much. Keven pointed out significant occurrences of the Lost River Chert.

"The Lost River Chert consists of nodules of chert – cryptocrystalline silicon dioxide. A concentration of sponges that form silica-based spicules, their support structure, provided the source for the silicon. The nodules extend from the limestone walls because the chert dissolves little in water, and it stands out from the more-soluble limestone. The name *Lost River* was applied by the geologist who first described it in Lost River Cave in Bowling Green."

"Can you go from here to Bowling Green through the cave?" said Rod. "Or asked another way, could someone come underground from Bowling Green to Mammoth Cave?"

"No. The cave passages trend toward the Green River, and no passage has been found that comes from the south close to Mammoth Cave Ridge. There are hundreds of miles of passage in Mammoth Cave, but none of them travel very far in one direction or the other," said Keven. He did not want to discuss the cave passages that radiated out east from the Frozen Niagara entrance.

As the tour straggled into Hawkins Pass, a loud buzzing made them all look around. The buzzing reminded Keven of a large electrical substation, but much louder. It hit its crescendo with an intensity that caused everyone to put their hands over their ears. The LED headlights that most of the tour was wearing went dark. Two of the tour were wearing the older style of lights with tungsten filaments. Keven wore his trusty carbide lamp that relied on chemical reactions, not electrical components. These three lights provided dim illumination of the passage.

"What the hell was that?" came a voice from the near dark.

The passage rang with everyone talking all at once.

"Listen up!" said Keven. He adjusted the lever on his carbide lamp, and yellow flame jetted out four inches in front of the reflector. He noticed that Rod lay face down on the ground. All four of his LED lights were dark. The group quieted to one or two murmurs. With forty years of guiding cave tours and teaching high school, Keven could control a group. "We have been through a very strong electromagnetic pulse. Some of you may have heard of an EMP? No? There are a number of things that can cause that phenomenon.

"The reason I know that's what happened here is that I can see only two other lights. The old ones. Those of you with the new, LED lights have no illumination. In an EMP event, integrated circuits that are not shielded burn out. The circuit elements are very tiny and unable to carry the voltage induced by the EMP."

"If this was a nuclear explosion," said Rod, now on his feet, "I'll have to take charge as a representative of Homeland Security."

"Thank you, Rod, for that information. This is still a National Park Service cave, and I'm still the cave guide. When we see some evidence of an attack, I will welcome your input."

"Input? This is …"

"Now, for those of you without light, stand by one of the people with a working light. Next, look in your fanny packs and take out the old-fashioned, hand-held flashlights. Turn them on. I want *everyone* to hold your position right here until I recon a little way ahead."

"Hey, Keven! My smart phone doesn't work."

"Another victim of the EMP," said Keven.

"Will the park service buy me a new one?"

"Probably not," said Keven. "We warned you not to bring them before we left, didn't we?"

"Yeah, I guess so."

The murmuring surged again, and boots shuffled while the tour members clustered around the two working lights, which provided a degree of security, and with that, a degree of calm returned. The extra lights improved the mood and settled the Wild Cavers.

In the passage ahead, Keven concentrated on the trail and the walls of the cave. They had heard no rock fall. Nothing had shaken. No earthquake. Nothing but the buzzing. Rod was right that thermonuclear explosions caused the main concern about EMPs. Had World War III broken out in the short time they were underground? He didn't think so. But what happened? *What's going on with me and lights today?*

He knew this area of the cave. The walls of Hawkins Pass looked familiar, but the floor of the passage didn't. He could see no sign of a trail. Not a single scuff mark or boot print. *Where am I?* The panic jumped into his throat. Keven forced it to subside. He knew Mammoth Cave when he saw it. He recognized Hawkins Pass. He had guided tours through here hundreds of times. But, what happened to the trail? He looked back the way he had come. He saw a single line of boot prints. *My boot prints!* Either he was going mad, or he was dreaming some elaborate dream. The dream intrigued him, and he would stay with it to see where it took him.

Keven knew enough science fiction to know that, at this point in the story, he would not be asking himself where, but *when* was he? He stopped at the point where Hawkins Pass changed to the next dome. Okay, SF movie, dream, or insanity, he would do what the situation demanded. He would focus on leading his tour out to safety and trotting on home to Myrna.

He strode back to the huddle of Wild Cavers.

"What's going on?" came one chorus of cries.

"I knew I should have gone out back there!" came another.

While he thought of an answer, he counted heads. Thirteen! "Who's missing?" he said.

Seven
The Other Side

"All right, settle down. Everyone yell out your name."

They went through the roll.

"Where's Craig?" asked Keven.

"He's not here," came a voice from the rear. "He stopped right back there just when we entered this passage."

"Who's that?"

"Josh."

"Thanks, Josh," said Keven. "We are safe. We have heard no rocks falling. We have felt no shaking or movement. There has been no earthquake. However, something unusual has happened. We just don't know exactly what. When the unusual happens underground, safety protocol says that we leave the cave by the quickest, safe route. For that reason, we are reversing course and going back the way we came to Snowball Dining Room. We just came through that passage, and we'll pick up Craig along the way."

"Keven?" asked Josh. "We've been talking. Rod said that nuclear bombs create an EMP when they detonate. Do you think we've been attacked?"

"No, I don't. But I'm not sure." Keven studiously avoided the glare from Red Hat Rod. "There are other ways to create an EMP, and there is a lot here that I can't explain. Like I said, I don't know for certain, but I think three hundred feet of limestone would shield us enough to prevent your LED lights from burning out." He didn't mention that close to the series of large domes at Hovey's Cathedral, the thin layers of rock overhead offered less shielding.

"The only thing electrical down here are transformers for the lights, and they are hundreds of yards away – through almost solid limestone. So, what caused it? I don't know. But we must take care of ourselves first." He worked back through the group, setting them up in pairs until he got to Josh. "Josh, I want you to be my trailer. Can you do that?"

"I'll do that," said Rod. "I'm a government official." He started shuffling toward Josh.

"Rod, I need you up here with me, in case we need to consult. And Josh has a working headlamp."

"Right. Good idea," said Rod, reversing course.

Keven saw Dan Ross smiling. He wondered what he was smiling about.

Josh stared into the darkness behind. Josh and one other had the still-working tungsten-filament headlamps. "Good. I want everyone to stay with your buddy. Keep an eye on each other and if you even think something is wrong, sing out. We'll find Craig up ahead."

"Keven?"

"Yeah, Josh?"

"I don't have a buddy."

"No. I'll be keeping tabs on you. Just in case, take your flashlight out, keep it off, but hold it in your hand. Any more questions? No? I'll lead us out," Keven said with a wave of his hand.

As he dealt with his tour, he struggled to not reveal too much of his own concern. He had no time to come up with an explanation, much less deal with a mutiny from Rod of the DHS. *Why my tour?* Events threatened to overwhelm Keven, but in a moment, he recovered. Thirteen people here, and one missing, relied on him to lead them back to the surface.

Going back to the Snowball Dining Room would allow him to look for Craig — he knew that Craig could not have got past them to Cathedral Domes and the passages ahead — and with any luck, they would be able to ride the elevator to the surface. He hoped the phone system still worked — it was an old analog dial system. Then he realized that an old analog system had a better chance to survive an EMP than a new digital system. He wanted to know what was happening on the surface before going up. He would have to call for the bus since they were making an emergency exit and not coming out at Frozen Niagara.

On the way along Martel Avenue, he thought it strange that the rocks now littering the trail could have fallen unheard. Even though he knew he was striding through Martel Avenue, rocks were scattered about the floor where the trail used to be. The ship's ladder that they had descended wasn't there. No one commented on this while they scrambled up the rocky slope. Were they disoriented, Keven wondered, or just scared? Or being good sports? They weren't complaining, and that was good. He noticed that they kept up in a tight formation. No stragglers now.

Up in Boone's Avenue, more virgin cave. No hint of a trail. Rocks covered the floor. They weren't big rocks. Few bigger than a volleyball. They displayed angular breaks on one side and rounded, smooth surfaces on the other. The rocks were broken from sections of wall or ceiling where the chemical action and passage of water had worn them smooth. Some stress caused them to fall to the floor. Keven paused until he could see his trailer.

"Hey, Keven!" Josh said.

"Yes?"

"I thought you said we were going back the way we came. This doesn't look familiar at all."

"I did, and we are. What's different?"

"I don't remember all these rocks. Have we strayed off the trail somewhere?"

"You're right, Josh. The rocks weren't here. There was nice, clean trail. And we *did* come this way. You've been looking at the ground or where the trail should be. Look around at the walls, and the larger rocks. Those are the same."

"I didn't hear any of these rocks fall," said Rod.

"No, Rod, I didn't either. Did anyone hear any rocks fall?"

No one responded.

"We have too little evidence to explain how the rocks wound up here. I don't know what happened, but I know we're in the right passage."

"The EMP induced a powerful current in the surrounding rock and knocked these loose." said Rod. "It's obvious." Keven noticed that with every pronouncement, Rod reached down to hitch up his belt and trousers, but was frustrated because he was wearing a fanny pack and coveralls. A hand shot up in the back of the group.

"Who's that?"

"It's me, Doug."

"What's your idea, Doug?"

"It's kind of far out, but I don't think these rocks fell since we passed through here the first time. They've fallen over a long period of time, one at a time.

"That's crazy, man. We haven't been gone from here much more than thirty or forty-five minutes. And none of these rocks were here when we came through," said Josh.

"Keven, I think we've somehow or other gone back in time. It looks like no one's ever made it through here. Not even us. I know it's crazy, but it fits the data," said Doug. Josh laughed. Nervous laughter rippled through the group, but they kept their eyes on Keven.

"That's the craziest thing I've ever heard," said Rod. "Whooee."

"Thank you, Doug — and Rod," said Keven, a little pleased to hear his own thoughts verbalized — by Doug. He went on, "I don't know if time travel is even possible. Maybe you are in my dream, or I'm in yours. I don't know if I am, or if we all are, under the influence of some sort of hallucinogen. I agree that we seem to be parading through virgin passage. You can see that for yourselves. Since, as you say, time travel is the best explanation, I am willing to go with that until we have more data. Doug, since you have the other headlamp that works, you lead for a while." It worked. The visitors chuckled and seemed to relax. Suspended disbelief in a surreal world seemed more comfortable than the tension and uncertainty of looking for a reasonable explanation.

However, the sense of time dislocation worried Keven. He knew that no one entered this part of the Cave before 1840 or so, and that would have been Stephen Bishop some time after he crossed Bottomless Pit, crossed Echo River, and discovered all of the cave on this side of the river. What bothered Keven more was that no one ever found a natural exit from the cave on this side of Echo River. After the New Entrance, the other entrances on this side of Echo River were blasted in the 1920s and 1930s. If they were back in time, back before Stephen Bishop crossed Bottomless Pit, it would be a hard, wet trail out of the cave. Enough strange speculation, he needed to get these people to the elevator.

When Keven got to the distinctive canyon, he had everyone look behind them at the way they had come.

"Now, look at that passage. Remember the arch of the ceiling and that big rock? Who remembers that?"

"I do," said Rod, eager to be the first.

"Me, too," said Josh. Murmurs of assent and a few awkward hands aloft confirmed what Keven saw.

Doug led them back up along Boone's Avenue. He stopped at the top of the climb. Keven came forward to study the passage. There were fewer rocks. The question became whether they would be able to go to the Snowball Dining Room the way they had come, using the nice concrete steps. Or, if the steps were not there, like the steel ladder at Pinson's Pass was not there, they would stay in Boone's and come back around through the Pass of El Ghor and in through the back by Mary's Vineyard. They saw no sign of Craig — or anyone else. *Where could Craig be?*

"Keven, where's Craig?" said someone right behind Rod.

"I don't know. I haven't seen any tracks. Have you, Doug?"

"No sign at all," said Doug.

Keven decided he would stop at the side passage that led left up out of Boone's and on to Washington Hall and Snowball. The lack of steps at that junction would tell him more. Would he even recognize the side passage without the steps? Dream, or not, this all seemed real and untouched. In which case, he MUST see the gypsum formations of the Snowball Dining Room in pristine condition. He didn't know if he would be able to restrain his tour — or himself — once they saw the splendor of the gypsum needles, stalks, rosettes, and cotton.

The going stayed rough at the bottom of the canyon passage. Over the years, Keven had spent many hours in genuine wild cave, but right now, he missed the tourist trail. He worried about the people on his tour, but they seemed to be coping — at least their stamina held up. They stepped from one breakdown rock to the next, balancing on wet boulders and slabs that tilted and slammed back down. The crashes echoed in the passage. They leaned on the walls for support. When they arrived at the place where Keven expected to bear left toward the Snowball Dining Room, he looked up at a muddy, rocky slope. Not today. No tracks in the mud. Craig had not gone that way. They could still go to the Snowball Dining Room, now it would be just the *Snowball Room*, but they would take the long route.

The passage curved left and right and left once more before Keven recognized the intersection. He stopped his group.

"We are now in the Pass of El Ghor, a part of the cave that you've never seen. The All Day tours came across Echo River and up along the right. In a short distance, we'll be back at the Snowball Room. If there are picnic tables and a cash register, that will settle once and for all whether Doug's idea about us being back in time is true or not." *Sorry Doug.*

"Now, here's the thing. Since we're letting our imaginations follow Doug's theory, in the event that his theory is correct, we should prepare for the Snowball Room to be *snowball* white. You know that when you saw it last, the grapes at Mary's Vineyard were gray. That is what one hundred seventy-five years of exposure to humans, their lights, and cigarettes has done. If we find gray formations, we will know that time travel is not what's going on here. However, if they're white, we will proceed with extreme care." *And we will be very, very confused.* "The gypsum formations will be in the same condition they were when Stephen Bishop first saw them in 1840 or thereabouts. You know in all the time-travel books and movies, what is it that they all warn about going back in time?"

"Not to mess with the past or you could affect the future," said Doug.

"Right. But here — and now — if we are back in the past, we're not worrying about interacting with people, but with the cave. What we will see if we are back in time will be amazing. The gypsum formations will be as delicate as they will be wondrous. We talked about how gypsum flowers form when we were back in Cleaveland's Avenue, right? Those were the merest remnants of what a passage full of gypsum formations laying undisturbed for millions of years looks like." *There.* Keven thought. *I have fed the adventure and eased my conscience. Now let's find Craig and get out of here.*

"We are going to *walk* single file, one step at a time. Once we're in as far as we're going to go, we will reverse and step back in the same tracks that we made coming in. Got it?" Everyone nodded. "Any questions?" Even Red-Hat Rod kept his mouth shut.

Keven lead them up the passage toward Mary's Vineyard. He recognized the cave *grape* formations at once. The grapes shone in white brilliance. Lantern and cigarette smoke had not discolored them over decades of tours. They followed the passage on the right through the hall leading to the Snowball Dining Room. A white and dusty-beige sheet of gypsum crystals and occasional rosettes covered the ceiling. The restrooms weren't there. He led the tour onward.

The passage opened up. Keven took one step, paused, and took another. His boots crunched in the layer of fallen gypsum crystals. He clicked the water lever on his carbide lamp, and the increased generation of acetylene gas shot the flame out six inches in front of the reflector.

"Oh my god!" Keven exclaimed.

He reached into his pack for his Mag-lite, glad that it used a tungsten filament bulb. In the brilliant white light, the crystals shimmered. The "snowballs" that cluttered the ceiling were recognizable first of all. But long, straight, shimmering needles of gypsum extended three, four, six feet. The needles shimmered with the mere presence of their bodies and lights. Tufts of white cotton gypsum cascaded along the walls and accumulated on the floor.

"This must be what it's like inside a geode in the early stages of formation," said Keven after the few minutes needed to compose himself. His grin was so wide, he spoke with difficulty. Seeing the Snowball Room, Keven accepted the time travel theory because, how else to keep going? *Now did that make any sense at all?* He still thought that he might be going mad, but he could think of no other explanation. And whatever it was, he had people depending on him to lead them out of the cave in safety, if not comfort.

The *wows* and other exclamations died down. Several disposable film cameras flashed. High-intensity fireflies. Members of the tour without cameras shuffled past the others to share in a photograph. They took pictures of themselves against the spectacular and unique backdrop. First they each snapped a picture of the room, a picture of them in front of the room, and last a picture with Keven.

"Remember! Take only pictures, leave only footprints. No souvenirs. Any gypsum souvenirs won't survive the way we're going since they're soluble in water." The groans from the group told Keven that some of them realized that they were going to be wading Echo River. "We have to keep moving. There's a long way to go." There followed the whispered explanations to the unaware.

"Keven where do you think you're taking us?" A challenge from Rod.

"I trust everyone has figured out that there is no elevator. No one has been here before us regardless of which way he or she might have come into the cave. We have seen no sign of Craig. We must assume that he is back where, or when, we left. Unless someone can give me a viable alternative, I am going to operate based on the information I have — improbable as it seems — we are going to have to leave the cave like the All Day tour used to. We are going across Echo River and out through the Historic entrance." No one in the group offered an alternative to the time-travel theory. Not even Rod. Keven led them back through Mary's Vineyard to El Ghor.

The path became easier, if still rocky and irregular. They slogged through long, sandy stretches in wide, high passages. Virgin stretches of river sand deposited over the millennia when Green River flooded and backed Echo River high into the cave. Keven let them rotate leading, "breaking trail."

He stopped when they entered the Echo River passage.

"Cavers dream of virgin cave. And there's no more virgin cave than this," Keven told the tour. But cavers don't start out in virgin cave and stride into timeworn passages, they slog through miles of known cave and tiptoe through virgin passage.

Keven, back in front of the tour, calls, "Buddy check. How are you?"

"Tired."

"Hungry."

"Everyone accounted for?"

"All present and accounted for," called Josh from the back.

"That's a check," said Rod.

"There are two passages from this point," said Keven. "I propose that we take the direct route and cross Echo River. The longer, more uncertain way is to try our luck in Ganter Avenue that comes out in the Wooden Bowl room behind Giant's Coffin on the Historic tour."

"We don't have any boats," someone called out. "Why not Ganter?"

"Ganter is a rough passage. There will be a climb up a steep cliff called Rider Haggard's Flight. From the other side, it stopped the Adena people from further explorations for thousands of years, and it stopped modern man's explorations up to the point when someone thought of piling rocks up from the base of the cliff. And that didn't happen until Stephen Bishop found this end of the passage. I'm not sure we can climb it with flashlights. On the other hand, Echo River should be a shallow stream with a series of pools. We will have to wade, but I don't think the water will be above anyone's waist. The dam on Green River hasn't been built, and remember, Green River controls the level of Echo River here in the cave. If we are lucky, it's not flooding. And, I don't think it is. If the river were in flood, the water would be backed up past here. Let's get ready to wade in the water."

He told everyone to take off their fanny packs, place the contents of their pockets in the packs, and secure them over their shoulders.

"Keven, I think we should split the tour in two. I'm an experienced rock climber. I could lead a small group of experienced climbers up through Ganter."

"That's very generous of you, Rod, but I think we need to all stay together." Keven suppressed the horror he felt if Rod stumbled into the midst of whoever might be on the other side of the river, provided he made it to the other side.

"Rod, how many caves have you been in before today?" said Dan Ross.

"None before today, but I received the highest score in route finding in Army Ranger training." Keven saw Rod's hands go for his belt.

"Okay. Keven, I think Sophy and I will stay with you," said Dan. There were sounds of agreement with some chuckling thrown in. Keven saw Josh talking to Rod. From Josh's gestures, he thought Josh was suggesting Rod try Ganter on his own. Rod shook his head.

The sand transitioned into thick mud, the oozy residue left from the dissolution of the cave, accumulated at the very bottom. Leading the tour through the shallow water, he saw three eyeless fish in the first ten minutes.

"This is so incredible!" said Keven. Knowing he had no less to worry about than before they saw the Snowball Room, he could do nothing but embrace what he saw.

"What?" asked the woman right behind him.

"You're Dot, right? Shine your light out to the side. See those little pinkish white fish darting about? Those are eyeless, cave fish. True troglodytes. Adapted to living in permanent darkness. They aren't blind. They have no eyes."

"Oh my!"

When they reached the far side of Echo River proper, the riverbank offered no place large enough to stop or dry off or rest. Keven led them in what seemed to be an endless slog through sometimes, knee-deep mud. He stopped several times to let everyone catch up. He waited until Josh signaled with his light that everyone had made it. Off he went. However slow he kept his pace, he knew the group would string out, and Josh, still at the rear, would wonder why he was running. Keven recognized the steep mud banks, the arch, and the small body of water that marked the next landmark.

"Welcome to the River Styx. In Greek mythology, the river separated the underworld from the world of the living. Charon the ferryman is not here to take us across. Never mind that he seldom, if ever, carried folks in the direction we're going. Back to the surface world. So, we will traverse along that mud bank on the right. I'll go first and establish footholds and hand holds. Follow me across one at a time. How is everyone's light?" Thirteen lights Bobbed. Everyone sounded good. "Josh, will you bring up the rear?"

Eight
Frozen Niagara

After forty-five minutes, Bob cranks the Suburban and drives along to the exit side of the loop in front of the Frozen Niagara entrance. He leaves room for buses or other vehicles to come and go.

"It's been too long," I say.

"Myrna, do you want to come with us?" says Bob. "We're going into check."

"No, Bob. Thank you. I have my phone so I'll talk to Daran."

"Good. Walt and I will go in back to Flat Ceiling to search for any sign of them. Maybe the Homeland Security guy has slowed them down. We'll go straight in, and maybe our presence will help speed them on their way. If there's no sign, they will be over an hour late and maybe Keven's having more trouble than just Homeland Security. We'll come straight out and call Denise."

After we pass through the airlock, Bob leaves the door closed, but unlocked. He switches on the first section of electric lights along the tourist trail. I look at the ancient passageway in a new light. A different light.

"These are more of the LED lights, right?" I say to Bob.

"Yeah. They claim this combination of amber and white gives a more natural light, but doesn't contain the wavelength necessary for algae to grow."

With the water that seeps into this part of the cave from the surface — the source of all the flow stone formations in this short section of cave — light promotes the growth of algae. Algae add unnatural greens and blues and cause damage to the flow stone formations.

"In this small passage, I think they work pretty well. You don't get so much of the spotlight effect. How do the guides like the new lights?"

"As you would expect," says Bob. "Some don't like any change, and others think it's great. I'm still considering whether I like them or not."

"But less algae, right?" I say.

"Yes. That part seems to work."

We follow the tourist trail past the Great Wall of China and the Temple, two flow stone formations on the right. Soon we bend over at the waist and pass along the Onyx Colonnade — an impressive 20-foot row of flow stone formations, which includes the Wedding Cake and what the guides called the honeymoon formation. A stalagmite with a distinctive shape. A fine-mesh fence protects the formations from the fingers of visitors.

On the other side of the Colonnade, we see Crystal Lake twenty-five feet below our trail. Two white, underwater spotlights illuminate this small body of water. The New Entrance guides *discovered* this man-made lake when they found the Frozen Niagara section. They needed a boat ride to compete with the Echo River ride in Mammoth Cave. The 1940 guidebook published by the Mammoth Cave Operating Committee spoke of Plymouth Rock being the location where the first man who discovered the lake swam ashore – in shallow water. More important than the boat ride, on the shore of Crystal Lake stands the white stalagmite that, when lighted from the appropriate angle, resembles *September Morn* the portrait of a young nude painted by the French artist Paul Chabas. The tour no longer features a boat ride or a glimpse of *September Morn.*

"I still think the green lights were the best," I say.

"I agree, but green light is not natural," says Bob.

"In a cave, no light is natural, so why quibble over the wavelength?" I jog-walk along to catch up with Bob who stands at the top of the forty-nine steps leading down along the stone cascade of Frozen Niagara to the Drapery Room underneath. The large flow stone formation called Frozen Niagara resembles a waterfall frozen and preserved in travertine. With these cave formations, George Morrison achieved a marketing edge over Mammoth Cave.

We ignore the steps leading under massive flow stone and hop down a set of stairs farther along the trail into a little valley where a side passage leads to the KEA Formations, named for the Kentucky Education Association, complete with a bronze plaque and some nice flow stone. No present-day tour takes you to either.

Up a short hill, we come to Flat Ceiling, a vast expanse of flat, smooth, limestone. The old Frozen Niagara Tour came in the same way. They came to this spot after the guide convinced the one hundred twenty visitors to file right past all the formations with the promise of time to look and photograph on the way out. The trailer at the back kept pushing the ones at the rear because the guide needed to get everyone to Flat Ceiling, where he would talk for five minutes.

The scheduling was critical because there were one hundred sixty visitors on the Half Day tour coming around the corner from Flat Ceiling headed out of the cave past the same Frozen Niagara formations. And often, those people on the Half Day tour were looking for daylight with a tad more anxiety than the Frozen Niagara visitors who had entered the cave a mere fifteen minutes earlier.

Once at Flat Ceiling, the guide climbed onto the rock and filled their buckets with information about the cave. After the lights-out/cave darkness demonstration, the guide took a few questions, and they reversed course for the trip out. The guide offered the visitors the option of the forty-nine-step trip down to the Drapery Room – with the *mandatory*, forty-nine-step trip back up to the main trail.

I stand on the rock and survey the room. Bob checks the passage going around the corner to the light switch. From this light switch, the guide on the Scenic Tour let the guide on the Frozen Niagara know that the big tour had arrived. Guide etiquette considered it bad form to hit the light switch while the Frozen Niagara tour stood in total darkness.

"Do you hear anything?"

Bob comes back around the corner. "No. Nothing."

"We call Denise?"

"That's the drill. It's been over an hour. They'll send in a four-man team with two rangers and two guides. One of the rangers will be an EMT and all that."

"I guess they practice for this," I say.

"I've heard that some of their drills in the cave were based on some pretty strange scenarios."

Nine
Up Through the Corkscrew

Once the last of the thirteen Wild Cavers slogged out of the mud and up to River Hall, Keven told everyone to scrape off all the mud they could. They rested. Keven noticed there were no footprints in front of their group. Stephen Bishop had not crossed Bottomless Pit yet. *Was he even born?*

"We are in River Hall. To the left leads to Mammoth Dome, for those of you who have taken the Historic Tour. To the right up those steps — no, there are no steps — up that rise to the right lies Odd-Fellows Hall, Great Relief Hall, and Fat Man's Misery." Keven considered the guides' belief that the Misery would have been a belly crawl through a very low, sandy passage when it was discovered.

"Which way do we go, Keven?" said Josh.

"Straight ahead. Up the Corkscrew."

"I've never heard of that," came a voice from the group.

"It hasn't been part of a tour since the sixties. We'll be climbing up through a breakdown area and come out in Main Cave up the hill from Methodist Church." Long after Stephen Bishop crossed Bottomless Pit, someone, quite by accident, discovered the Corkscrew. The cave visitor who discovered it entered from the bottom.

Keven checked on everyone's physical condition. This climb would be their last physical obstacle, but everyone had to be able to make it to the top. He feared that their reserves were ebbing.

"We have a bit of a climb, and I may take a little time to find the way. I've never been through this maze without ladders and some scuff marks to follow," said Keven. "The alternate route would be a belly-crawl through sand, a winding passage around Bottomless Pit, and more crawling. This is the easier route. You two with the functioning headlights, space yourselves at regular intervals. You with the handhelds be sure to secure them in a pocket before climbing. Light the way for the folks behind you. It's not all that far, so let's be slow and careful."

Keven led the way past what would become Vanderbilt University Hall, with a large, brass plaque bolted to the rock, into the entry of the Corkscrew. The way up from River Hall to the start of the Corkscrew appeared much the same when Keven last led the Historic tour, but with one important exception. No torch smoke blackened the walls and ceiling. He led everyone to the upper level at last, with no more than one dropped flashlight, two dead-ends, and one scary balancing act he wanted someday soon to forget.

Still the tour guide, Keven asked, "How did you like the corkscrew?"

"Awesome!"

"I'm hungry!"

"Do we know *when* it is, yet?"

"No, not with any accuracy. We know it's before October 1838 when Stephen Bishop crossed Bottomless Pit. But how far back before that time ..." said Keven. He stopped when he caught a glimpse of light on the cave ceiling near the Rotunda. He didn't know if it came from cane-reed torches carried by Early Woodland cave explorers or from lard-oil lanterns carried by a cave tour. But, it would be one or the other. Archaeologists found evidence of only three groups ever coming in the cave: Early Woodland people, saltpeter miners, and cave tourists. Keven thought this group did not make enough noise for Early Woodland gypsum miners — or saltpeter miners for that matter. And he hoped for a cave tour.

"Quick! All lights out. Total silence!" Keven hoped his stage whisper conveyed the urgency he felt. He extinguished his carbide lamp and eased into a comfortable crouch with his right knee on the ground and his chest leaning along his left thigh.

The yellow-orange glow of light on the cave ceiling increased in size and intensity. The dawn of a clear day. A new day. A new day in an old time. *What was Myrna thinking right now? Were they looking for his lost tour? How would they ever find a tour lost in time?*

He thought he could hear voices, but no distinct words. Keven tried to play out the sequence in the theater of his mind. If a cave tour, they would be stopping and discussing the saltpeter leaching vats in the Rotunda. If the Early Woodland people, they would come on back into the cave. From his vantage point at the top of the Corkscrew, Keven couldn't tell anything about the state of gypsum mining in this part of the cave. The Early Woodland people scraped gypsum deposits off the walls of the cave to the height they could reach from the cave floor and from ladders improvised from trunks of slender cedars.

The glow of the light moved toward them. Keven knew Broadway offered little in the way of features for a tour to stop at before the wooden pipelines at Methodist Church, which was down the hill past where he crouched. They would amble by right under the ledge he and the Wild Cave tour occupied.

"Now, ladies and gentlemen, prepare yourselves. Over this next rise, we will enter the Church ..."

A cave tour! Keven relaxed – a little. Strange though it was, he knew when. Some time after the cave became a tourist attraction in 1816, but before that day in October 1838 when Stephen Bishop and Mr. Stevenson crossed Bottomless Pit. Keven relaxed a little because his cave tour wouldn't have to forage for hickory nuts, sunflower seeds, or steal squash and pumpkins from the earliest of cave visitors.

Up the hill, on the other side of which lay Methodist Church, strode a black man of medium height wearing a black frock coat and carrying a lard-oil lantern. He led with the steady, fluid pace of an experienced cave guide. Six visitors with lanterns strolled along behind the guide. A little farther back two men carried baskets, jugs, and more lanterns.

Stephen Bishop! Keven contained his excitement with great difficulty. Now was not the time to reveal themselves —

indeed, to scare the very devil out of everyone below them on the trail. *But ... Stephen Bishop! In the flesh!*

Someone close to Keven dislodged a small pebble. It fell six feet onto a lower ledge, struck a limestone rock, and bounced back onto the ledge.

At the distinct click of the pebble hitting the rock, Stephen Bishop paused but a second, looked left over his shoulder. The pause was missed by his visitors, but not by Keven.

After the party of visitors with their famous guide had examined the wooden pipelines and assembled at Methodist Church, Keven kept his charges quiet and still. They didn't know the half of how hard it was to sit still. He could no longer see the tour, but he could hear the voice of Stephen Bishop. The plaintive notes of a "country alto" female voice soon overrode the other voices straining in a hymn. She was better recognized for her volume than for her pitch. A loud *Amen* ended several minutes of silence.

Keven imagined that when they finished praying, they would head up the next hill to the second set of saltpeter leaching vats and the entrance to Gothic Avenue. After a few minutes to examine those vats, they would climb the stairs and spend thirty or forty minutes exploring Gothic. That would give Keven and the Wild Cavers time to move. He followed the tour in his mind. The visitors feeling the timbers of the vats, kicking around in the dirt — things that today's visitors, visitors in the twenty-first century that is, couldn't do in this National Park Service cave. Keven realized that Edwin Booth, the famous Shakespearean actor, would not have visited the cave yet, and so would not have tested the cave's acoustics with Hamlet's soliloquy from the big rock overlooking the leaching vats. Keven spent several minutes thinking about what to do next. The visitors on *his* cave tour were getting fidgety.

Sitting in the perfect blackness of the cave, Keven strained his eyes for any flicker of light. No spark. No note of sound other than the breathing of Dot right behind him and the ringing of blood racing through his eardrums.

Keven whispered to Dot, "That was a cave tour that just passed below. I think we're in 1838. I don't think anyone will be behind them, but just in case, we need to jog to our next point. It's not far, but we can't loiter. If we do run into anyone, please let me do the talking. Pass it on."

Ten
Rangers to the Rescue

Myrna puts on a brave face when Bob and I emerge from the Frozen Niagara airlock into the shadows of late afternoon. She shows confidence in Keven's ability.

"Nothing?" she says.

"No, not a sign," says Bob. "I need to call Denise." He punches a few buttons on his cell phone and tells Denise what we did not see. He faces us.

"Denise already alerted everyone. She felt that, if they were needed, the sooner the better. And even if they're not needed for a search, Keven may need help with a sick or injured visitor. The team should be here any minute. Denise wants us to wait until they arrive, brief them, and then we're free to go." He glances at Myrna.

"Can you give me a ride back to my car at the elevator?"

"Of course."

Five minutes drag by before a green, Park Service Suburban pulls into the loop followed by a civilian pickup truck. The two emerging from the Park Service vehicle are dressed in black tactical gear with climbing helmets and backpacks. I notice that they are not wearing side arms. These are the caving rangers. The two in the pickup are wearing standard-issue Park Service coveralls carrying white caving helmets and fanny packs. They are the guides. The rangers unload a Stokes litter from the roof of the Suburban. The rangers had modified the litter for use in caves. They will carry it to the first crawl way.

We approach the group assembled at the door to the airlock. Bob identifies himself and introduces Myrna. He summarizes the little that we know. One of the guides asks Bob about the route Keven took between Snowball and Flat Ceiling.

"Well, we can do a little better than that. Walt and I saw Keven and the tour down in Martel Avenue. He was headed to Cathedral Domes," says Bob.

"You were down there?" asks one of the rangers looking sort of sideways at me.

"We were photographing the Wild Cave tour." Bob does not bring up the lantern.

"They were okay?"

"They were fine. Keven was in his usual high spirits," says Bob.

The guide follows up, "How about coming out of Cathedral Domes?"

"I'm not real sure about that. It's been a long time since I led the Wild Cave. I think the options are not all that varied. Most of the time, you're focusing on the time, trying to get in behind the Grand Avenue tour right after they leave Grand Central."

"Right, But you don't know of any variations Keven runs?"

"No. I think he takes Robertson to a bridge that runs into Nickerson, and Fox to Grand Central."

"Okay. Thanks, Bob. Are you guys leaving?"

"Yes, it's been a long day for us old folks. Do you have our cell phone numbers?"

"No, I don't guess I do."

I take my notebook out. "Myrna, what's your number?"

She gives it out, I write it down above Bob's with mine at the bottom, and give the page to the guide.

"Thanks. We'll call Myrna first."

The team heads in at a trot, but I know there are few places in the cave where they could do that for long. Getting the litter down the ship's ladders at Big Break would be tough. Getting a loaded one back up boggles the mind. Even an easy carryout requires a lot of folks. That one would be anything but easy.

Once we're back in Bob's truck, I call Barbara to update her on events, and that we're dropping Myrna off before heading back to the Cetera house. She reports they've been busy getting supper ready. Barbara prompts me to ask if Myrna will come with us.

"No. Thank you," she says. "Keven has been a lot later than this from much more remote parts of the cave. When he was still caving with FRC he would be gone for over twenty-four hours. I'll be fine." The Flint Ridge Coalition conducts research and maps the cave.

I relay this to Barbara and ask her to pass it along to Zona and Mary. I punch out on the phone.

"We're having steak for supper," I report.

"Sure you won't come along, Myrna?" asks Bob. "Walt is grilling, so you know they'll be good."

"Thank you, but no. I have a quilt to finish, and he'll be along soon. It's just the Wild Cave." She smiled. We wait while she gets her car started and follow her on to the Cave City Road.

"Here's the thing about the Wild Cave tour," says Bob. "If something goes wrong, the guide is the only one who knows how to get help. Up to a point, that is. He can take a couple of the visitors to the nearest main trail and send them to the next telephone with a written message explaining the problem and their exact location. He can go back to the victim or problem or whatever. He — or she — can also take the whole tour to the phone leaving a visitor there to man the phone and run right back to the problem area."

"Unless Keven is the one out of commission and can't tell the tour how to get out. And they can't remember how they got there." I say.

"Yeah, but with this amount of time, they could have backtracked to the Snowball Dining Room at least. I don't understand how all fourteen visitors and Keven have failed to get some word out to the surface."

Eleven
Little Bat Avenue

Keven led what was now the *first* Wild Cave tour down from the ledge onto the trail of Main Cave, Broadway. Once everyone was down, he increased the pace and studied the narrow trail of packed dirt and rock slabs. If this was what the Civilian Conservation Corps had to work with back in the thirties, they accomplished a great deal in creating the wide, easy trail of Broadway. The CCC established four camps of workers in the park during the Great Depression. They did all their trail building with hand tools and wheelbarrows. Keven led the group up to the rotunda, which seemed strange without stainless steel handrails around the leaching vats. They crossed the rotunda at different elevations than the modern-day, smooth trails – never mind the pavers and boardwalk.

"We're going to Little Bat Avenue because no one will be coming that way. There will be little traffic there until they discover Mammoth Dome at some point after they cross Bottomless Pit."

"You mean, they haven't crossed it yet?" asked Josh.

"No. That's why we had to come the way we did. The bridge hasn't been built yet. If my sense of time is correct, they will build it soon. They haven't discovered the Corkscrew passage either."

"Wow!" says Josh. "More virgin cave."

"True enough. There was no evidence of aboriginal activity in the Corkscrew," said Keven. He wondered about the bats and their residue in the avenue up ahead. He hoped the Indiana brown bats were still out of the cave for the season. He led the tour left out of the huge expanse, of Audubon Avenue, into the narrow, square cross section of Little Bat Avenue.

"Ah! We're in luck," said Keven. "The bats are still out. Let's get back in here and have a little meeting." All of the Wild Cavers sprawled out in a clean patch of dry sandy cave dirt facing Keven who knelt in front of them.

"First thing. Switch your lights off and conserve your batteries. Second thing. We are in the year 1838. Stephen Bishop came to the cave earlier in that year — this year — but he hasn't crossed Bottomless Pit yet.

"Now to the logistics. In 1838, we can't go prancing up to the hotel and announce that we've just dropped in from the twenty-first century. It won't work."

"Keven, do you really think we've traveled back in time? I mean, like, for real?" said Josh.

"For real. Have you ever been to the Rotunda before today?"

"Yeah. Lots of times."

"Did it ever look like this? With no handrails? And where is the boardwalk?"

"Well, no, but holy crap, man! I mean, time travel?"

"The Department of Homeland Security has never acknowledged that time travel exists. There has to be a more natural, simpler explanation," said Rod.

"Can you give me any other explanation?"

"No, but ..."

"For now — or until whoever is dreaming this wakes up — we deal with where and when we are. Anyone see our situation any other way?" No answers. "Okay. I believe that the guide we saw was Stephen Bishop. He fits the description, and the one portrait that exists in the future favors this man. And that is to say nothing of the absence of lights, ladders, footprints, and the presence of the pristine gypsum in the Snowball Room. I think we have to accept 1838. I'm going to try to catch Stephen Bishop on his way out of the cave and see if he can arrange for accommodations and so forth."

"And some food," someone says.

"And supper," agrees Keven. "You folks have been great. Thank you. But our situation is this. We have no clothes for this period, and – more importantly – we have no money. It's not going to be easy." He counted on the levelheaded intelligence of a cave guide to not panic when he meets another cave guide from the future. What if it had been during the Civil War or 2,000 years earlier during the Early Woodland period? Or even worse, when various tribes of Native Americans called Kentucky the *Dark and Bloody Ground.*

"Keven, I think I should go with you to be the official representative of the government."

"Rod, that is very generous of you, of course. Right now, your department doesn't exist, and we want to win over their cooperation, and frankly, I think you would scare the hell out of them. I'm sorry."

"Keven, we need to talk about another problem," said Dan Ross, cutting off any further protest from Rod. "What about us being in 1838 — in Kentucky?"

"Ah, Dan. Yes. I understand your concern. We're going to have to be very careful, but understand, none of us will be accepted right off the bat," said Keven.

"Right. But Sophy and I are the only ones that risk being enslaved and sold to a Louisiana plantation to chop cotton." There were murmurs of support for their situation from the group.

"I know. And I think we can avoid that. If it comes down to it, part of the Underground Railroad runs through here, and we're only a hundred miles south of the Ohio River. We all must be very careful." The Underground Railroad – even at Mammoth Cave – was not under the ground in a cave.

"Thanks, Keven," said Sophy.

"No problem. Did anyone bring any candy or other food?" asked Keven.

"I brought some power bars," came one voice.

"I have some food bars," chimed in another. And so it went. Everyone pulled something from a pocket or pack. Keven took four Snickers bars in a zip-lock bag out of his fanny pack — a bit mashed, but the wrappers were intact — and tossed them to Josh. "Chow down. I'll be back quick as I can. Remember there's a hundred-foot drop at the back of this passage along with plenty of bat guano to slip on. Be careful and keep quiet." He was surprised that Rod didn't have a couple of Meals-Ready-to-Eat.

What a time to be without a camera! Keven berated himself on the way back to the Rotunda. He strode through the total darkness, looking past the pool of yellow-orange light cast by his carbide lamp. He decided that the best place to wait lay behind a pile of leached cave dirt on the left of the entrance to Houchins Narrows — and remembered that it wasn't "Houchins" at this particular time. Even in Hovey's book, it was "Hutchins." For the first time, he realized the importance of *how* he was going to be able to talk about the cave to Stephen Bishop.

Keven settled in behind a familiar pile of dirt and realized it must have been left by the saltpeter miners. If he recognized it, that meant the CCC had not moved it during their trail building.

He couldn't guess what tour Stephen Bishop was leading. He didn't even know what time it was. He supposed it might be morning, and if so, the tour could be going deeper into the cave for hours. According to his wristwatch, it was 7:15 in the evening. He was sure they planned at least one stop based on the two trailers with their baskets and jugs. Thinking about the fried chicken he had smelled in those baskets, Keven's stomach told him it was indeed late.

"Hello, Mr. Bishop, I'm Keven Neff, Mammoth Cave guide. How are you today?"

That sounded stupid. How did he approach a fellow cave guide from one hundred seventy-five years ago? The world's most famous cave guide and a slave?

Twelve
The Chief Ranger

We arrive at the Cetera's house out on the Sinkhole Plain east of Mammoth Cave National Park at seven-thirty, twilight.

"I'm going to take my camera gear on to the studio," says Bob. "Do you want to get out here?"

"I'll go with you," I say.

Bob said nothing until he punched in the code to switch the alarm system off.

"With Keven and the Wild Cave tour gone missing, I'd almost forgotten about the ghost lantern. Have you ever seen anything like that?" asks Bob.

I shake my head. "No. We went to see a ghost light along a railroad track in Crossett, Arkansas, when I was in high school, but the police picked us up before we saw it. How about you?"

"Seen? No. Several guides have said they felt things while in the cave."

"Things?" I say. "What kind of things?"

"Well, I've felt something — or someone — brush past me. When I was trailing a tour. There were those footsteps when we were in the Grand Canyon of Floyd Collins' Crystal Cave. Don't forget that," says Bob.

"No, I haven't forgotten the footsteps or the yelling at a tour. But has anyone seen anything? I mean in the last twenty or thirty years?"

"You know I'm out of touch with the guide lounge gossip over there, but I haven't heard that anyone has seen anything."

As we file into the kitchen, Zona, Mary, and Barbara are preparing a grand spread.

"Now, Bob and Walt, what's the news about Keven?" asks Zona.

"We haven't heard anything since we left the search party at the Frozen Niagara entrance. Did anyone call?" asks Bob.

"No, no calls. Are you hungry, Walt?"

"Yes, thank you. Very hungry." I hug and kiss Barbara.

"Well, you know where the grill is. Why don't you start, and Bob will bring you a Scotch."

With a strong sense of déjà vu, I lead Barbara through the French doors out to the big stainless steel gas grill on the deck. Bob always enlists his guests for the grilling. Cuts down on complaints, he told me.

"What's going on?" asks Barbara.

"I don't know. First that ghost lantern, and now Keven's being late."

"Why is there always something going on when we come up here?" says Barbara.

"Either planned or unplanned. That's the truth. How are you?"

Before we become too involved, Bob arrives with a tumbler of single malt in each hand.

"Here you go, your well-earned reward. How's the grill?"

After an incredible meal of New York strips, loaded baked potatoes, broccoli, salad, and Derby pie, we are all sitting around the dining room table staring at the damage. We catch up with Mary and her many activities, local theater, and other Cave Country news. Mary retired from teaching school and built a house a couple of sinkholes west of the Cetera's.

"Walt, you did a great job with those steaks," says Zona.

"Thank you, Zona. It's an easy grill to cook on, and I was lucky."

"Mine was perfect," says Mary. "And you said that all you could cook was hot dogs. I know better now."

"Thank you, Mary."

"Bob, what's going on with Keven?" asks Zona.

Before Bob can answer, his cell phone rings.

"Wait. This may be the park." He stands up and takes his flip phone from his pocket and answers. He steps away from the table into the kitchen. In less than five minutes, he's back.

"They found one of the Wild Cavers. He's been in the dark a long time. He's so upset, the rangers couldn't learn much from him," says Bob.

"Where was he?" I ask.

"Hawkins Pass on the way to Cathedral Domes. That was Denise. She wants us in for an interview with the rangers since we were the last to see the tour," Bob says, looking at me.

"What about Daran? He was there, too."

"I'm not sure she knows Daran was with us and not with Zona," says Bob. "I'm not going to drag him into this if they don't bring him up."

On our way back to the park, Bob and I theorize on what happened. Why would one visitor be there and not the rest? Why was he in the dark? *Where the hell was Keven?*

We race through the light traffic to the ranger offices in record time. In the paneled lobby that used to be a living room in an employee's house, we see Denise and her boss, Anne, who is the chief of visitor services.

"Hi, Bob, Walt," says Denise. "Walt, you know Anne, right?"

"Hello. Yes, we met last year during that bacteria thing," The reason Barbara and I are here this weekend is to attend Bill Soonscen's wedding. Bill led our small band of retired and former cave guides in that escapade. Before becoming a cave guide, Bill had been in the army, where he was in an elite, biological warfare unit. After we saved the bacteria, Bill moved on to direct the sponsor's research program in the cave.

"They found one visitor by himself?" asks Bob.

"Yes. The search team you talked to before they went in found him sitting on the trail banging a rock on the wall, laughing, and saying, 'There's another Wild Cave tomorrow, isn't there? Isn't there?' and so on. He would have been there at least five hours," says Denise. "His name is Craig … something. The rangers can fill us in on him when we talk to them."

"Bob, when did you and Walt leave them? And where?" asks Anne.

To me, Bob says, "When would it have been? About one or one-thirty?"

I nod my head. "We left the Snowball Dining Room no more than fifteen minutes ahead of them."

"Where did you see them last?"

Bob looks back at me and at Anne, "We saw Keven in lower Boone's. He passed us while we were setting up a shot at the bottom of the first set of steps. And then ..."

"You saw him after that?" asks Anne.

"Yes. We watched the Wild Cave descend the canyon. We didn't hold them up for another shot. After they left, we were setting up our shot with John and Pam playing Wild Cavers, and one of the visitors – it was Craig – from the Wild Cave tour came running up. Keven sent him to get Walt and me."

"What did he want?" says Anne.

"We promised Keven we wouldn't say anything, but let him explain it, if it ever became necessary. I guess under these circumstances, we need to tell you all about it," says Bob.

"I agree," I say. "Although I doubt it pertains to his delay in getting out of the cave."

"What happened?" asked Denise with a sharpish edge.

"As soon as they came into Martel Avenue, Keven and the tour saw a lantern moving along the passage."

"A lantern? Who held it?"

"That's just it," says Bob. "He said that no one held it. It floated about two feet above the ground. Keven described it, and he asked us to look around for a projector or something that could create that image. He led the Wild Cave off toward Cathedral Domes. I sent Walt back up to Pinson's, I stood around that bend to the left in Martel, and Daran waited over on the right in the dark," says Bob.

Bob nods in my direction, and I pick up the story, "When I came down into Martel, a lard-oil lantern floated at about the height you would hold it off the ground. It didn't give off any sound, smell, or light, but the flame did flicker. I followed it around the bend to where Bob was standing. It disappeared."

"Did you see it, Bob?" says Anne.

"No. I saw nothing until Walt came up. His eyes were wide open. I remember that." They were wide open, he shined his big flashlight right in my eyes.

"Was there anything else?"

"No. Well, Daran didn't see it either. Just Walt. We looked around. You know, for a projector or something, like Keven asked us to do. Even when we took our photography group back for a look, we didn't find anything," says Bob.

"Okay. Well, I don't know," says Anne. "I know this might not be ethical, but I don't want the rangers and whoever else is involved to think Keven — or the guides in general — are loony. For now, let's say that you last saw them in Martel headed for Cathedral Domes. What do you think, Bob?"

"That sounds good. I don't have a problem with it. Walt?"

"I think it's the way to go. I can't see how it's related to the missing tour because Keven led them on past the lantern spot; although, I don't understand either event," I say.

"Anne, I think you're right," says Denise. "We keep this to ourselves."

"Good. Let's go see the rangers."

The interview with the rangers goes better than we expect. A short man from Homeland Security gives a long harangue about putting the park under his jurisdiction if his agent doesn't show up before midnight. The chief ranger tries to re-assure him that extreme measures won't be necessary.

"This event has the distinct feel of a terrorist attack," says the short man.

"They'll be out pretty soon. Keven is an experienced cave guide," says the chief ranger.

"Has he ever been to Afghanistan?" There is general laughter in the conference room.

"Well, has he?"

"I believe he taught high school science before guiding full time," says the chief ranger.

They obtain a written statement from each of us — in separate rooms — and appear to be satisfied. As we leave, Bob asks the chief ranger about the member of the Wild Cave tour they found in Hawkins Pass.

"Ah, that's a sad story. He doesn't make any sense. I'm afraid the experience of being left alone in the dark — and whatever else he may have gone through — was too much for him. Poor guy."

"Does he say anything at all?" says Bob.

"Well, it's all gibberish," says the other ranger. "He does talk about stopping to turn his cell phone on, hearing a loud hum, and his headlamp burning out. He starts yelling for Keven and saying, 'It's me, Craig.'"

"We've checked the roster, and there was a man named Craig on the tour," says the chief ranger. "His ID matches up."

"Yes," says Bob. "He was the first one we photographed on the tour coming out of the Snake Pit."

"Right. I thought he was a good kid. We talked to him at the Snowball Dining Room when Bob got the model releases signed," I say.

"The strange thing about that was, this kid Craig also asked where Creighton had gone to. He wanted to talk to Creighton, but there's no one named Creighton on the roster. He's still in shock," says the chief ranger.

"You said his light burned out," I say. "What kind of light?"

"More strangeness," says the other ranger. "It was an almost brand new LED headlight. They're supposed to last for years."

"We don't think this kid Craig did anything to Keven and the tour because he left himself with no way out of the cave," says the chief ranger. "He's in pretty bad shape."

"Where is he now?" Bob asks.

"We got him a room at the hotel. He came here alone. He called his parents. He's tired, but he seems to be okay otherwise. Denise asked Alan to stay with him in case of nightmares. At least he didn't run berserk through the cave in the dark," says the chief ranger. "Thank you two for coming in tonight. Thanks to you, too, Denise. Keven wandered off track and got himself disoriented. We'll find them tonight, tomorrow at the latest. Not to worry," says the chief ranger with a smile that was not quite reassuring.

"Keven is not lost," says Bob. "He knows that area too well. Something else has happened." Bob's eyes are shining orbs of Lost River Chert.

"Now, Bob, I understand what you're saying," says the chief ranger, demonstrating that he has no understanding. "Believe me, I want to find these folks as much as you do. Anne, can I see you for a minute?"

Bob, Denise, and I step out into the parking lot to let Anne talk to the rangers. Light from the moon casts shadows from the oaks and hickories on the western edge of the clearing. The night air is dropping to near cave temperature.

"Keven is not lost," says Bob.

"No, I don't think he is either, but what else can the chief ranger do? He's got four two-man teams plus he's being dogged by that fellow from Homeland Security. But what happened to Keven?" Denise says.

"You're right," I say. "Is Craig talking about the Creighton I'm thinking about?"

"I've never heard of a ghost associated with him. Nothing strange ever happened to me back in that section of the cave," says Bob.

"Except for this afternoon," I say.

"Well, remember, it didn't happen to me. Just you."

"Right," I say. "Creighton's the guy who carved his name on a rock, and who may have left his footprints near Gerta's Grotto? Not much is known about him, right?"

"As far as I know," says Denise. "There is Creighton's Dome that is also on the other side of Cathedral Domes. I think that was where they found his name. But Anne is the one to ask. I do know that the footprints and the name were there when Kaemper and Ed Bishop mapped that part of the cave."

"But why would, for the sake of discussion, why would his ghost be roaming around down there?" Bob asks. "He didn't die in the cave."

"I don't know. I'm not sure I believe in ghosts anyway," says Denise. "I'm going to talk to Craig. I don't think the rangers are giving his story any credence. I'll follow up with Anne."

"That sounds good," says Bob. "Do the rangers have guides with them like this afternoon?"

"Yes. Anne tried to get people with Wild Cave experience. One on each team. They're still searching from Martel out to around Frozen Niagara," says Denise.

Bob frowns, hesitates, and says, "I don't believe that Keven's lost in the cave — and certainly not around Frozen Niagara. It doesn't make any sense."

"What can we do?" says Denise. She stares at Bob's face. I look from her to Bob. "Bob, can you and Walt make a trip into the cave?"

"I don't know about this sort of thing. I'm too old for cave rescue," says Bob. "What do you have in mind?"

"Are you guys available tomorrow?" asks Denise. "For a Wild Cave trip?"

"I guess we are," says Bob. "But if we're going in, can we afford to wait until tomorrow?" He looks at me.

"I don't think we should wait." I say. "We need to go now because we have the rehearsal dinner tomorrow night. Friday night, right?"

Bob says, "Right. Bill and Courtney's wedding rehearsal. And I'm supposed to take pictures. The rangers are going all out, but they don't seem all that upset, not upset enough anyway. Keven and his folks don't have food, water, or a way to stay warm. They're inexperienced, except for Keven. And who knows about the Homeland Security agent? So, there's nothing to be gained by waiting, but there could be a lot to lose. Denise?"

"Let me talk to Craig. We're going to need to eat and pack our gear. Why don't you two go home, eat or whatever, and talk to your wives. Meet me at the elevator at ten. We'll go in from there." I don't mention that Bob and I had huge steaks for supper.

"Sure. Walt?" I nod my head. "We'll be there," says Bob, glancing at Denise and back at me.

Thirteen
Stephen Bishop

"Mr. Bishop, excuse me?"

"Who's that?" said the famous guide whirling with a lard-oil lantern in each hand. After waiting with ever increasing anxiety for two hours, according to his watch, Keven had watched the small group of visitors trudging up the slight rise toward Houchins Narrows. They shifted into an anxious gait, appearing to sense the closeness of the surface, blue skies, and the green of the outer world. Stephen Bishop kept to his normal, regular, guide's pace, letting Mat and Nick take the tour on out. Leaving the pile of dirt, Keven ignited his carbide light with the characteristic pop and placed it on his hard hat.

"I said, 'Who is that?'"

"My name is Keven Neff, and I'm a cave guide." Keven understood what he said right after it came out of his mouth. He did manage to keep from bouncing up and down.

"Sure you are. You come up out of the darkness with a pop, there's fire spurting out of your head, and you call me mister? Tell me why you aren't Old Scratch himself — come to torment poor Stephen Bishop."

"Mr. Bishop, I can't believe I'm meeting you. Where I come from ... well, that's a long story. I know I seem a little strange to you."

"More than a little strange. And I'm not sure I want to hear your story. How'd you get in here?"

"I'm a cave guide. We've come a long way, and we're going to need a place to stay and something to eat. Will you help us?"

"Well, I can't let you go up to the hotel looking like the devil ... especially if you're not. And — more important than that — I have to catch up with my guests. You wait here, Mr. Neff, and I'll send someone to fetch you directly." Stephen spoke in an even tone and an articulate manner. He was used to sizing up people at a glance. His position – both as slave and as cave guide – required it. Keven did not think Bishop thought he was talking to *the* devil.

"Thank you, Mr. Bishop. I appreciate it."

"And if you don't quit calling me mister, you're going to get both of us in trouble. Call me Stephen like everyone else does. Wait here, I'll send someone for you. How many besides yourself?"

"Right. There's just me," said Keven. He thought it would be better to break this to Stephen Bishop in stages so that he didn't feel like Mammoth Cave was being invaded.

"But you said, 'us.'"

"Just a figure of speech. I'm used to guiding groups of people through the cave."

"Uh huh," Stephen Bishop shook his head. "Wait right here."

Stephen Bishop's outward evidence of excitement showed in his urgent pace up the Narrows. Keven had forgotten to ask him what time it was. But he had seen Stephen Bishop, the greatest cave guide of all time! Spoke to the man! In The Mammoth Cave! *If I don't calm down, I'm going to die of heart attack in 1838 and never make it back to Myrna.*

By Keven's watch, another two hours passed. He waited with Buddha-like patience, his carbide light extinguished, and a single stub of a plumber's candle for light and company — and heat. He worried about the others. At least they could huddle together to stay warm. While he waited, he went through his pack to see if it held anything he could trade for food. He rejected his Swiss army knife and his hand-cranked LED light to be too valuable to the group's survival. He had one spare pair of wool socks. He slipped them in the pocket of his overalls. *What would he ask Stephen Bishop? What could he tell Stephen Bishop?*

He heard voices growing louder in the Narrows. One sort of a clear tenor and quick. The other, a deeper, double bass rumble. He couldn't tell what they were talking about, but he could guess.

"Mr. Neff?" came the voice of the tenor, with nervous tremolo in it, from about 50 feet up the passage. Keven could tell they were more than a little apprehensive. He didn't know what Stephen Bishop told them about him. When the two men had come closer, Keven saw that the man with the deep voice stood taller than he, with a full beard. The other man was shorter, and also had a beard.

"I'm here," said Keven standing and holding his candle in his left hand. "I'm Keven." He approached the two men in the overlapping circles of lantern light and held out his hand.

"See? Stephen told us there was fire shooting out of his head!" said the tenor. "I knew he was just joshing us."

"Mr. Neff, Stephen sent us down here to bring you back up top." He paused and looked Keven over. "You're not from around here, are you?" said the man with the bass voice. He shook Keven's extended hand and stared at the Park Service coveralls and hardhat.

"Well … that's a complicated question. But, call me Keven. Mr. Bishop — uh, Stephen — said he would send someone. You must be Mr. Materson Bransford and Mr. Nicholas Bransford. I am very pleased to meet both of you."

"See? He called us 'Mister!' And he knows our names. I'm not sure Stephen should have told him our real names." Nick talked in a stage whisper and looked at Mat when he spoke.

"Hush up, now, Nick. That's right. I'm Mat, and this is Nick. Mr. Neff, that's mighty kind of you, but if we slip up and call you, a white man, by your first name in front of another white man, we'll get in trouble. So, if it's all the same to you, we'll keep calling you Mister Neff. Now, one thing Stephen got right is that you can't go around in those clothes. Here. Stephen sent this old coat for you to put on. Does that white thing on your head come off?"

Keven laughed. "Yes, it comes off. It's a hard hat. Some protection if a rock falls." He rapped on the hat with his knuckles after he took it off.

"Well you won't need one here. We haven't had a rock fall since the earthquake back in 1812. That's what they say anyway. And that's what we tell the people we take in the cave," said Mat Bransford.

Mat took the hardhat with the Park Service arrowhead emblem and hit it with his own fist. "Sure is hard, to weigh no more than it does. It might do better than these old hats we wear." He stuck the hard hat in a cloth bag and twisted the neck of the bag shut. Keven wanted to ask a thousand questions, but he could not settle in his mind what he could ask without revealing too much about the future.

"So, Mr. Gorin still owns the cave?" asked Keven.

"Yes, Sir. When he bought it, he brought Stephen over from Glasgow. After that he brought Nick and me over here, too. Do you know Mr. Gorin, Sir?" asked Mat.

"No. No, I never met him," said Keven, laughing to himself. "I have heard a lot about him, though." Keven worked out that Franklin Gorin was the owner, having bought the cave in early 1838 and brought in Stephen Bishop to guide tours. Gorin owned the cave for a few months before he sold it and Stephen Bishop to Dr. Croghan late in 1838. So the date was about right, and he thought he'd find out the time of day soon enough.

"How do you like working here in the cave?" asked Keven.

"We like it just fine," chimed in Nick. "Don't we, Mat?"

"That's true enough. We spend a lot of time trailing after Stephen. You know, carrying dinners and oil for the lanterns, stuff like that. Along the way, we're learning about the cave. We don't know as much as Stephen. Don't nobody know as much as Stephen," said Mat.

"But, I bet Mat here could give a visitor a pretty good trip. Couldn't you, Mat?" said Nick, staring at the ground while he spoke.

"We will soon enough, Nick. Mr. Neff, Nick here knows as much as I do about the cave, but he's still a little shy about talking in front of white folks. Mr. Archibald – he's the manager here – told us we'll be taking folks in the cave on our own soon. He's expecting a lot of folks to come here to see The Mammoth Cave," said Mat.

Keven asked about their favorite parts of the cave. He thought they were taking his sudden appearance with amazing calm compared to his own reaction to the floating lantern that morning. In a few minutes, they were at a dry-stacked, stone wall with a wooden door. The wall surprised Keven, but even in the early days, they must have valued security. Mat motioned Keven and Nick to the side behind the door. When he opened the door, a gust of wind exiting the cave blew out Mat's lantern. It wasn't quite a gale, so Keven knew the outside temperature was just a little warmer than the fifty-four degrees inside the cave. Appropriate for early fall. It might be warmer out here for the Wild Cavers. But where to put them? He and Nick went through the door shielding their flames, and Mat locked the door behind them. Once past the dripping spring over the lip of rock at the entrance, Keven saw stars blazing in a brilliancy limited to mountaintops in twenty-first century America.

In the feeble lantern light, negotiating the irregular stone steps was difficult for Keven. The two cave guides took them in their stride.

"Are you taking me to the hotel?" asked Keven.

"No, Sir. Can't take you there. Stephen said to bring you back to the back, by where we stay."

"Of course. I guess that would upset everyone."

"Yes, Sir. It sure would. And Mr. Archibald sure don't like surprises. Not that that keeps him from being surprised all the time. But he sure don't like them."

"No, he don't," said Nick.

Keven reflected on his knowledge of Archibald Miller, the man Franklin Gorin hired to manage the cave and hotel. Keven thought every visitor that made it to the hotel was a surprise. And their improbable demands of a remote hotelier must have cascaded into a series of ever-larger surprises. Keven followed

Mat up a narrow trail along the right side of the ravine. Nick brought up the rear. Vines hanging from the trees cast weird shadows from the swinging lantern light. Keven wished for his fanny pack, with the Mag light and the backup LED light. *Time enough to scare hell out of them later.*

At the top of the ridge, they emerged into a small clearing. The smell of wood smoke was the next sensation he experienced. Across the way, he saw lantern light filtered through a window and an open door of the hotel. No moon shone. Deneb, a bright star in the constellation Cygnus, the swan, blazed overhead. Vega blazed even brighter nearby. It was September. September 1838. He had gone back one hundred seventy-five years, a few days more or less. He was going to Stephen Bishop's cabin. He was going to eat supper with Stephen Bishop!

Fourteen
Back to Boone's Avenue

On the way back through Cave City to Bob's house, we talk about where Keven and the Wild Cave Tour could be.

"Do you think the ghost lantern is connected with Keven being late?" asks Bob.

"I don't know," I say. "We really don't know why Craig got separated from the group. But, I don't see how the lantern in Martel — or whatever is manipulating it — could be involved."

"Yes. There would be no reason to think anything else. When we saw it, the lantern didn't suggest anything beyond the ghost who was carrying it. So I guess it shouldn't suggest any more now that we know about this other stuff. So you think it was a ghost?"

"It's either a ghost or a projection like Keven and John said," I say. "I mean, have there been any apparitions in the cave? I haven't heard of any. Well, I guess that extra light on that after-hours tour sort of counts. But that was back in Main Cave, wasn't it?"

"It was. Near Blue Spring Branch. And those were Coleman lanterns, not lard-oil lanterns. But to answer your other question, I don't know any historic stories about other apparitions that weren't explained once the facts were known," he says.

We ride the rest of the way talking about what we will do when we're back in the cave. Coming up with no good answers, but with several observations about DHS. They felt that their search exhausted the possibilities around Cathedral Domes and moved the focus of the search to the Frozen Niagara section. Some bureaucrats cling with desperation to preconceived ideas even when surpassed by new data. I am sure they are doing their best, but I'm convinced – as is Bob – that they have missed something.

The house sits well off the road behind a small hayfield. Bob pulls into the garage and closes the door using his remote. Inside the kitchen, we are greeted with hellos and a barrage of questions.

"Have they found Keven?" asks Zona.

"I guess we better skip the Scotch?" says Bob. I nod. "Walt, you do the briefing."

I explain that the search team found one Wild Caver, Craig. Zona and Barbara remember Craig from our photo shoot at the Snake Pit, and he was the one who came back for us in Boone's Avenue. When I explain what little the rangers learned from Craig, there are exclamations all around.

"What happened to Keven and the rest of the tour?" asks Barbara.

"According to what Craig said, there was a loud hum followed by darkness because his headlight burned out. And silence," I say. "He was alone in the dark."

"And it was dark after that? That must have been scary. Those few seconds that the lights were out in Snowball were bad enough for me," says Barbara. Bob and I stare at her.

"The lights went out? What lights? When?" asks Bob.

"The lights in the Snowball Dining Room, Bob," says Zona. "They went out for five or ten seconds. Long enough for John to pull his flashlight out."

"When?" asks Bob.

"Well, we were still putting out the food. It seemed more like five minutes to me," says Barbara. "That's why John pulled his flashlight out."

"This may be important," I say. "It must have been some sort of electrical surge. That would account for Craig's headlight burning out and the lights in Snowball flickering. Maybe a pulse." That blackout may explain why Barbara and Pam seemed nervous about the elevator, I realize.

"What could cause a surge like that?" asks Bob.

"I don't know. Nothing in the cave that I can think of," I say.

"We ate about two-thirty. The lights blinked about thirty minutes before that. Where would Keven have been?" says Zona.

"It's been a long time since I guided a Wild Cave, but I guess he would have been close to Cathedral Domes," says Bob. "And that's where the rangers found Craig. In Hawkins Pass."

"Bob, does this flickering of the lights have anything to do with Keven's being late?" says Zona.

"I'm not sure, but it sure seems that it could have happened at about the same time as Craig was left alone in the dark."

"Any more about the lantern?" asks Zona.

"No. Walt and I talked about it on the ride back. No answers."

"We're going in about ten to look around," says Bob. An intense discussion begins, and it covers everything from what will we carry to when we will be out.

"Bob, we need to tell them about Creighton," I say.

"Who's Creighton? You're not talking about Craig, are you?" asks Barbara.

"Creighton was a visitor to the cave in the late 1840s," I say. "He was in the Cathedral Domes area, carved his name on a rock, and maybe left his foot prints in the mud. The name is still there."

"I remember that," says Zona. "Barb, I never guided the Wild Cave, but I've been back to Cathedral Domes with Bob several times."

"So, what about Creighton?" asks Mary. "Did you see him, too?"

"Well, we didn't, but Craig asked about Creighton when he was rescued." By the time we fill in the history on Creighton, it's almost nine.

"Bob, I better change into something suitable for Wild Cave," I say.

"No, you won't need anything. We'll change into Park Service gear because of the white nose syndrome."

"Right." I say to Barbara, "The bat disease. In case visitors or cavers carry the vector, they don't want it to spread any more than it has. So, we'll wear specially decontaminated Park Service coveralls and hard hats."

"You'll need something to eat and drink when you come out. Zona, can we fix a cooler?" says Barbara.

"Of course, we can. Good thinking, Barb. We can make some sandwiches with that ham I bought last week, and we can put some fruit in. How does that sound?"

"Sounds great," I say. "I'm thinking we won't be out of the cave before dawn. Not if we do much looking around."

"And coffee, Zona," says Bob. "Don't forget the coffee."

"How much do you want me to make?" asks Zona.

"Enough for Walt and me. Denise is taking care of the Wild Cavers."

While Mary and Zona pack the cooler, Barbara comes with me to our bedroom.

"What's your plan?" she asks.

"Well, Denise is trying to talk to Craig and maybe she can understand what he's saying, without the rangers' interpretive overlay. He's talking about some strange stuff. She's also packing supplies for taking care of the Wild Cavers if we find them. I'm hoping the rangers missed something, and we find all of them in good shape."

"You're worried that Keven's hurt. Otherwise he would have made some contact with the surface," says Barbara.

"Well, that's one worry. But, it makes no sense that the rangers couldn't find Keven and his tour. He's too good a guide and caver to be that hard to find."

"Walt? You know I love you and trust you; but you do realize that you have told me about seeing a floating lantern? You can't all be hallucinating, can you?"

"It's bizarre, I agree with you there. The thing about hallucinations is they're hard to identify when you're the one having them. I don't know."

"I'm scared. You do know I'll never forgive you if you don't come back?" She says with not-so-mock anger and puts her arms around me.

"I believe you. I'm coming back," I say and give her a big hug.

"What are you going to do?"

"We won't do anything stupid. At least I hope not. But we don't know how long we'll be gone. Trust me, I will come back to you. The rangers haven't believed anything Craig has said except that he's not with the tour, but they don't suspect him of foul play. Keven's missing and for some reason that I can't explain, I don't think we can wait. That means it has to be Denise, Bob, and me."

"Sounds like a good team," says Barbara, her arms still around my waist.

At nine fifty-five, Bob and I pull into the parking lot of the little building sitting atop the Snowball elevator. Denise sets four Coleman lanterns on the concrete porch. Before she sees us approach, she ducks back inside. Instead of Denise, a tall, slender man dressed in Wild Cave coveralls emerges.

"Hello, Bob. And you must be Walt. Remember me?"

"Hello, Craig. Of course. How are you doing after your ordeal?" says Bob. We shake hands.

"A lot better after some rest, a steak in the hotel dining room, and someone – Denise – listening to what I'm saying. That made the most difference."

"And you're going with us back to that same spot?" I ask, taking in his coveralls and boots.

"Yes, I am. All I can think of is trying to find Keven and the others. So, I'm ready to go."

"He wanted to come," says Denise, walking up. "And I thought that since he was there when the lights went out, and because he knows what happened better than anyone else, he might be some help. He's got all the same gear he took on the Wild Cave tour, including a new LED headlamp to carry – in case it has a bearing on this – but an old headlamp to wear. Is that everything?" she asks Craig. Light-emitting diodes are solid-state devices that operate on low voltages. Compared to traditional flashlights with tungsten filaments, LEDs are sensitive to any voltage surge.

"Just took my cell phone off the charger," says Craig. He holds up the phone and the charger.

"That's good, Denise," says Bob. "If nothing else, Craig can re-enact the five or ten minutes before they disappeared."

"Craig, tell us what happened," I say.

"Well, before I left for this trip, I studied a map of the cave. Based on that and what Keven told us, I knew that when we got close to Cathedral Domes, the rock overhead would be thinner, and I thought I would try to see if my new cell phone could get a signal."

"Did it?" I ask.

"No," says Craig.

"And then what?"

"I thought, 'Well, what the hell,' and punched in the number for a friend of mine in Atlanta. As soon as I hit send, that loud buzzing started. My cell phone shut down. My light burned out. When the buzzing stopped, it was dark. I mean totally dark! I was scared. And no one would answer me." Panic was back in his voice.

"I've been alone in the dark myself, but not for as long as you were. I'm sure it was scary," says Denise. "You handled it very well. You did just what you were supposed to." Craig seems to benefit from Denise's encouragement.

"That's right, Craig. So the buzzing started right when you hit send?" says Bob.

"Yeah. Right then."

"Walt, do you think the buzzing is related to the power surge that blinked the lights in Snowball?" says Bob.

"It seems to be."

"So, let's start with the buzzing, go back to Hawkins Pass, see what we can find, and go on from there," says Bob. "You're the scientist. Since this is technology, you figure it out."

"Thanks a lot," I say. "Craig's the one with the new cell phone. Maybe he should study his operator's manual to find out what kind of apps are available." Everyone laughs. The laughing helps relax us — a little.

"First, we have to go over to the dormitory so you two can change," says Denise. "We'll come back here and go on down. I'll fill you in on the way. I know bringing Craig along has thrown you a curve, but I couldn't tell him, 'no.' It seemed so important to him. I thought his mental state would be more compromised by leaving him behind. And he seems okay. The minute I told him I was thinking about letting him come, he calmed down and started making real sense. At least it makes as much sense as any of this. So, like I said, I couldn't refuse."

Bob says, "I agree, but I'm a little worried about taking him back into the cave so soon after he sat in the dark all that time. But if he loses it, we'll deal with it. Otherwise having him re-enact what happened might be the best option we have." I nod in agreement, and Denise relaxes.

"Thanks for understanding."

Craig emerges from the elevator building, and we load up in Bob's Suburban for the ride over to the dormitory.

At the dormitory that used to house seasonal employees for the hotel, Bob and I change into Park Service coveralls and find boots that fit us. We find hard hats, old style headlamps, gloves, and knee pads.

While we change, Bob voices my thoughts, "I wonder if Denise is right to bring Craig. He seems strong enough, but his manner is so different from when we met him earlier today and later in Boone's Avenue. I think his time alone in the cave traumatized him more than Denise realizes."

Just knowing Bob and I see things the same way makes me feel a little better about it. "Yes," I say. "In the cave, this afternoon, he was a puppy loping around eager to fetch whatever was thrown. Now he's subdued. In spite of that, he wants to go back in the cave."

As we rejoin Denise and Craig, Bob says, "Before we go in the cave, let's make sure we have everything, and we are all on the same page. Denise, you have first aid equipment and hot drinks, right?"

"I've loaded backpacks for each of you at the elevator. We're carrying all kinds of first aid supplies, space blankets, Thermoses of hot chocolate and coffee. Water, of course. Spare coveralls and socks. And sandwiches. If we find them, we don't know what shape they'll be in. At the very best, they will be cold and hungry. There are also spare, regular headlights. All set?" says Denise.

"Craig, do you have everything you carried this morning?" asks Bob. Craig gives him a thumbs-up. "Walt, did you give Denise the Snickers bars?"

"Yes, and I have my rock hammer and the whistle you gave me," I say.

Bob asks, "Anything else?" A round of head shakes, and we pile back into the Suburban.

Bob makes the left onto the Cave City Road. "Correct me if I'm wrong," he says. "We assume that the rangers made a thorough search of every logical location up to the point where they found Craig. And, we know that something extraordinary must have happened to keep Keven from getting out of the cave, or at least, getting his Wild Cave tour to a place where the rangers could find them. So, we need to be on the alert for anything extraordinary, anything outside of a logical explanation." I agree, and Denise and Craig smile.

"Given those guidelines, we need some illogical and outlandish thinking. I propose that on the way to Hawkins Pass, we let the cave help us brainstorm. No idea is too wild. Voice any idea. But at the same time, we should move as fast as we can to Hawkins Pass. While we go along, let's alternate periods of quiet, so that we can listen for Keven and his group, with our yelling for Keven, so that they can hear us."

Craig says, "My friends will tell you that I'm the right one to provide outlandish ideas. And I can start right now. Kidding about the apps on my phone aside, it seemed like I pushed the send button and made them vanish. One reason I'm so grateful that Denise let me come is that I feel sort of responsible. I know it's nuts, but I really feel that way."

Denise pats Craig on the shoulder. "Whatever happened, Craig, we know you aren't that good a magician. If you were, you sure wouldn't be pulling stunts of this sort in front of fourteen other people."

"Let's continue with the story," says Bob.

"So, Craig sat down right where he was, in the dark, and yelled for Keven. How long did you yell?" asks Denise.

"Not long. They had been right there in front of me. After a while, I realized that they weren't joking with me. They were gone," says Craig.

"What do you think happened to them?" asks Bob.

"I don't know. I figure it must have been a huge power surge to burn out my LED headlamp. I think the humming went with a power surge. But I don't know why it didn't blow up my phone."

"What happened next?" says Denise.

"Nothing for quite a while. You have to promise you won't send me out of the cave when you hear this." Craig glances from one to the other of us.

"We want to hear what happened. Go ahead with your story," says Bob.

"Thanks. Well, then this guy showed up dressed in old timey clothes carrying an old lantern that smelled of bacon. He said his name was Mr. Creighton," says Craig.

"You could smell bacon cooking?" I ask.

"Sure could. And it made me hungry, too."

"Did you talk to him?" asks Bob.

"Sure. I told him I was separated from the Wild Cave tour — he didn't seem to understand that part — and that my light was burned out. He asked where my light was, and I showed him the headlamp. He held up his lantern, shook it, and said, 'No, where is your lantern? Your light?' Like I didn't understand English.

"I asked him if he could take me back to the Snowball Dining Room. He said that was too far for him to go. He said for me to wait right there, and he would be back."

"Did he come back?" asks Bob.

"No. He didn't. I thought I was hallucinating. And so did the rangers when I told them and Anne about this guy. They thought I was crazy. Denise understood what I was saying. She listened. How could I hallucinate about some guy I didn't know about? And he didn't look to be a ghost neither. And his lantern was more real than that one we saw this morning," says Craig, excitement in his voice.

"No, your description doesn't sound like he's a ghost, does it?" says Denise. She seems to calm Craig.

"But if he wasn't a ghost, just what in the world was he? He can't be *the* Creighton," says Bob. "There aren't Creighton reenactors, are there?" I laugh.

"Go on, Craig," says Denise.

"Well, I just sat there. I ate a candy bar. Got cold, so I ate the other candy bar. I think I dozed off. When I woke, I saw flashes of light. So, I yelled for Keven. And I yelled for Creighton for a while. But no one answered."

"The flashes of light," I say. "Did they light up the cave, or were they bright flashes with nothing behind them?"

"Just flashes. I'm not ever going anywhere without a cigarette lighter or some matches and a candle. No where."

"The mind sometimes creates things to keep us occupied, particularly in a sensory deprivation condition like this. But the mind rarely comes up with Mr. Creightons complete with a smelly lantern and period clothes," I say.

"Go ahead, Craig," says Bob.

"It lasted forever, but my ears were ringing. It was so quiet. I remembered the story about that guy who was lost in the cave for 39 hours? So I started banging a rock against the wall. I started out banging randomly, but in a little bit, I tried banging out S-O-S in Morse code. That got me to laughing." The Charles Harvey story dated from 1838. He became lost in the cave when he tried to go back to where he dropped his hat. He tripped, and his lantern went out. When they found him, he sat in the middle of the trail banging two rocks together.

"When did you hear the rangers?" asks Denise. Bob pulls up to the elevator building, and we get out of the Suburban before Craig can answer. We lift the packs Denise has loaded, and head into the elevator to begin the descent of 267 feet to Marion's Avenue behind the Snowball Dining Room.

"These are heavy," says Bob.

Craig continues his story.

"While I was laughing, I stopped banging the rock, and then I heard footsteps. Several people this time. So I yelled for Keven, and Creighton again. The rangers blinded me with their lights when they came into the passage. I guess my pupils were wide open. Worse than the strobes this morning. I became so excited I asked where Keven was and where Creighton was. The rangers acted like I was crazy, and I guess I was a little. Crazy with relief."

"That's an amazing story, Craig," says Bob.

"The rangers think he's in shock, hallucinating, and is really hiding what he did with the thirteen other visitors and Keven," says Denise. "All at the same time."

"Yeah, Craig, what did you do with all those people?" I ask.

"I sure don't want to talk to that guy from Homeland Security. He's creepy, and I don't think he's very bright."

I laugh. "He has a very narrow focus."

"Do you remember the precise sequence when the buzzing started, and when they disappeared?" asks Bob.

"It happened at the same time I hit the send button on my phone. When the buzzing stopped, I was in the dark. There was no light at all."

"No light from your phone?" I ask.

"No. It was dead," says Craig.

"I think the cell phone may be important," says Bob.

"When we leave the elevator, we're going straight through the Snowball Dining Room — there shouldn't be anyone there at this time — and on to Cathedral Domes. Bob, you know that area better than me. You lead," says Denise.

"I haven't been there in years," says Bob.

"Well, it's been thirty-seven years for me," I say. That time for me was an after-hours Wild Cave tour within the first couple of weeks of arriving at the cave in 1976.

"I think I remember," says Craig.

Bob marches to the front. "Come on Craig, we'll break trail for these other two." Craig smiles, and we fall in behind the leaders.

Everyone seems to be concentrating, whether on listening or on ideas of where Keven might be, I'm not sure which.

Bob switches on the electric lights, and we hurry down the passage past the serving line, go left past the restrooms, past the concrete and stone benches of the waiting area, and unhook and re-hook the chain across the trail. I'm trailing so I cut the lights behind us. A little past Mary's Vineyard, we descend the steps into Boone's Avenue.

Along Boone's Avenue, Bob calls for a stop. "I want to try something. Everyone spread out along the walls." We fan out, and once we are all in position, Bob yells, "Keven! Keven!" We all listen. Nothing. Bob fishes his whistle out of his shirt pocket and gives three sharp blasts. No response.

As we collect ourselves and move out, I say, "I want to contribute to this out-of-the-box thinking. Craig may not be a well-paid magician, but the description he gave resembles a disappearing act except there's no smoke or noise, but someone is still gone. Do we need a magic word – and maybe some smoke and mirrors – to bring them back?" I expect at least some laughter, but everyone keeps hiking in silence, considering what I have said with more solemnity than I intended.

When we reach the fork with Rose's Pass where the Grand Avenue tour goes up and to the right into the narrower passage, our route angles left and down to follow Boone's Avenue. Bob leads the others down Boone's, and I break off to jog ahead to kill the light switch. With the cave lights out, I switch off my headlamp and scan all around, but my eyes pick up no mote of light. None.

I switch on my headlamp. Headlamps are more convenient when walking than carrying lighted lanterns. Also, we're conserving lantern fuel for later when we might need all we have for area light and heat. I catch up to the others who are tramping down the steps.

"This is where we set up for the photograph. Keven and the Wild Cave caught up with us before we were set, so we let them go on without any additional delay," says Bob.

"Right," says Denise.

"Guys, I haven't been honest with you," says Craig. "I tried to talk to the rangers, and they thought I was nuts. I was afraid if I told you about all this, you wouldn't let me come with you. Some of the guys – well two guys and one woman – and I have invented this app for our phones. Not the one you said, Walt. But it is a sound amplifier. What comes out of the phone is amplified – a lot. We have another app that is a signal amplifier. I won the toss to bring it on the Wild Cave tour. We picked out a couple of places in the cave, that if a tour took me to them, I would see if I could amplify the signal enough to call the team back in Atlanta."

I interrupt. "Georgia Tech?"

"Yep, a rambling wreck, but right now I don't feel so much like a hell of an engineer. Anyway, that's why I knew where I was when I made the call, and how I know where they were when they disappeared. I hoped that the signal would be amplified enough to transmit through the thinner layers of rock.

"I don't know what that might have to do with Keven and the others vanishing – if you want to hear my team's theories. I want to share, but you can't send me back." There was a little panic in his voice.

Bob looks at the rest of us, and we consider what Craig has told us. "We won't send you back. No matter." says Bob.

Bob fans us out along the wall, and Craig calls through his phone, "Keven! Keven!"

Again, nothing.

"That's a good app," I say.

When we relax, Denise says, "Surely Keven got the tour past here, didn't he?"

As we resume, I say to Craig, "I assume the theories your Yellow Jacket friends put forward have to do with alien abduction, parallel universes, or time travel."

"Only the less crazy ones. Maggie thinks I sent a signal to something deep in the cave, sort of like when the dwarves delved too deep in Tolkien's story, but in this case, triggered by technology. That wouldn't scare me so much if Oscar or John said it, but Maggie is the one with her feet on the ground – most of the time."

At the reminder of shadow and flame from deep in the Earth, I stop, and I see a look of fear cross Denise's face. Bob, our leader, breaks the tension.

"I've been trying to think of how this would work as a *magic trick*. I'm at a loss, and I can't think who would be the magician. Keven would never pull a stunt like that – even if he knew how – and I can't see a Wild Caver convincing a whole tour to go along with him either. Wild Cavers often get along because they share the interest of the cave experience. Up on the surface, they seem to be pretty independent types. So, I prefer the technology theory, but I'm out of my depth."

"Ugh," we reply together, so that Bob knows the pun is not lost on us.

I say, "We don't have magic to help us, but if puns will put it down, we are well armed. No one has reported scorch marks in the cave or any other evidence of that sort of devilment." We play our flashlights around the cave walls, finding nothing. "I think our best shot at solving this is to go with a technology-based displacement of some sort. It fits the circumstances better than anything else I can come up with. And, you said it earlier, Bob, Craig's phone fits in with that theory. If we don't come up with anything that makes more sense, we'll see where that takes us."

Denise shakes her head. "I'm willing to go along if we don't come up with a better theory, but I'm going to rack my brain for something else and hope we find a here-and-now, twenty-first century explanation. In fact, I would take a nice twentieth century answer if it comes to that."

Bob chuckles, but he takes on the abstracted look of someone lost in his own thoughts. Denise, too. Craig smiles. Bob, ever the leader, moves us along and shares a bit of cave lore to help us put one foot in front of the other. I think about Barbara and wonder if Craig's phone would let me call her, but I put that thought aside when I realize if the phone contributed to Keven's disappearance, using it could be bad. Denise seems to be checking behind us more than before. Unlike the rest of us, Craig seems chipper. I assume that's because he's shared his concerns, and Denise didn't send him back to the surface.

With Bob still in the lead, we descend the slope that leads toward Martel Avenue.

"Whoa! What the hell's that?" says an excited Denise who is right behind Bob.

I am right behind her, and see the lard-oil lantern moving down the passage. It's a plain, lard-oil lantern. It gives off no odor, no sound, and no light. I'm excited that it's still *hanging* around.

"That's the lard-oil lantern that Keven saw this morning." says Bob with agitation in his voice. "And, now we've all seen it."

"Tell me this again," says Denise.

"When we got here with Craig, Keven was standing over there," I point to the right. "He was telling the Wild Cave tour a story about Cathedral Domes. He took us aside and told us about the lantern and asked us to check on it after they left," I say.

"And?" says Denise.

"Bob went on around the bend over there on the left, Daran down on the right, and I climbed back up the slope and left the Coleman lantern. When I came back down with my flashlight, the lantern just floated on by. I followed it over there down the passage. When I rounded the bend, I saw Bob's light, but no lantern."

"And you didn't see it before?" Denise asks Bob.

"No. But I saw it just now."

"Okay. Walt, I understand now what you said about no sound and no odor."

"Right. And the lantern did not light up the cave. You saw it, but its 'light' illuminated nothing."

"I understood what you had told me, and I guess I believed you, but oh my God, it was still a shock to see it like that," says Denise. "Let's go. Bob, I think you should continue up front, but I'll be right behind you," says Denise.

We give up calling out for Keven. But we reach a sort of tacit agreement that we will not be conducting a straightforward search and rescue activity. I start composing a note to Barbara in my head.

Fifteen
Questions in the Cabin

Mat led Keven to a small log cabin beyond the clearing at the rear of the hotel. They were almost at the cabin before Keven saw a sliver of light leaking around the edge of the door. Mat lifted the wood latch and went in with Keven right behind him.

Nick said, "I'll be right back with supper," and started to close the door.

"Excuse me, Nick?"

"Yes, Sir?"

"When you're at the hotel, could you check the clock for the time? I want to see if my watch is right." Keven was thankful he still wore a self-winding watch and not an electronic one that would have failed in the EMP.

"Yes, Sir. I will do that," said Nick, and he closed the door.

"Mr. Neff, you do look less fearsome without that fire spouting from your head and with regular clothes," said Stephen Bishop sitting in a chair in front of the fire — the only illumination in the one room. The fire burned in a small hearth of sandstone masonry.

"Thank you, Mr. — er — Stephen. I appreciate all the trouble you're going to. I assure you, I didn't plan this."

"I believe you are telling the truth. I do. Here, Mr. Neff, you sit. With the one chair, we're used to sitting on the floor."

"You don't live here alone?" asked Keven.

"A single, male slave with his own, private cabin? Mat, wouldn't that be something?" Mat nodded his head in agreement. "No, Sir, the three of us share this cabin. We get by all right. I've never been on a plantation, not even on a big farm. Mat tells me we have it pretty good." Keven studied the room in the dim light from the fireplace. Three pallets were lined along the wall opposite the fireplace at one end of the cabin. A shuttered window about two feet by two feet cut the center of the end wall. Clothes hung from pegs in the logs of the wall. On shelves on either side of the fireplace, sat a pot, a frying pan, a couple of gourd bowls, some tin plates, and a wooden bucket with a gourd dipper. And there were two books. Keven was dying to find out what books were on the shelves of Stephen Bishop's cabin.

"That's right, Stephen. This is a good cabin, Mr. Neff. The roof don't leak, the chimney don't smoke, and we've got it chinked pretty good for the winter."

"Well, good," said Keven. "I guess I need to explain myself and where I come from. Maybe I should say, when I come from. And we have to see to the others." Keven went with his instincts here. He saw no easy way to break the news.

"The others?" said Stephen Bishop. "I thought you said it was just you."

"Well, I did say that, but I thought it would be better for you to get used to all of this a little at a time."

"Okay. Go on then."

"There are thirteen members of my cave tour waiting down in Little Bat Avenue."

"Thirteen? They all come with you?"

"That's right. I was taking them on a cave tour when something happened to us deep in the cave. And – and here we are."

"What happened?" asked Mat.

"I'm going to get to that," said Keven. "Stephen, have you ever experienced something strange or scary in the cave? Or you, Mat?"

"Well, I have," said Stephen Bishop. Mat nodded his head. "Every time I'm far back in the cave, and my lantern goes out. I'm nervous until I get it lit. When I'm near a drop off or a pit."

"Yes, I know what you mean about that. I've led tour groups in the cave when the lights went out and the visitors get pretty nervous until the lanterns are lit," said Keven.

"You mean, all your lights go out at once?" asked Mat.

"Uh — Yes, sometimes. I'll explain later." Keven realized he wasn't thinking everything through before he said it. Maybe if he concentrated on the Lantern tour or the Star Chamber tour, it would be safer. No electric lights there.

"But what I'm talking about is this. Do you ever feel there's something else there or someone else with you, but you don't see them. You can't see anyone else?"

"You mean a ghost? A spirit?" asked Stephen Bishop.

"Yeah, a spirit."

"No, Sir. I can't say as I have. You know, when I'm down in the cave, I feel safer and calmer than I do up here on top of the ground. I guess that's because I know that ground down there in the cave better than I do the ground between here and Bell's Tavern. I know what's where, and it don't ever change. White folks are nicer, at least in the cave. They're more predictable, too. I can't say that about out here. Why are you asking? You're not a spirit, are you, Mr. Neff?" asked Stephen Bishop.

"I'm no spirit, but some strange things have been happening around me — and to me. That's how I got here. This sounds strange to me, and I know it's going to sound strange to you."

"Go ahead on, Mr. Neff," said Mat, sitting on the floor.

Keven stood up and pushed the chair aside. "I can't sit on a chair while Stephen Bishop and Mat Bransford sit on the floor at my feet." He sat down on the packed-dirt floor and completed a semi-circle in front of the fire.

"You seem to know about us, Mr. Neff. More than we know about you for sure. What are you trying to get at?" asked Stephen Bishop.

Keven paused, trying to corral his thoughts, but they scattered like sparks from a Roman candle. "I know a lot about you, that's true. The reason I do, is that — there's no other way to say it — I come from the future." There. It was out. He had said it.

"The future? What do you mean?"

"I have tried to explain to myself what happened every way I can. I still might be dreaming, or out of my head, but I think

I've been carried back in time. When I woke up this morning, the year was 2013, one hundred seventy-five years from now — in the future." Stephen Bishop shifted, not quite rearing back. Mat leaned forward on one knee and stared at Keven.

"We were a ways back in the cave when we heard a loud buzzing. When the buzzing stopped, we were in the same passage — for the most part. One of the visitors was missing, and the cave looked a little bit different. There was no trail. There were lots of rocks that had not been there before. But we didn't hear any of them fall."

"What part of the cave were you in?" said Mat.

"Mr. Neff was in a part of the cave we don't know about, weren't you, Mr. Neff?" said Stephen Bishop.

"You're right," said Keven.

"What happened to your other visitor?" said Mat.

"We don't know. When the buzzing stopped, he was gone."

"Do you believe that, Stephen?" said Mat. He leaned forward again and stared at Keven in wonder.

"All right," said Stephen Bishop, skepticism in his voice, his hand motioning to Mat to sit back down. "Where were you this morning?"

"I was over on the other side of the ravine at the visitor center of Mammoth Cave National Park preparing to take fourteen people on a cave tour. I work for the United States National Park Service as a cave guide. I know this is hard to believe."

"You're right about that. A hundred and seventy-five years? And the cave is still there? I guess you've explored it all out, and you know every little tunnel out to the end of the cave," said Stephen Bishop.

"We know a lot more than you do at this time. Yes. But we still have found no end to it. It goes on for quite a ways."

"You say you are a cave guide. At Mammoth Cave?"

"Right."

"How do you get to Blue Spring Branch?" asked Stephen Bishop.

"Ah! A test," said Keven. "Well, you go out Main Cave, and it's the first major passage on the left after the biggest room in the cave, what we call Chief City."

"That's right. What do you find at the end of Blue Spring Branch?"

"Sandstone break down," said Keven.

"Where did Mr. Hyman Gratz scratch his name in the cave?"

Keven knew this one, too. "On the back of Standing Rocks between the second set of leaching vats and Giant's Coffin."

"Okay, where does the passage on the other side of Bottomless Pit go?" asked Stephen Bishop with a big grin on his face. He looked at Mat who grinned at Keven.

Keven did not hesitate when he saw the grins, "It doesn't go anywhere. It stays right there."

They all three erupted into laughter.

"Mr. Neff, you *are* a cave guide. I don't know yet if you're from the future, but you have most definitely shown people through a cave. And it seems to me that it was this cave. You have proved you've been deep into Mammoth Cave without either me or Nick or Mat here with you. And you were in there this evening without anyone knowing about it." Stephen Bishop crossed his arms and stared into the fire.

A knock at the door interrupted the short reverie. Mat stood to let in Nick who was bearing a wood tray covered with a piece of sacking.

"I talked them into some extra helpings, and there was plenty," said Nick. He sat the tray on the floor in front of the hearth and joined the others on the floor.

"Got enough for thirteen more?" asked Mat.

"Thirteen? Is Jesus and the apostles coming? I mean, are they coming tonight?"

"Just as mysterious, Nick, but maybe not so holy. Mr. Neff, here, has told Mat and me that he traveled back in time from the Mammoth Cave that is in something called a National Park one hundred and seventy-five years in the future."

"He is the devil! Stephen, what are we going to do?" said Nick, jumping to his feet.

"Well, now, I haven't ruled it out that he might be the devil. But right now, I think we're going to give Mr. Neff credit for his story. I don't think he seems slick enough to be old Lucifer. But he may be a sneaky old white man trying to put an uppity slave back in his place – in the cotton fields down south." Keven didn't like the sound of that and started to protest. Stephen Bishop waved him down. "But I don't think he's that either. Since he answered our questions right, he must be a cave guide. By the way he's dressed and all this stuff he has, we know for sure he's not from around here … or maybe I ought to say, from around now.

"Here's what we do. Let's eat supper ourselves and then go see what we can do about feeding the multitude down in the cave. Nick, did you get the time from the clock?"

"The clock in the dining room said ten o'clock."

Keven pulled his sleeve back to check his watch. It read eleven-fifteen. Close enough. He had no idea what time they kept at the cave in 1838. *When did time zones start?*

"What's that on your wrist, Mr. Neff?" asked Mat.

"Oh. It's my watch."

"You don't carry it in your pocket?"

"No, wrist watches are more common than pocket watches. It's easier to look at the time."

"Time must be pretty important where you come from," said Stephen Bishop.

"Unfortunate. It really is."

Mat took down a tin plate and a spoon from the shelf and put portions from each of the three plates Nick brought and handed it to Keven. Keven accepted the plate of boiled pork, turnip greens, and corn pone. While they sat in front of the fire eating, Keven formulated a hundred questions for these guides that he knew as legends.

Before he could start with question number one, they hit him with questions from three sides.

"How many visitors come to the cave?"

"What's on the other side of Bottomless Pit?"

"Are slaves still guiding in the cave?"

To this last question, Keven answered, "Slavery ended — will end — in 1865."

Stephen Bishop said, "In twenty-seven years. So I should live to see it."

"Us, too," said Mat. Nick nodded.

"All of you will die free men." Keven was going through agony. He knew that Dr. Croghan, who would buy the cave from Mr. Gorin later in the year, would give Stephen his freedom. Through his will, Dr. Croghan provided for manumission of all his slaves seven years after his death. So, in 1856, Stephen Bishop and his wife Charlotte – whom he had not yet met — would become free persons. However, Stephen would die in 1857. Because Mat and Nick were leased from their owner, they would continue working as slaves along side the freed Stephen Bishop and later by themselves. Their freedom would come at the end of the war. Keven thought that this time travel was harder than he ever could have imagined.

"So," said Stephen Bishop, "There are no slaves in the future. That's good."

"Well, there is no institutionalized, legal slavery, but there are people still forced to work for no wages against their will in certain parts of the world. But no, not what you're talking about, not in the United States," said Keven.

"That is good news. Good news indeed, even if it does take too long. I'm glad to know it's coming. From the look on your face, Mr. Neff, I'd say you were in some difficulty in your mind. What's the matter, Sir?"

"I could tell you a lot about what happens. But I don't want to influence what you will do on your own. I may have done too much damage already. The three of you accomplish a lot all on your own. If you talk about my coming back in time, I'll receive the credit for having shown you the way. The history of the cave that I know tells us that you did it all on your own, and

I don't want to diminish your accomplishments. The reason I know who you are is that you are still admired a hundred and seventy-five years from right now. I would feel terrible to take the credit that belongs to you. Do you understand?"

"What you're saying is, we have to keep you a secret. And you have to keep what you know about the cave a secret. Is that it? For our own good?"

"That's right. But I want to ask you some questions. May I ask them now?" said Keven.

"Go ahead and ask."

"How are you treated? Is Mr. Gorin good to you?"

"Yes, Sir. He treats us as well as I've ever heard of slaves being treated. Well, that is except some house staff. Some butlers and housekeepers, I hear, are treated like family. But folks that work in the house get no time to be private, except maybe if they can go to their own church service," said Stephen Bishop.

"I think I understand," said Keven. "So, you're happy, content?"

"Mr. Neff, I wouldn't want this to get back to Mr. Gorin or anyone else. You understand?" Keven nodded. "We still want to be free. I want to guide people through the Mammoth Cave because I choose to do so, not because if I don't obey Mr. Archibald, I risk being sold down the river to a plantation in Tennessee — even Mississippi."

"You haven't crossed Bottomless Pit, have you?"

"Bottomless Pit? No, no one's ever crossed it. Not yet, anyway."

"Have you been around it yet?" said Keven. He leaned forward watching the guide's face in the light from the fireplace.

"You mean, is there a way around it without having to cross it? That's what you mean, isn't it?" said Stephen Bishop.

Keven could see from the expression on Stephen Bishop's face that he was no longer with them in the cabin, but in the cave, going through the passages of the Lower Chambers.

After a pause, Keven said, "I've said too much."

"No, Sir. You haven't. You haven't told me anything. You reminded me of something, but nothing I didn't already know. Not really."

"Good." Keven remembered the socks and rose to his feet to pull them out of his pocket. "The only thing I have to trade for food is this pair of wool socks. They're good socks, but I have no money, none you would recognize."

Stephen Bishop took the socks. They were Vermont Merino wool with reinforced heels and toes. He rubbed them between his fingers. "Mr. Neff, these are amazing. Miss Ellie up at the kitchen is always complaining about cold feet. She'll love these socks."

"Good. I hope she does."

"The five thousand are still down in the cave starving to death. You go on back down there with Nick. Mat and I will go over to the kitchen and see if we can find some loaves and fishes."

Sixteen
Hawkins Pass

In Hawkins Pass, Craig says, "This is it." He goes over to the wall of the passage and picks up a rock. "Here's the spot I banged out the S-O-S." I see a small area of chips in the limestone wall. He doesn't seem to have damaged the cave very much. I don't know what I would have done, but about the same I expect. I think about the times I've been alone in a cave, but I always had two or three light sources or reasonable assurance of companionship within a short time. And fourteen caving companions never vanished before my eyes – leaving nothing but the dark.

We are in a level passage ten to twelve feet across that looks to be fifteen to twenty feet high. It runs straight for about forty feet and ends in a wall that slopes upward to the first of the five domes comprising Hovey's Cathedral. I kneel on the damp rock of the cave floor and go through the procedure to light one of the Coleman lanterns. The glow of the lantern dispels some of the gloom and the tension that I felt approaching the point of departure for Keven and the tour. I can sense some relaxation in the others, too. The light shows the brown of the irregular layers of the limestone and the black nodules of the Lost River Chert protruding from the walls. I rise from the lantern and step over to touch the nodules.

"That's the way to Cathedral Domes," says Bob. "But you stopped here?" He looks at Craig.

"Right here. Keven was about half way to that wall when I turned on my cell phone."

"All right," says Bob. Let's leave our gear here. Once we finish lighting the lanterns, we'll split up into two groups and check the different passages leading out of Cathedral Domes. Denise?"

"That sounds good to me. How far do we go?"

I light another lantern.

"You and Craig go down Bishop's Way. See if you can find any signs. Walt and I will head down Becky's Alley. I know the rangers and the two guides were in here, but you can miss little stuff when you're searching for fourteen people."

"And we're not sure how far they went after they found Craig," I say. I study Craig for a moment. He doesn't seem agitated or at all upset to be back at this place in the cave. I take that to be a good sign.

"So, Walt and I will take Becky's Alley to Lida's Pass and on to Gerta's Grotto. I think that Creighton's footprints were on the other side of the grotto. That's the way I expect Keven would have gone. We'll meet back up in Cathedral Domes after thirty minutes."

"Let's go," says Denise. She and Craig pick up the first two lanterns that I've lit. Bob and I take the other two and follow into Hovey's Cathedral Domes. They are breathtaking. In his 1912 edition, Reverend Hovey acknowledges his gratitude to the cave management for attaching his name to this incredible area of five majestic domes. At the end of the fifth dome, we admire Bridal Veil Falls, a small, but beautiful cascade.

At the falls, we split into our two teams. Denise and Craig enter Bishop's Way at the fifth dome. Bob and I backtrack to the first dome and head into Becky's Alley. After the height and grandeur of Hovey's Cathedral, Becky's is well named, and we emerge from its narrow confines to the place where it intersects Lida's Pass. We pause here to look for signs the group may have gone to the right, but that way shows no promise. We study the damp trail and see no footprints or other signs. At Gerta's Grotto, there are multiple passages leading on. Bob knows the way and leads us up Robertson to a bridge over a canyon passage in the floor. We have seen nothing to indicate Keven and his tour passed this way. Not that there would be much.

"We're a little over our time," I say. "I guess it would be too much to expect to find him right away."

"Yes, I think so," says Bob. "I haven't been back here in years, and we don't have the time to follow all the passages back in this area right now. Keven would leave a note or some sign if he diverted off his regular route very far."

"Would he?" I ask.

"Well, maybe. I don't know if I would have thought of it. Maybe not," says Bob. "I know the way I'm feeling right now, I want to leave breadcrumbs everywhere I go. Let's go back and see if Denise found anything." I nod and about face.

"Bob, what did you find?" asks Denise. We are in the first dome from Becky's Alley. Her expression is hopeful.

"No sign of anything. And you?"

"No. Nothing. What now?"

"I'm thinking that we should retrieve our packs and follow Keven's normal route to Grand Central Station. We can check side passages along the way. But I think we need to go in that direction."

"Sounds good to me," says Denise. "Walt? Craig?"

"We're with you," I say. Craig gives a thumbs up.

We climb down to Hawkins Pass and head for the packs. I haven't gone twenty feet when I trip and sprawl out face first, managing to roll onto my right side, holding the lantern above the floor with my left hand. After useless appeals to various deities, I lie there on the floor of the cave, my head twisted to the left, resting on the edge of my hardhat.

"Walt! Are you all right?" asks Bob. He crouches on my right.

"Am I hurt? No. Am I all right? No, just as clumsy as ever. But, look at this." I set the lantern on the floor and point with my left hand to a two-inch high ledge in the rock. It runs in a curved line along the passage.

"What? What do you see?" asks Bob.

"See this ledge?" I rise with a little groaning. I glance behind me. There's a precise series of arcs that intersect a three-quarter circle at the end closest to Cathedral Domes. I follow the three-foot circle on around to the other end of its arc, and succeeding arcs continue away from Cathedral Domes. The larger pattern is a series of overlapping circular cutouts. "Did you see this before?" The floor inside these cutouts feels smooth to my gloved hand. I take a glove off and feel with my bare fingers. The floor and the edges are glassy smooth. "This is not the result of a natural depositional – or erosional – environment."

"I'm not sure what I'm supposed to be seeing now," says Bob.

"It's a very clean series of precise cuts in the limestone floor. See it? Put your lantern over there. See the curving edges?"

"Yes, there they are. I've never seen anything like this," says Bob.

"What?" asks Denise.

"Denise, stop where you are and set your lantern on the floor. Craig, step over about ten feet to Denise's left and set your lantern down," I say. As they position their lanterns, the irregular – not quite amoeboid – shape appears.

"Walt – literally – has stumbled over our first sign of something unusual. See this cutout in the floor?"

"Oh, my."

We stare at the cutout in the rock floor about eight or nine feet wide at its widest and twenty-five feet long extending to the three-quarter circle at the end. A large, three-foot diameter cookie cutter cut about two inches deep, in precise, overlapping slices of limestone.

"What in the world did that," asks Craig of no one in particular.

"This must be it," says Bob.

"What do you mean?" asks Denise.

"Craig, is this where Keven and the tour were standing when you were using your phone?"

"Yeah, more or less." Craig scuffs over to the wall where he banged with the rock and looks back at us. "Yeah, that's about it."

"I think that when the Wild Cave tour left here, they took some of the cave floor with them," says Bob. "Or, rather, whatever it was that took Keven and the Wild Cave tour, took some of the cave floor, too."

"Incredible!" says Craig. "No one else noticed this."

"Are you thinking they were beamed up — or out?" I ask, still believing that science fiction must follow science fact.

"It's crazy," says Bob. "But consider the evidence."

"Holy cow!" says Craig. "Just like in the movies."

I groan.

"Bob, do you think this is it?" asks Denise.

"If my crazy theory is correct, Craig activated some sort of energy field with his cell phone. Back there where Craig stopped is too far away for the field to affect him, but close enough for his cell phone to activate it," says Bob. "And it caught up a cylinder of space around each person or object, which accounts for this pattern in the floor."

"You think Keven and the tour were caught up in an energy field? And you think the energy field carried them somewhere else? Please tell me you don't think they were disintegrated," says Denise, shaking her head.

Bob shakes his head, too, "I don't know what happened, but some of the pieces to the mystery are the buzzing followed by Craig's blown light and cell phone with a dead battery — and where it happened. And now, this missing slab of limestone."

"If Craig's LED light burned out, why didn't his cell phone burn out, too?" says Denise.

"Good question. Walt, any ideas?"

"No, not any good ones," I say. "If this is a *transport mechanism*, whoever designed it, would not have set it up to burn out their remote control every time it was activated.

Maybe the phone circuits are better shielded than the lights. I don't know, but that's a good question."

"Well, this shows us where the active area is," says Bob. "You can see what could be thirteen interlocking circles for the tour group – minus Craig – was standing. And I guess that circle at the far end was where Keven stood."

"I don't want to waste time on some insane theory when we should be looking for Keven, but this otherwise unexplainable area supports Keven's unexplainable absence," I say. "Let's see if it works."

"You want to try to *disappear* one of us?" says Denise, incredulous.

"No. Let's use something else for the first go around," says Bob.

"Too bad, we don't have a kitten," I say, smiling.

"Walt, that's not funny," says Denise.

"How about a bottle of water?" I say.

"Good," says Bob. "If this is an energy field, it seems to take whatever is inside some standard volume around whatever, or whoever, is being transported. The question is, does it always take the same depth below the passenger or cargo?"

"You mean," I say, "Will it take two more inches with the water bottle, or will it cut two inches off the bottom of it? Right?"

"Right. Craig, set it on a rock. Make sure all of it sits above the original level of the floor. We don't want a water bottle with no bottom in it."

Craig takes out one of his Nalgene water bottles and picks up a six-inch piece of limestone. He sets it on the rock right in the middle of the cutout.

"Scratch a circle around it," says Bob. "We want to know where it was — is ... wherever." Craig draws the circle with a smaller piece or rock and withdraws from the cutout area to where we are gathered at his original spot.

"Craig, let's see your cell phone — don't turn it on yet. I want to compare it to Zona's, which I brought with me. She has the latest model — as of last month anyway."

Craig digs out his cell phone from his pack and hands it to Bob. "They look identical. Walt, what do you think?"

I study the two phones, but smart phones show so little information on the outside. "They're the same brand. But we don't know if Craig's modifications make his phone the one phone that will work.

"Why don't we try Zona's phone and see if the water bottle disappears. If it does, Zona's phone is close enough," says Craig.

"Is all our stuff out of the zone?" says Denise

"We're clear," I say.

"Right. Here goes." Bob powers up the phone. Nothing happens.

"Craig, give me that number you punched in before," says Bob. Craig recites the number from the 678 area code in Atlanta. Bob's finger slides across the face of the small black rectangle.

"Damn! Give it to me again."

Denise looks at me and mouths, "Old man." We laugh, but loud buzzing cuts our laughter short.

"That's it!" says Craig, waving his arms over his head, yelling above the noise. The water bottle and the top two inches of the rock it sat on disappear. The buzzing cuts off. Our lights stay on. I see no evidence of the bottle. No dust, no smoke, no crackling electric arcs. It vanished. Nothing else. The top of the rock left behind looks smooth.

We stand stunned for a moment. Denise shakes her head as if to clear it, narrows her eyes, and says, "Craig, I brought you here because I thought you could help. This is *not* funny. Where is Keven?"

Craig, shocked almost to tears by Denise's accusation, denies that he has hidden Keven and the tour. "Not me!"

Denise stares at me. I walk along the edge of the cutout and pick up the now four-inch thick rock. The top is glass under my fingers. It's warm, not hot.

"Denise, I can imagine a conjuring trick that hides the bottle, but slicing off two inches of limestone from the top of this rock and polishing it? All in the blink of an eye? That's a bit much, don't you think? Who could have anticipated all this and set it up for a water bottle to disappear? No, it's something else," I say.

"Sorry, Craig. That frightened me. I know you didn't do it."

"It's okay, Denise," says Craig.

"What does our little experiment with the water bottle tell us? 'Just the facts, Ma'am.' No theorizing yet."

"Whatever it is, it still works," I say.

"Craig, is that the way it happened before?" asks Denise.

"Oh, yeah! It's the same noise, but I don't think this one was quite so loud. And it's a lot better this time. It's not dark, and I'm not alone." He nods his head.

"Bob, you were right about it taking a standard volume," I say.

"What do you mean?"

"It took the top two inches of the rock."

"Do you think if we put the water bottle on the floor of this cutout area, it would take two more inches of rock with it?" asks Bob.

"I'm not sure about that. There'd have to be a floor to it somewhere."

Bob nods and ponders the rock left behind in the cutout.

"How's the charge on Zona's phone?" I ask.

"It's low, but still on," says Bob. "Let's try it with Craig's phone and see if the bottle comes back. Craig, is your phone still working?"

"It's got a full charge."

"You think this is a revolving door?" I say.

"I'm thinking about a hidden door in a revolving bookcase in a Gothic mystery – set on a space ship – but on that same order. Yes."

"It can't hurt to try," says Denise.

"Wait till I'm clear of these circles," I say, scrambling when I notice Craig pushing buttons on his phone.

"I wasn't going to send with you in the target area," says Craig without raising his head from his phone. "Ready, Bob?"

"Give it a shot."

The same buzzing started again. And it stopped without any fade. The water bottle was not there one second, and then it was there.

After a moment or two of rapid breathing, Bob says, "It came back."

"Where's Keven?" says Denise. "Why didn't they come back with the water bottle?"

"They must have moved out of the active area," I say. "This is incredible! The bottle disappeared and then reappeared." I paused. "Just like magic."

"We know where the revolving bookcase is. We know where the secret switch is — the cell phone number — but we don't know what's on the other side," says Bob.

"Well, we can't do anything else until we recharge these phones," I say. "How about a charger?"

"Right here," says Craig. He produces the 120-Volt charger/adapter we saw at the elevator building. "Where can we plug it in? I have the 12-Volt adapter, too."

"The Snowball Dining Room," says Denise.

We enter the dim Snowball Dining Room, with the concrete floor, picnic tables, and serving line. When it's lit up, and there are people all around, it's identifiable as a fast-food joint. However, one that's two hundred sixty-seven feet below the surface of the earth. A lot of air moves through here, and it feels chilly after our hasty march from Hawkin's Pass.

"Craig, there's an outlet at the cash register stand," says Denise. "Let's plug in and get it charging. How long will it take?"

"Shouldn't take more than twenty minutes per phone," says Craig, plugging in the charger. "Pity we don't have a second one."

I stop at one of the picnic tables and unshoulder my pack. Under the security light at the checkout counter, the fresh cut looks polished. I remember cutting a section of Ordovician limestone in graduate school to expose some fossilized red algae. The saw left a rough cut that had to be polished and etched with acid. The top of this rock looks cut and polished.

I don't need to wet it to see that it has the oolitic texture of the Ste. Genevieve Limestone and not the crystalline, dolomitic texture of the underlying St. Louis Limestone. The one- to two-millimeter diameter spheres of calcium carbonate called ooids stand out in the polished section. A dramatic recess in the wall marks the contact between these two rock units in the vicinity of Cathedral Domes. This piece of rock came from somewhere above that recess. Over some unknown number of millennia, it had fallen from a spot higher on the passage wall, and we happened to pick it to support the bottle. And to act as a bridge across another, less well defined line. Or plane, or whatever.

Still holding the rock, I look around the dining room and think about my job here trailing tours in 1976. How there used to be a pay phone near the serving line, where you could call someone collect and say, "Hey! I'm calling from two hundred sixty-seven feet below ground!"

Calling from deep within the Earth reminds me of the question Denise asked earlier. "Is this a transporter, or is it a disintegrator. I think we know it's not a disintegrator, but is it a transporter?"

I join Bob sitting at the small, round table behind the serving line. "Yes, it didn't disintegrate the water bottle, but we don't know where the bottle went when it left our sight. Can anyone explain this in twenty-first century technology instead of as a science fiction story?" says Bob, a note of pleading in his voice.

"Please think of something that will not get me fired or all of us committed to the state hospital," says Denise.

When no one answers, Bob gestures for me to proceed.

"We demonstrated that some sort of device in Hawkins Pass makes objects, and we assume people, disappear. And by that, I mean they no longer occupy the space where they started out. They are not covered up or hidden. They have moved. It makes me think an advanced civilization produced this device. What would be the logic of placing such an advanced device in Hawkins Pass?"

"That's a good question," says Bob. "Why would such a civilization put anything, much less a transporter of some sort, in this remote area of the cave?"

"With what we know, it makes no sense," I say. I can see that Bob is considering our next step. His expression says that he is having trouble with it.

"So, what do we do next?" asks Denise.

"We follow the water bottle," says Craig. "We boldly ..."

"Yeah, yeah, I know," I say. "But follow it, boldly or otherwise, to where?"

"If Keven is alive on the other side, he has little chance of having a way back," says Bob. "And that is only if he landed among the folks who know how this thing works. And he is free to return. Without that piece of luck, he has no way of even knowing which way is back."

"You're right," I say. "If we can find him. But, can we get Keven, the tour, and ourselves back to the here and the now?"

"To coin a phrase, 'That is the question,'" says Bob. He looks at each of us. "We have a chance to bring everyone back. Keven has none. He has no way of knowing about the cell phone or any of this. I want to try."

"What about the rangers and Anne?" says Denise. "Shouldn't we call them?"

"I understand you're thinking," says Bob. "We have a chance to get to Keven and the tour quickly, and we 're pretty sure we know how to bring them back. If we call in the cavalry, all of that will be delayed. Maybe by days. That is if we could get them to entertain any of our ideas. Craig didn't have much luck with that." Craig nods. "They certainly had little use for anything Walt and I tried to tell them about Keven not being lost in the cave."

"I'm really going out on a limb here. It's my butt in the sling," says Denise.

"I know," says Bob. "But it's Keven. We have to try."

"I don't see that we have any choice," says Denise. "But you all have to back me up on this, right?

"Of course," I say. "We won't leave you hanging."

"All right, then. Do we go?" says Bob.

"At least we can try. That Homeland Security guy won't. If *my* tour is just lost in the cave – which I don't believe – they will find them. If they're where the bottle went, we're their only hope," says Craig.

"I'm in." I set the rock on the table and pull out my notebook to start composing a letter to Barbara.

"Writing a letter?" asks Bob.

"Yeah. A note to Barbara. You know, in case we can't come back right away."

Bob pulls out his own notebook.

Denise pulls out her notebook and pen.

"I'm going to write a separate letter to Myrna and Daran that describes what we think happened to Keven and the Wild Cave tour. And what we're going to do. I'm not sure what to do with them. They could overlook these letters here in the dining room. I think at Hawkins Pass, they'll stand out," I say.

"We have a full charge on Zona's phone," says Craig. He holds the black rectangle to show Bob and Denise.

"Great!" says Denise. "Let's charge up the second phone. I'm cold." She's smiling. So is Craig. The mood improves.

"And there's no chili to warm us up," I add with a smile. Even the hardiest of guides ate the Snowball Dining Room chili only when their hunger was overpowering. The resource folks for the park determined that the steam tables in the Snowball Dining Room were affecting the gypsum, so that resulted in microwave chili. While the visitors on the Grand Avenue tour have the restrooms at Mt. McKinley about an hour ahead of them, the Wild Cavers don't. It wasn't the chili anyway; some cavers wouldn't wash their hands before they ate. Too few went to the trouble.

"No chili, and no coffee for us either. We're saving it for Keven and his group," says Denise.

"Wait a minute," says Bob. "Are we going to wherever this device sends things and people and counting on making the trip back on one charge on one phone?"

"It doesn't sound good, put that way," says Denise.

"How about taking a twelve-volt battery with us to charge the phones?" says Craig. "We could take a battery out of one of the vehicles."

"Good thinking, but I think I have a better idea. Let's take a twelve-volt gel cell battery from one of these emergency lights," I say.

"Sounds good," says Bob.

"And we can use Craig's twelve-volt adapter," I say.

"Walt, can you get one out?" says Bob.

"Craig and I should be able to do that." Craig grabs a chair for me to stand on.

"Do we have an adapter to connect the twelve-Volt charger to the gel cell?" No one answers for a minute.

"If nothing else, we can strip the wires from the cigarette lighter end of the adapter and wrap them around the battery terminals," I say.

"That should work," said Craig, but he doesn't sound convinced.

I take the cover off the emergency light at the cash register. I pull the leads off the battery terminal one by one and lay them back well away from each other. The battery slides right out.

"Great," says Bob. "How do we carry it?"

The rock goes behind the checkout stand to make room for the battery in my pack.

"Walt, do you think the ghost lantern will be there when we go back?" asks Bob. The lantern stayed hidden on our trek back to Snowball Dining Room.

"It's been pretty consistent," I say. "Going in that direction."

"Can I go first?" asks Craig.

"Sure. Why not?" says Denise.

We string out in single file in Boone's Avenue using our headlights in the narrow, twisting passage. With our repeated trips through this passage, we make the left fork before I expect it. In a few minutes, we're at the slope leading down to Martel Avenue.

"I want to try an experiment," says Craig stopping us at the top of the slope. "Can we spare a couple of minutes?"

"Just a couple," says Denise. "I have to work later today." And she nods her head to reinforce her consent.

"What are you going to do?" asks Bob.

"I want to go into the passage as slow and quiet as I can with only a little light. I bought this little key-chain light in the hotel gift shop." He holds up a tiny light in the shape of a yellow hardhat on a key chain. "I can see to climb down, but not wash anything out with too strong a light, and alone, I can hear better, too. To see if I can tell where the lantern appears first. I'll whistle for you to come on down."

"Okay," says Bob. "Give it a shot. We'll switch our headlights off and keep quiet until we hear your whistle." Bob clicks off his headlamp. I think Craig has his confidence back, which is good. And, he's not afraid of the dark – not now anyway. I hear a sigh of compliance from Denise. She's working on a long day and wants this to end well, and be over and done with. And, she thinks this will be over tonight?

We stand in the dark and quiet. I hear Denise shuffling her feet and sniffling. Bob hums the tune "To Each his Dulcinea" from *Man of La Mancha*. I resist the temptation to do squeaky bat imitations.

Time seems to stop while we wait in the dark. At last, we hear a faint whistle.

"I thought he lost his way or ran off," says Denise, switching on her headlight.

"How long have we stood here?" I ask.

"Almost ten minutes," says Bob.

"Let's go," I say. I'm worried about what Craig has been doing.

"As we half leap down into Martel, we see Craig's hardhat on the floor. He sits beside it.

"Craig, what happened?" asks Denise.

"I'm not ... not sure." He shakes his head and holds it with both hands.

"Sit right there, and don't move," says Denise. She drops her pack and takes a pen light from her pocket. "Walt, light a lantern." She kneels beside Craig and unclips her fanny pack from her waist. When I light the Coleman, I see the red cross on the green pack.

Denise goes through the routine of checking pulse, pupil reaction, and the how-many-fingers-do-you-see routine. Craig checks out well.

"Now, how do you feel?" she asks.

"A little fuzzy, but okay," says Craig.

"Can you tell us what happened?"

"I crept along, real quiet like. When I stopped right here, I saw the lantern moving to the left. There was no sound. Nothing."

"Then what?" asks Denise.

"This black shadow fell across my field of vision, and I felt something brush against my shoulder. When I jumped, I lost my balance."

"Did you hit your head? Why is your hardhat off?" asks Denise.

"I'm not sure. Well, I didn't snap my chinstrap. I think it came off when I fell."

"Can you stand up?" asks Denise. Bob and I crouch on either side of him.

Craig nods. Bob and I each grab an arm, and in so doing, hinder his standing, but he makes it to full up right. Denise goes through another series of checks and seems satisfied.

"Are you dizzy at all?" she asks.

"No, I'm fine." He shakes loose of our grips. "Woo! What was that?" He's just come to himself. Craig is having a pretty rough day. I'm wondering how much he's reporting and how much — if any — he's embellishing. The focus has been on him a good bit since the photo shoot at the Snake Pit in Cleaveland's Avenue. Then being the one left behind. All in all, quite a day.

"You need an emergency room," says Denise.

"No! I'm all right," says Craig. "We have to find Keven."

"Bob, what do you think?" asks Denise.

"I don't know. I'm not a doctor, and I'm not on duty."

"It's not far to Hawkins Pass," I say. "Let's see how he does. We can cancel any time before we ... uh, go too far. As it were."

Bob and Denise nod. Craig smiles and puts on his hardhat, careful to snap the chinstrap in place. Bob pats him on the shoulder, and we head off.

"When Hovey wrote about coming back here, he mentioned seeing the automobile headlight and battery that Mr. Pinson carried into the area in order to see the domes better. I now have a better understanding of why Pinson left the light and battery in the cave," I say.

Back in Hawkins Pass, I set my lantern down near Craig's
original spot. The contrast of the cutout with the regular cave
floor stands out now that we know about it.

"Denise, how do you want to do this?" says Bob.

"I'm sorry to say this," says Denise, "But we all can't go.
I'm not sure Craig should go even if we could ..."

"I'm not being left behind again! Alone, in the dark, or
otherwise."

"You're right, Denise, the letter to Myrna could be useful,
but we need more than that," says Bob. "We need someone to
stay behind to bring in the cavalry if things don't work out and
to explain in detail what we have discovered, what we think
this machine is, and how we think it works. The letter alone
could be dismissed as the ramblings of a crazy geologist. We
need some backup."

"Thanks, Bob. I think Craig has a valid position," I say.
"And I agree, Denise, someone should stay."

The discussion runs on for five minutes. In the end, Denise
agrees to stay after I point out only she has official status, and
as such, has no permission to leave this universe, set of
dimensions, star system, and go to wherever the hell this
contraption will send us. Of the four of us, she alone has a
chance of convincing the rangers that we're not just a bunch of
old cave guides gone loony. And they already believe Craig is
delusional.

We agree that if the three of us disappear, Denise will wait
for two hours in case we come back right away. If, after two
hours, no one appears, she will go to the surface and arrange
for Anne to provide relief and backup. If after twenty-four
hours, we're not back, Anne will call in serious support. I hand
her my letters. Bob and Craig give her theirs.

"All right, folks," says Bob. "I don't want to take a chance
on this two-inch margin thing. Let's find some rocks to stand
on. Try for at least six inches thick. And then we'll give this
machine a go." The three of us wind up with two rocks apiece.
Craig sets the battery on three other rocks. All meet Bob's

dimensional requirements and are slab-shaped to give us secure footing.

"Denise, let's double check. In case we don't come back in a reasonable time, and the rangers decide to come behind us, they will need the phone number of Craig's Atlanta friend and the model number of the smart phone. Right?" says Bob.

"I have it, and I will write down the exact time you disappear – or whatever," says Denise.

"I have Zona's phone, with the number stored in it. We have the battery and the adapter. Are we set?" He checks with Craig and me.

"My phone has a full charge," says Craig. "And here's the charger. Bob, I think it would be better to use your phone to send us out, and use my phone to bring the large group back since we know mine will handle a large group. What do you think?"

"Sounds reasonable," says Bob. He takes Zona's smart phone out of his pocket and powers it up. He brings up the phone number.

We are standing on our rocks about six feet apart in triangle formation.

"Good luck," says Denise.

Bob smiles and pushes *send*.

Seventeen
Feeding the Five Thousand

"Nick, how do you like guiding cave tours?" Keven asked while they followed the narrow path along the side of the ravine leading to the mouth of the cave. Keven carried a lard-oil lantern in one hand and the bag with his caving helmet in the other.

"I like it just fine. But you know, I'm still learning all this while Mat and me go along to help Stephen with all the stuff for the guests. You know, the food, and the wine, and oil for the lanterns. It's like Stephen says all the time, 'Down here, we're in control. It's our world. We have the attention of white folks, when we're down in the cave.' Most of them, rich people. I mean poor folks can't afford to come to the cave."

"What about Mr. Miller, how do you like him?"

"Mr. Archibald is a good man. He likes the cave as much as anyone, except maybe Stephen. He keeps up with what Stephen and we are doing. He gets Stephen to show him everywhere he's been."

"Does Stephen show him all of his latest discoveries?" asked Keven.

Nick stopped to stare at Keven before they went through the gate at the entrance. Once the lanterns were re-lit, he said, "Stephen says he does. When he takes Mr. Archibald in the cave, the two of them always go alone. So I don't know what he shows him and what he don't."

"What about the Indian mummies? Do you know where they're buried?"

"This is no place to be talking about dead people. No, Sir," said Nick. They trod on in silence and exited from the Narrows into the Rotunda. Keven detoured to retrieve his fanny pack from behind the mound of dirt where he had waited for Stephen Bishop.

"What's that you got, Mr. Neff?" said Nick.

"This is my pack. It carries my stuff on cave trips." Keven held it out for Nick to examine. Nick rubbed the material with his fingers.

"It feels funny. What kind of hide is that?"

Keven repressed the inclination to say, *Naugahyde*.

"It's not from an animal." He was close to being baffled by how to explain plastics when an idea struck him. "You know how some oil will set up like a wax, but if you heat it a little, it changes back to oil?" Nick nodded. "Well, some scientists figured out how to make threads and cloth from oil that stays solid except when it gets very hot."

"Uh huh. Scientists," said Nick. "So, you don't carry baskets in the cave?"

"No, no baskets."

"What all you got in your pack there?"

"The light on my helmet — my hardhat — burns a gas, and I carry water and carbide — uh — fuel for the light, a candle, a spare light, and a few things like that."

"If you carry a candle and a spare light, what is the spare light?" asked Nick.

Oh, brother, thought Keven. How am I going to dig myself out of this hole?

At that moment they entered Little Bat Avenue.

"Hello, I'm back," said Keven.

"We thought you left us to starve to death here in the cave."

"Where the hell have you been?" That came from Rod.

"We are starving to death!"

"I knew I should have gone back when we saw that lantern."

"Who's that with you?"

He was pleased that the group stayed together and was no more than a little grouchy.

"Hold on a minute. I'm sorry we took so long, but there's no burger place right around the corner. Or anywhere else for that matter. But they are bringing food in a few minutes." Keven surveyed the thirteen faces. They looked hungry, tired, and he thought, more than a little frightened. Those were natural reactions. Everyone sat or laid on the cave floor. They had taken their hardhats off, and green and orange glow sticks provided dim light. Rod knelt at the rear of the group.

"This is Mr. Nick Bransford, the famous guide. Mat Bransford and Stephen Bishop are bringing you something to eat."

The group stared at Nick. He grinned and said, "Welcome to The Mammoth Cave. Just call me Nick, okay?"

A voice from the back, "Nick, what year are we is it?"

"Well, young sir, it's the year of our Lord, 1838."

"Holy crap!"

"I'm mighty sorry that I offended you, Sir. Please accept my apology," said Nick.

"Nick, please understand," said Keven. "He's not upset with you. In our time, that expression means that he finds what you said to be incredible. There's nothing religious about it. He was amazed when you confirmed what we had guessed." Keven instructed everyone to introduce himself or herself. It occurred to Keven that Nick wouldn't know the word "crap" either.

Rod made a production of it. "I am with the U.S. Department of Homeland Security on detachment to evaluate weaknesses for terrorist attacks."

"Yes, Sir. I'm mighty proud for you. Mighty proud, Sir."

The last to introduce themselves were the black couple from Atlanta.

"I'm Dan Ross, and this is my wife Sophy, from Atlanta, Georgia. We are honored to meet you Mr. Bransford. You are an inspiration."

"Mr. Ross, I am excited to meet you, Sir. And you, Miss Sophy. May I ask? Are you working for the tour? You know, servants?"

"No, sir. We are visitors on the tour," said Dan.

"Are you free?" asked Nick.

"My great, great, great grandfather was a slave on an indigo plantation in South Carolina. He was freed in 1865 at the end of the war. My father is in the Georgia legislature," said Dan Ross.

"War? What war?" asked Nick.

"Nick, there will be a war between the southern states and the U.S. government that starts in 1861. It will be over slavery. The federal government will win in 1865, and all slaves will be set free," said Dan.

"Hallelujah! Then what Mr. Neff told us is true. Now, Mr. Neff, I didn't doubt what you said, but it's good to see some flesh and blood evidence – as they say," said Nick. "In the legislature with all the white men?"

"That's what he means. You will be free, Nick. And for a long time," said Keven.

"And what happens to me?"

"You keep working here at the cave, and you are respected and honored by those you guide into the cave."

"My, oh my. Praise the Lord."

Nick went around and shook hands with everyone again. Keven organized them a little better out in Audubon Avenue in preparation for the picnic. He rummaged through his pack and found four wet-wipes sealed in individual packages. He passed them around for people to wipe their hands and share. It was the best he could do. Nick lingered with Dan and Sophy Ross.

Keven prepared to settle down and wait for Stephen and Mat when he saw the glow of light and heard voices from the Rotunda.

"Mr. Neff, is that you?" It was Stephen Bishop's voice.

"Here we are." He saw Stephen and Mat carrying baskets and buckets in one hand and lanterns in the other."

"May the Lord have mercy on our souls," said Mat. "You were telling the absolute truth, weren't you, Mr. Neff?"

"Everyone, this is Mr. Mat Bransford, the great, great, great grandfather of a cave guide in our time at Mammoth Cave

National Park," said Keven. "In the time that we come from, that is."

The expression on Mat's face was unbelievable. He was astonished. "My great, great, great grandson? He's a cave guide, like you?"

"He is indeed. His father wasn't a guide, but that generation of your descendants was the only one not to guide cave tours. But he is. And a good one, too." Stephen Bishop looked at Keven. The look on Stephen Bishop's face brought Keven near to tears.

"What about me, Mr. Neff?" asked Stephen Bishop.

"Stephen, you die a free man with a wife and a son. History tells us a lot about you. You are well known and respected. But we know very little about your descendants." Keven paused and swallowed the lump in his throat. He knew that Stephen Bishop would die in 1857, one year after Dr. Croghan, granted Stephen his freedom in his will. And his son does not survive the Civil War. But Keven says, "No more. We can talk no more of the future without causing more trouble than all of us put together can sort out."

"I bet you folks are hungry," said Stephen Bishop.

"Yes! We're starving."

"Mr. Neff, we did the best we could, but it's pretty slim. We brought burgoo and corn pone."

"Thank you," came the chorus from the group. As they brought out the food, a question came up.

"What's burgoo?" asked Dylan.

"Where I come from in Harlan," says Josh, "it's stew made from whatever you have to hand. It might be squirrel, might be deer, whatever. And it's always kind of spicy." The two iron pots of burgoo were steaming. It was thick. Keven thought he recognized pieces of turnip or potato. The corn bread was a little stale. Stephen Bishop passed out an assortment of spoons, most of them wooden.

The Wild Cavers divided into two groups: one around each pot. Dylan dug in with enthusiasm, and the others followed his lead and took turns dipping out spoonfuls of the stew. Mat carried two buckets of water, each with its own gourd dipper. The group ate with gusto, and their appreciation showed in the empty pots. With the way they drank the water, the burgoo must have been spicy.

Keven remembered a number of Wild Cave groups that he was so glad to be rid of when he came out at Frozen Niagara that he wanted to ride back to the visitor center on another bus, but not these folks. They were real troopers.

"Mr. Neff, Miss Ellie liked the socks so much, she said she's going to fix you a 'possum tomorrow."

Keven smiled with genuine appreciation, which masked his concern. *If we had been dining with the Adenans, a 'possum would be a luxury.*

Josh said, "Mr. Bishop, please tell Miss Ellie she makes real good burgoo."

"I will, Sir. She will appreciate that."

Eighteen
Sleeping in Church

With immediate needs met, Keven's visitors relaxed into a more comfortable and somewhat less anxious state of mind, other questions surfaced.

"Keven, where are we going to sleep?"

"When can we go outside?"

"Keven, we need to get organized," said Rod.

"Those are good questions," said Keven. "This is 1838. The cave hotel is small. Tiny. And even if with adequate room, can you imagine the uproar we would create marching in claiming to be from the twenty-first century? Remember, we have no money. We don't look normal for 1838. If we weren't strung up or burned at the stake, at a minimum, we would be locked up. No, we're going to have to stay down here for now. Stephen, do you think we could run them out on the surface around sunrise before most people would be down around the mouth of the cave?"

"Yes, Sir. We can take them up the bluff behind the mouth of the cave. Most of the guests at the hotel are leaving in the morning. I don't think anyone will be coming down around the mouth."

Rod came to stand by Keven and Stephen Bishop. "Steve, I'm with the U.S. Department of Homeland Security and should be officially in charge of this group."

"Nice to meet you, Sir. I am glad you are here," said Stephen Bishop.

"Why can't we go outside now?" said one of the Wild Cavers. Rod was frittering all around, but no one paid any attention to him.

"This is an environment that you are not familiar with," said Keven. "There is no moon tonight, so it is very dark. Not quite cave dark. There are stars. The background noise is very low. The people who live around here are not watching TV or listening to electronic gizmos. Because of these conditions, the light and noise we would make would be noticed at once. Dawn will be safer."

"I'm not sure about what all you just said — I know we don't have any gizmos — but if we take even a few of you out of the cave in the middle of the night, everyone will know about it," said Mat.

"Thank you," said Keven. "Put the pots and spoons back into the baskets. Just so you'll know, it's September, if I'm not mistaken. While the temperature wouldn't be too uncomfortable, there's nowhere to bunk fourteen strangers. However, I think we can find a more comfortable spot than this to sleep here in the cave. I was considering the Church. What do you think, Stephen?"

"That's about as good as any. There are some benches there, but I don't know how good they are for sleeping. Are you going to come out with us, Mr. Neff?"

"No, sir. I'll stay with these folks for now. You've been very kind. Thank you."

"Yes, thank you, Mr. Bishop," came a voice followed by eleven others.

"You are welcome. I'm sorry we can't take you to better lodgings. You should all be honored guests, but I see the sense of what Mr. Neff has said about not stirring things up."

"As an unauthorized, unofficial mission, we have to remain completely clandestine," said Rod.

"Yes, Sir. I'm sure you do," said Stephen Bishop. "And we'll help you all we can."

"All right, grab your gear and prepare to move. We're going over to Methodist Church," said Keven.

"Did you say Methodist?" asked Mat.

"That's what we call it. I'm not sure when that started," said Keven.

"Why is it called Methodist church?" asked Mat.

Keven grinned until he thought his face would crack. "Because it's too dry for Baptists." The laughter from the three guides overwhelmed the groans from the Wild Cavers.

"Yes, Sir. You are a real cave guide, Mr. Neff. There is no doubt about that."

The whole group ambled along at a comfortable pace, Keven and Stephen Bishop in the lead. For the first time since the tour left the visitor center, Keven didn't have a schedule. He relaxed. Mat and Nick talked to the Ross couple at the rear. Things became a little unsettled when the two Wild Cavers switched on their headlights. Keven explained to the guides that it was not magic, but he was too tired to try to figure out how to explain electric lights. He was familiar with the third law of Arthur C. Clarke, the great science fiction writer, which says *Any sufficiently advanced technology is indistinguishable from magic.*

There were four wooden benches about six feet long each at Methodist Church. In addition, there were four sections of wooden pipeline lying along one wall. The ground wasn't sandy soft, but the clay was smooth. It wouldn't be comfortable, but it would be bearable. The guides left them two lard oil lanterns and a jug of oil. Mat and Nick said goodnight and left the Wild Cavers to try to rest the best way they could.

Keven and Stephen Bishop strolled up the hill past the second set of leaching vats and the entrance to Gothic Avenue. They said nothing until they reached Standing Rocks.

"There is so much I want to tell you, and there are things I want to give you," said Keven.

"I understand why you can't, Keven." Stephen Bishop looked him straight in the eye. Keven grinned in the dim light of the lanterns. "If I show up talking about wild ideas, I won't ever live to achieve what you claim I will. And I'd rather be ignorant of the future than to know all about it while I'm chopping cotton in Mississippi ... or worse."

"I'm glad you understand. I don't know how long we'll be here. We may be gone when you come in the morning. We may be here forever. We have no more way of knowing that than we did that we were coming back in time a hundred and seventy-five years.

"In case something happens before I see you again, I want to give you one thing." Keven reached into his fanny pack and pulled out an LED light powered by a hand-cranked generator. He had been saving the light for an emergency, and hoped that the original aluminum-foil packaging provided enough shielding from the EMP. After he unfolded the foil wrapping, he demonstrated how the crank folded out, cranked it, and pushed the button. It worked!

When he switched it on, he heard an intake of breath from Stephen Bishop. The five LEDs emitted a bluish white light much brighter than both their lanterns combined.

"How did you do that?" asked Stephen Bishop.

"We call it a flashlight, but some folks call it a torch."

"It's not like any torch I ever heard of," said Stephen Bishop.

"No, it won't be heard of for a very long time. I'm giving this to you for emergency use or when you are all alone in the farthest reaches of the cave." Keven paused and thought of the line from J.R.R. Tolkien's *The Fellowship of the Ring* when the light of a star is given to the main character.

"And this is not magic?" said Stephen Bishop, pointing the light all around, seeing the cave in detail he had never seen, even with multiple lanterns.

"No, but I couldn't begin to explain it to you. We don't have time." He paused. He had an idea. "You have heard of Morse's telegraph maybe?"

"Why, yes, Sir. Some guests were talking about messages sent using electricity. They were here earlier this year. I understand it has something to do with lightning. When I asked them about it, they said it was like lightning stored in a bottle. Is that it?"

"Close enough. This has a little electricity generator in it. When you crank it, it generates electricity that it stores inside. When you push the switch on, electricity runs through these bulbs at the end, and they give off the light. That's as good an explanation as I can give."

"Good enough. Thank you for this gift, Keven. I will keep it and all the rest of this secret. And so will Nick and Mat. Don't you worry none. But, before we go back, I want to do one little thing."

"Okay, what's that?" asked Keven, wondering what Stephen could be talking about.

"You knew about Mr. Gratz's name being back here. No one but a Mammoth Cave guide would know that. We don't show it to the folks we bring through the cave. I want you to scratch our initials right below his name."

"In our time, we call that vandalism, and it's against the law," said Keven.

"But, we aren't in your time, Keven. And I want a more permanent reminder that we stood here together. The torch is a wonder, but our initials will last for a long time, and I can come here and be confident that it wasn't a dream." Keven could see how important this was to Stephen Bishop, and combined with the honor, he couldn't resist.

He pulled his Swiss Army knife out of the fanny pack and stood behind Standing Rock. Stephen Bishop held his new light to illuminate the section of limestone. With the awl attachment, Keven scratched "K N - S B" in one-inch-high letters. He thought it looked like radio station call letters.

"There." Keven stepped back to let Stephen Bishop see the letters.

"Good." He smiled at Keven.

"There are some other things we need to talk about, Stephen," said Keven. "You are going to push into the long reaches of the cave. You will be the first person to walk in those areas."

"This is amazing. I'm dying to know all that you know about the cave," said Stephen Bishop.

"I know. And I know you understand why I can't tell you more. We haven't left much sign that we have been here, but we have left tracks. You will need to brush out our tracks and make sure you leave only your tracks."

"I'll remember that. What's the other thing?"

"If we're stuck here, we need to get Dan and Sophy headed up to the Ohio River as soon as possible. They are in real danger."

"Oh, Lord. You're right about that. Kentucky is no place for folks that were born free. I hadn't given that any thought. You know about that, too?" Keven nodded. "I'll talk to the right man about that as soon as I can. You know, we call it the River Jordan."

"I didn't know that. Good name for it though. Have you ever thought about leaving?"

"You mean running north?"

"Yes. About running to freedom."

"I think about being free all the time. But crossing Jordan is dangerous work. Most folks try for it only if it's really bad. Like whipping or breaking up a family. And ... I really like the Mammoth Cave. I really like finding new cave! Do you understand that part?" Keven nodded. "I have it pretty good. Taking it all into account, anywhere else, I wouldn't have what I have here, would I?"

"No, not in 1838, I guess not," said Keven. "No cave certainly."

"No. Not the Mammoth Cave. Only one of them is right here. And I feel like I have things to do here. Important things." Stephen Bishop smiled. "What about the rest of your folks, Keven?"

"I don't know. If I'm going to be in 1838, there's no place I'd rather be than Mammoth Cave. But, we have to focus on Dan and Sophy first.

"I agree," said Stephen Bishop. They started back toward Methodist Church. Keven heard the loud snoring of the Wild Cavers before he could see them.

"Stephen, I am honored to have met you."

"Keven, one more thing. Dan Ross said he was from Atlanta like it means something special. I've never heard of it."

"No, Stephen, there is no town with that name yet, but it becomes very important in black history."

"Black history?"

Nineteen
Is this Hawkins Pass?

The loud buzzing stops. It must not have worked, because I'm in the same place. Our lights are still working. But, I see that Denise and her lantern are gone. I look around to see Bob and Craig still standing where they were before the buzzing started, standing on their own pieces of limestone. The gel cell battery is right where Craig put it. I see that a portion of our rocks are now on top of the cutout section that we assume came with Keven and the Wild Cave tour.

"Did you feel anything, Walt?" says Bob.

"No, nothing. How about you?"

"No. Craig?"

"The lights blinked, but I didn't feel anything. The buzzing was right." Craig shines his headlamp all about the passage. "Everything feels the same to me, but Denise disappeared. Did we make it?"

Bob shines his headlamp up and down the passage, "We're at the same place. Hawkins Pass," says Bob. "There are more rocks on the floor. Trail maintenance has fallen off."

Or not yet begun, I think.

"If we didn't move in space, what did happen?" says Craig.

"Well, to be technical, we did move in space because we are not where we were — only — we moved to a space that is very similar to where we were," I say. "In the science fiction I've read, we would either be in a Hawkins Pass of a parallel universe or in the same Hawkins Pass, but in a different time. I don't know how to tell the difference. Either way, we had to move in space as well." Bob and Craig are still standing on their pieces of limestone. I'm not sure why, but I stay on my rocks, too.

"Okay. Where's Keven?" says Craig.

"Good question," says Bob.

He looks at Zona's smart phone. "It still has some charge."

"We don't want to take a chance of re-activating this thing until we're ready," I say.

"There, it's off." says Bob. "At least we're not on board a star ship or something even stranger."

"Craig, let's wire your charger to the battery," I say. Craig cuts the cigarette lighter plug from the cord of his charger and strips back the insulation. Bob hands him Zona's phone, and he plugs it in.

"Is it charging?" I say.

"Roger, that," says Craig, and he loads the battery and the phone into my pack.

"Are we in the future or in the past?" says Craig. I think we're both a little hung up on this *when* question.

"Let's hope we've been sent to the same Hawkins Pass that Keven and the others went to," says Bob.

"This amoeba-shaped piece of limestone makes me think we are," I say, looking at the curvy slab of limestone we're standing on.

"Keven!" yells Bob. We wait for an answer, but the silence holds no answer.

I hesitate a moment and step off my limestone.

"It's all right," I say. "You can leave your rocks."

"Walt, which way should we go?" says Bob. He looks around for tracks. The wet rock floor shows no sign.

"I think we should go to the Snowball Dining Room. That may help us get oriented. From there we may be able to figure out which way Keven went," I say.

"Sounds good to me. Should we leave a note?" says Bob.

"Good idea." I pull out my notebook and scribble down our names, the date and time, and that we have headed to the Snowball Dining Room by way of Martel Avenue and Boone's Avenue. I leave it anchored by a rock outside the active area.

"Craig, you want to lead us to Snowball?" says Bob.

"No, someone else lead. I don't want to walk point into the weird."

I start to chide him about being young, fit, resilient, and so forth, but decide against it. He has been through a lot and with very little rest.

"I'll take a shot at it." Rocks litter the way, and it seems that the walls are a bit fresher, cleaner. I'm unsure.

As we emerge up into Boone's Avenue, I say to Bob, "There's no tourist trail through here, but the rocks have been scuffed, and there's some mud on some of them."

"So you think we're following Keven's path?"

"We're following someone," I say.

The ship's ladder is missing, and the steps up to the intersection with Rose's Pass, too. At the intersection, we stop to look around.

"I'll run up Rose's to check for a light switch," I say and take off my pack. I enter the narrow passage, but the rock fall that chokes the passage soon stops me. If we are in the future, it lies so far ahead that there has been plenty of rock fall, and no tourists have passed here for a very long time. If it's a parallel universe, no visitors have been to this part of the cave. I back up, collect my pack, and trot back to join the others.

"Light switch?" says Bob when I emerge into the intersection. I notice he has taken his pack off and is sitting on it.

"No. No switch. And there is no trail. Lots of rock fall," I say. "Sure hope we can make it through."

"Well, all we have to do is find Keven and the Wild Cavers and get to Hawkins Pass," says Bob. "And hope that thing works in reverse."

"Yeah, that's all we have to do," I say.

"Did you see any sign that they followed the Grand Avenue tour route?"

"No. It doesn't look like anyone's been that way. Ever."

"So, we're in the past?" says Craig. "How far back do you think?"

"It's hard to say with any certainty that we've traveled in time. We could be in a parallel universe that differs a little, but not much. Say, one in which no one discovers the cave. Or another one, in which the Bering land bridge never happens and humans never settle the North American continent. On the other hand, if we have traveled to the past of our own universe, we've been sent back before anyone made it to this part of the cave."

"So that could be from the late eighteen forties on back," says Bob.

"Oh," says Craig in a near whisper.

I worry about how Craig may react if we don't find Keven and the others. I worry about my own reaction if we can't get back to the twenty-first century that we just left.

"This is pretty neat. Just think what the Snowball Dining Room will look like before anyone has trampled through it," I say, not finding it hard to sound enthusiastic.

Craig smiles and nods, "Yeah."

Bob loads up and leads us on into Boone's Avenue toward Snowball Dining Room. I ease into my pack straps and trail. The going continues to be rough with wet rock debris on the floor. We balance on the rocks with one arm out on the nearest wall and the other holding a lantern. The large backpacks snag on rock projections threatening to throw us for a spill – some of us for a second spill. Boone's narrowness won't allow side-by-side perambulation.

After about ten minutes, Bob stops. "I'm not sure, but I think this passage up on the left is where the tour comes down into Boone's." A small, but steep, wet ledge slopes up to a passage about ten feet above where we are standing. No one has ever climbed it. The rocks appear pristine in that direction. "If he didn't climb out here, he went around to the Pass of El Ghor. From there, he could have gone to Snowball Dining Room by way of Mary's Vineyard. We should be able to see his tracks at El Ghor."

"Good idea," I say. "I would have missed that turn without the steps there. Craig, does this look familiar to you? Remember those wet steps after you passed the cave grapes? You came down the steps that were here then and then right into this passage."

"Yeah, it does look familiar. So we're that close to the Snowball Dining Room?"

"Right, but we're going to follow Boone's a little farther and see if we can find Keven's trail," says Bob. He pushes on, Craig follows, and I bring up the rear.

Bob leads us into a chamber formed by the confluence of several passages. Off to the right lies the way to Echo River. We stop at the center of the intersection.

"I've found tracks!" says Bob. "They are the same pattern as ours, the one that the Park Service boots have. The tracks show they went up to the Snowball Dining Room and also went toward the river. I think I understand what happened.

When Keven got here, he had already recognized that he was in virgin cave, and he couldn't resist a look at Snowball — maybe even Cleaveland Avenue. But, I doubt that he went that far. He would be conscious of damaging too much. The condition of Snowball would give him information about when and where he was. And it will for us, too."

"So then, they backtracked and headed to the river, where they could cross and go out through the Historic entrance?" I say.

"Keven left Hawkins Pass because something unusual happened," says Bob. "Standard operating procedure requires that if something unusual happens, and if everyone is ambulatory, get to the surface by the quickest, safe route. I don't think he realized for sure what happened until he saw Snowball. If the Snowball Room looked pristine, he realized that this part of the cave was unexplored, and that there was no exit from the cave on this side of Echo River.

"Keven must have realized that they were in virgin cave – how great is that? – and, that his one chance to get out lay through the Historic entrance, the one natural entrance that we know about. Also he would need to keep the tour moving before they panicked far away from food and warmth."

"Why didn't they go out the way we came in this morning?" asks Craig.

"That's a man-made entrance," I say. "Virgin cave means no Carmichael entrance. Stephen Bishop discovered this part of the cave after 1840, but it was not until 1931 that Mr. Carmichael engineered the entrance at the other end of Cleaveland Avenue. So the one way out of the cave, there is any hope of, is the Historic entrance on the other side of Echo River. And there's no boat on the river," I say. "If there was an entrance at the far end of Cleaveland Avenue, we would expect to see evidence of people or water or something."

"Right," says Bob, "but remember, there's no dam on the Green River, so Echo River may be very low compared to what we're used to. Craig did you ever go on the boat ride on Echo River?"

"No. Keven told us it was closed for the last time in the nineteen eighties, before I was born. I would like to see it though. Will we have to swim?"

"No. At least I hope not," says Bob. "But, it's going to be cold." I nod my head.

Bob leads us into what Hovey described as "… an uninviting hole …" Our packs are a bit tight squeezing through this passage and we climb without benefit of the concrete steps of the twentieth century. We emerge beside Mary's Vineyard, a floor-to-ceiling, shiny, white stalactite covered with cave grapes. Calcium carbonate precipitates to make cave formations. Under special circumstances, these formations take the shape of small spheroids up to a half-inch or so in diameter. Cave grapes.

"We are going in here to make sure no one from the tour is still here. So we take a quick peep and keep moving," says Bob.

"I will, if you will," I say. To the right, we enter Washington Hall and sure enough, the restrooms are not there. The passage leads straight into the Snowball Room.

The last time we saw this room some unknown number of years in the future, there was a concrete floor, a serving line, and colorful picnic tables. Now the whole room dazzles pure white with pockets of beige and brown. A thousand "snowballs" plastered against the ceiling, formed from the purest white gypsum. Interspersed needles and tufts of cotton gypsum shimmer in the slight breeze we generate by moving and breathing.

"See their footprints," says Bob pointing to a short trail into the room. "Craig, you go first, and do not stray beyond where they went or to either side."

Craig nods his understanding, and with his eyes popped out and mouth wide open, steps with care along the path. "This is amazing! What happened to it?"

"These delicate gypsum formations, the long needles and cotton, don't survive the presence of people or lanterns for any time at all. And in the early days, collecting souvenirs *and scientific specimens* was considered a part of the tour. There is another section of cave that the park never opened to the public. It resembles this. But even it has suffered from the few people who have been in there," says Bob.

I go next, mouth gaping, too. "I am overwhelmed, Bob. I can't believe it."

After I ease back, Bob steps along the narrow path, with a small Canon point-and-shoot camera at the ready. "Watch your eyes." He takes half a dozen shots and comes back to us. "I don't know whom I'll ever be able to show these to besides Zona and Mary, but I couldn't pass it up."

"And Barbara, too. You're right," I say. "The Wild Cavers were here, but left. Back to Mary's Vineyard and on to El Ghor?"

"Lead on, MacDuff!" says Bob. "I'll bring up the rear this time." All charged up from seeing the Snowball Room in pristine condition – and confident that we are on Keven's trail – we march on with renewed vigor.

On our way toward Echo River, Bob plays tour guide pointing out Victoria's Crown and the Sheep Shelter among other features. From the Pass of El Ghor, we progress into Silliman's Avenue and Ole Bull's concert hall. The Norwegian violinist gave — will give? — a recital here in 1845. We pass the Stern of the Great Eastern, named for an ocean liner.

"This is the Hill of Fatigue," says Bob. "Up ahead at Serpent's Hall, we'll come to an optional route, a connection to Ganter Avenue."

"Ganter leads to the Wooden Bowl Room, doesn't it?" I say.

"Is Serpent Hall named for all the snakes found there?" asks Craig.

"No snakes in the cave," I say.

"Ganter does lead to the Wooden Bowl Room and the Historic tour route and the Historic entrance. Echo River leads to River Hall on the Historic route. So there are two paths out, from Serpent Hall. We'll see which route Keven chose," says Bob. "Don't you think we should follow their trail, whichever way they went?"

"Right. We don't know how far they've gone, and if they tried Ganter, they could be stuck at Rider Haggard's Flight. But I'm guessing the river," I say.

"I hope so," says Bob. "He must have been thinking the same thing I am. Ganter is a long, rough passage, plus there's the near-vertical climb at Rider Haggard's Flight." The cliff at the Flight stopped exploration from the other side for quite a long time. Ganter remains the only other path to the other side of the river. No other way exists. Bob has been through it, but I never have. Archaeologists found a lot of aboriginal artifacts in Ganter, but not on this side of Rider Haggard's Flight. The cliff's namesake, Rider Haggard, wrote a series of adventure novels, including *King Solomon's Mines*.

From Serpent's Hall, the passage runs in the direction away from the Wooden Bowl Room until it comes to the cliff. From Rider Haggard's Flight, it is still a long way to the Wooden Bowl Room. And, it's not a straight, obvious shot either. Even with wading, Echo River seems to me to be the easier route.

When we come to the junction with Ganter, Bob studies the cave floor for tracks of the Wild Cavers. "I've been here a few times, and it sure looks different without a nice CCC trail. But we're in luck, Keven took the river route."

"That's good, right?" says Craig.

"Yes," I say. "We'll be wet, but we won't be lost. And we won't have to climb a sheer cliff with heavy packs."

We come to the high-water mark of Echo River. Footprints, some of them deep, mark the churned-up sand changing to mud. We slip in the mud — and in places — we sink in up to our knees. Everyone struggles, but no one falls.

Bob leads. We wade in Echo River at the very bottom of Mammoth Cave.

"Hey, Walt. The water is still muddy."

"That's a good sign."

The ceiling looms close over our heads, maybe ten feet. Water extends the full twenty-foot width wall to wall. No bank offers a place to pause and rest. And we soon experience the reason for the name. Every word and splash echoes.

"Keven," calls Bob. The name rebounds time after time. We stand still, thigh deep in the river. The sound of water sloshing echoes against the cave walls. There is no answer but echo.

We minimize the splashes by raising our feet only enough to clear the muddy bottom before we slog forward. Bob leads us in a slow, careful pace. He's moving forward, but if he could spot some of the eyeless fish, we would all be thrilled. The water may be too muddy.

"There's one!" Bob points off to the right.

"I see it!" says Craig. He shows the first sign of enthusiasm since leaving the Snowball Room.

"There's another," says Bob. I'm too far in the rear to see, and no fish would hang around after such a disturbance.

After what I thought was an hour, on the other side of the river, Bob recognizes the limestone ledge that one day will be the boat dock. Bob and I climb out with help from each other. Craig, the seal, leaps out onto the limestone bank. We keep moving because we are even more wet and cold than we are tired. For a little while, the going becomes easier, and we regain some body warmth. We hit more mud when we negotiate around Lake Lethe and the River Styx. The dark brown mud sucks up all the light. At long last, we slog up the slope into River Hall.

"Look. You can see where they cleaned the mud off their boots and pants," says Bob. He sits on a rock with a pile of mud all around.

"They're not here, so I guess they were able to get through Fat Man's Misery," I say. My legs are weak, but I focus on the route going forward. Going backward on the Historic route, we can go to Great Relief Hall and into the Misery, a duck walk and crouch. The packs will be interesting. I always wondered if Stephen Bishop found that narrow channel filled with sand and dug it out. We will soon know the answer.

Twenty
Living a Nevada Barr Novel

The buzzing stopped. Denise pulled her hands away from her ears. Bob, Craig, and Walt were gone. The little slabs of limestone they stood on were sliced lengthwise leaving a smooth top. She looked at the watch on her wrist and marked the time. Two hours to go. She set the alarm.

She trotted around the edge of the cutout. The scratched circle was still there. There were the pieces of sliced and polished limestone in the active area. What if they come back and hit those rocks? She picked up the pieces of rock, stacked them, and set her lantern on top.

What if Creighton comes to check on her? Had he been here before, or had Craig been hallucinating?

She couldn't go wandering off. Some or all of them could come back at a moment's notice. No, there would be no notice. They would just be here. Does it buzz out there, or just on this side? *Does the light go out when you close the refrigerator door?*

Well, she was not worrying about hallucinating. She had scrambled and crawled in remote parts of the cave, alone for extended periods, without a care at all. To paraphrase the Reverend Hovey when he sat alone on the mound of breakdown rocks at Chief City, "… fancy had *not* peopled the darkness with all manner of shapes."

Denise scuffed her way back to her pack, pulled out her Crazy Creek Chair, a Nevada Barr mystery in paperback, and a bottle of water. She sat her chair beside the stack of rocks, sat down next to the Coleman lantern, and opened the mystery to page one. *I'm living a Nevada Barr mystery!*

"Excuse me, madam."

Twenty-One
"Hey, Ranger!"

The mud comes off our boots with ease, but cleaning the mud off the coverall pants takes forever. We made no provision for this activity. We are filthy, wet, cold, and bone tired with it.

"I think that's all the mud we can get off," says Bob.

"Good," says Craig. We're all sitting on rocks, our packs at our side.

"That's the way to Great Relief Hall," I point off to our right.

"Correct, but Keven's tracks lead up through the Corkscrew," Bob says and points his headlamp up toward Vanderbilt Hall and the lower entrance to the Corkscrew. That's going to be a tough climb even with following their mud trail. I am definitely too old for this."

This section of cave lacks all the blackening of thousands of torches and the smell of the old pit toilets that endured for years after the flush toilets were installed in Great Relief Hall.

"Right. Me, too. If no one has built a trail here, they haven't built a bridge over Bottomless Pit. And, no chance of finding slender cedar poles on this side of it either. I guess Fat Man's Misery will have to wait." One of the versions of Stephen Bishop's crossing of Bottomless pit says he crossed on slender cedar poles. I can't imagine why he would have done that – or in this case, maybe – why he *will* do that.

"Can we rest a little longer? I'm beat," says Craig.

"So am I, but only for a few minutes," says Bob. "We can't sit still too long, wet the way we are. We need to keep moving."

"Here, Craig. Have something hot to drink, and eat a Snickers bar. I pull out a Thermos of cocoa and a bag of candy bars. "Better eat one ourselves, Bob," I say. In this first pause since we left Bob's house, I think about what we're doing.

How far from Barbara I am. How we need to put this show back on the road and head for home.

"Do you guys have any idea of where or when we are?" asks Craig.

Bob nods toward me. "I don't think we are in the future because we have seen no sign of trail, light fixture, hand rail, concrete fragment, anything. That leaves either a parallel universe or the past. If it's the past, we are before October 1838 when Stephen Bishop crossed – or will cross – Bottomless Pit. But how far back before that I don't know, and I'm not sure it makes a difference at this point. Later on it might. And I don't have any idea how you identify a parallel universe from geological evidence alone. Some of my geology professors gave the impression of being from different universes, but they didn't cover it in our coursework."

We climb through the edge of a breakdown area. We pull the packs up with a section of climbing rope. According to Hovey, someone discovered the Corkscrew around 1871. Other sources say that the black guide William Garvin discovered it. Either way, visitors to the cave descended to the lower levels on the same route through pits and domes, but returned from River Hall to Main Cave through the Corkscrew to avoid retracing their steps, and not of minor importance, allowing a second tour to start without the two tours having to pass in the cave. Wooden ladders and steep steps made the passage possible for visitors. We wish for ladders as we scramble and negotiate the climb.

We move in one short, but complicated, climb from near the bottom of the cave to come out in Main Cave near the uppermost level, Gothic Avenue. When the Park Service installed the stair tower in Mammoth Dome, the risk of the Corkscrew and the expense of replacing the ladders became unnecessary.

About half way up, we perch on a narrow ledge to rest. Bob and I are breathing hard. Craig is a little red in the face. "It's a good thing Keven knew where he was going. I don't think I could find my way through here on a good day," says Bob.

"I've never been in here. It's different from Big Break at Grand Central Station." That pile of break down boulders — big as houses some of them — took the New Entrance guides five years of probing to penetrate, but it resulted in the discovery of the Frozen Niagara section. The part of the cave with most of the traditional formations or speleothems, the stalactites and stalagmites. We move out again.

"We're at the top," says Bob in a whisper. I hear his labored breathing, along with my own. "Let's take it slow and quiet until we can figure out what or who is here. We might be pretty startling to a party of Adena cave explorers."

"Right!" I whisper between breaths. The Adena people were part of the Early Woodland culture who — based on archaeological data — spent thousands of years going in and out of the cave. Whatever else they did, they scraped a lot of gypsum off the cave walls for up to two miles from the natural entrance.

"I hear some faint buzzing, not the loud sound of the transporter, but more gentle. It's coming from Methodist Church," says Bob.

"Are there bees in the cave?" says Craig.

"Not that I've ever heard. Walt told you, noooo snakes," says Bob with a chuckle.

I laugh at the reference to a well-loved former cave guide's answer to whether or not there were any animals in the cave. "Does Keven snore?"

"That could be it. I'm sure the Adena people must have snored, too. Well, here goes," says Bob.

After we climb down, I recognize the trail. "Bob. There's a trail!"

"Thank goodness. Well, we won't be running into any Adenans."

Our lights shine onto the cave trail, somewhat narrower than what the Civilian Conservation Corps made, but still a recognizable tourist trail. "Hey, Walt, the pipeline!" says Bob. "It might be our universe, but not our time." The fatigue drops away. He isn't jumping up and down, but he looks energized. My fatigue eases, but I still feel it.

At this location, in our Mammoth Cave in the twenty-first century, we have these same two wooden pipelines, one suspended above the other supported on tripods of wooden poles and cairns of rock. These are things that we are familiar with. They are reassuring. As we descend the hill toward Methodist Church, the buzzing becomes louder and multi-tonal. When we round into the alcove of the church, we spy bodies lying on benches, the floor, and sections of wooden pipes.

"Hey, Ranger."

Twenty-two
Ranger Neff, I Presume

"Great Jumping Jehoshaphat!" says Bob in a voice loud enough to wake the Wild Cavers — and even the dead.

"Bob, are you all right?" asks Keven. Having scared the ever-living hell out of Bob, now he's concerned about Bob's heart.

"I'm fine, Keven. But, Holy Crap! You scared me enough to cross on over — but not quite."

Keven explains that he had been sitting against the wall of the Main Cave opposite the church contemplating 1838, when he heard us exiting the Corkscrew and saw our lights coming down the hill. When we rounded into the alcove, he tiptoed up behind Bob and put his hand on Bob's shoulder at the same time he uttered his greeting.

"How are you? Where are we?" says Bob.

"You mean, 'When are we?' don't you?" says Keven.

"Yes, I do."

"Well, I ate supper with Stephen Bishop, Mat, and Nick last night in their cabin. It's 1838. September. Are we ever glad to see you!"

The rest of the Wild Cavers descend on us with great joy and excitement. They appear to be over being in 1838, seeing the famous cave guides, and are ready to go home. Craig fields a hundred questions from his fellow Wild Cavers.

"Bob, I'm the representative of Homeland Security. I need to know how you managed to follow us here. All of this is classified. You don't have security clearances."

"Hello, Rod. Good. You have it all under control," says Bob.

I ease my pack off and start lighting the three Coleman lanterns. The Wild Cavers hover around the lanterns trying to warm up. Once we can see, I pour hot coffee and cocoa into paper cups. Bob brings out more Thermoses, bags of Snickers and energy bars. Craig dispenses hand sanitizer, paper towels, and sandwiches.

"1838? That's incredible," says Bob.

"Keven, what time is it here?" I say.

"The best I can make out, it's about four-forty-five in the morning. How did you get here? How did we get here?" says Keven.

"Be careful. What you are discussing is highly classified — or will be as soon as I get back," says Rod.

"Right, Rod. Thanks. There's not much to it. We just followed you. You leave a pretty good trail in virgin cave," says Bob.

"No, I mean how did you – all of us – leave the twenty-first century and arrive in this here and now? 1838?" says Keven.

"We don't know for sure." Bob spends a few minutes explaining about Craig and his phone call attempt, the rangers' ongoing search, and how we left Denise back in Hawkins Pass. Rod darts around like a wasp that can't figure out who to sting.

At the end of that monologue, Keven asks, "Can you take us back? I think these folks are ready to go home. I've dreamed about doing this very thing, but when we got here, I realized living in this time would be very rough. I still haven't figured out a way to blend in without either being hanged or burned at the stake or on the other hand messing everything up beyond all redemption. And, more to the point, I want to get back to Myrna. How is she?"

"She's worried, but not too much. She says that you've been late before from deeper parts of the cave. None of us was thinking about deeper in time. I thought you'd be intrigued with all this," says Bob. "But, yes, we think we can take you all back." I look at Bob, but he ignores me.

"From here?" asks Keven.

"No, we have to go back to Hawkins Pass. That seems to be the active area," says Bob. "The small active area is why Craig was left behind."

"What about the Homeland Security detachment in the park?" says Rod.

"They are working with the park rangers and searching between Cathedral Domes and Frozen Niagara for you guys," says Bob. "They think Keven is lost in the cave." Bob laughs. "Rod, Homeland Security wanted to restart the search tomorrow morning come first light. Something of a disconnect there, I think." Rod's look says he does not yet grasp how you can search at night as well as in the day in a cave.

"How was it out on the surface?" I say to Keven.

"Well, it was dark, but the sky was clear. There were thousands of stars. I caught Stephen at the end of a tour. I stashed these guys in Little Bat and waited for him at the entrance to Houchins Narrows."

"What's he like? How'd he react?"

"He's a cave guide. A *real* cave guide. I had a little bit to do to convince him I wasn't the devil — well, that carbide flame was shooting out of my head. I had to pass several tests, but after that, he seemed to accept me all right. I went out after dark and ate supper with him and Mat and Nick in their cabin. This is all unbelievable! It's a dream come true."

"Mat and Nick? Oh, great!" says Bob.

"I thought they didn't come to the cave until 1839," I say.

"Well, they're here now," says Keven.

"He hasn't crossed Bottomless Pit, has he?" asks Bob.

"No. And I've been going crazy trying not to tell him too much. I want so much to know if he found that passage at Richardson Spring that goes around the pit, but I think I gave him a hint, or rather, a reminder. He and Stevenson are supposed to cross it next month, so I didn't want to ruin that."

"What did you talk about?" says Bob.

"Not as much as I thought I would. We talked about how they're treated. They seem to think pretty well — for slaves. But they want to be free, and being sold down the river to chop cotton in Mississippi is always on their minds. Stephen quizzed me on the cave and where certain things were."

"And, of course, you passed," says Bob.

Keven is on a first-name basis with the great guide.

"Yes, I passed. Wouldn't that have been something, if he asked me about something I didn't know or something he called by a different name?"

"Yes, something indeed," says Bob.

"Walt, thank you for coming to rescue us," says Keven. "You guys were – are – taking quite a risk."

"Bob stood up for you in front of the rangers," I say. "He knew you weren't lost. Something else had to explain why you were missing."

"We were lost, in the cave, but not *when* they could find us," says Keven with that laugh he uses with cave tours.

"Well, the rangers were not moving in the right direction — or right dimension — as soon as Bob thought they should," I say. "They thought Craig was raving about you having just disappeared, and they were searching closer to Frozen Niagara. We knew you weren't lost."

"What if you'd been beamed onto a space ship or something?" asks Keven.

"I don't know. Bob and I talked about it a little. We just came after you — and the Wild Cavers, of course. If cave guides kept showing up in the transporter room on the star ship, I guess they would have figured out that someone had left the gate open, and more would be following at any time. And maybe it would prompt them to send us all back."

"We sent a water bottle out first, and we managed to bring it back. Since human bodies are mostly water, we tried it ourselves," says Bob. "We had a pretty good chance of getting back, but unless you were on that star ship, you had none." He smiled at Keven.

"Thanks, Bob. Thank you for taking that incredible chance," says Keven.

The Wild Cavers are finishing their meals, and they look happier and healthier. Bob takes out a handful of incandescent headlamps and passes them around. "Craig's light burned out when you left, so Denise figured you might need some replacements. Man, is she going to be mad when she finds out *when* you've been in the cave — with Stephen Bishop, no less. Did you take his picture?"

"No," says Keven. "I couldn't do it. Didn't seem right. What could I do with it if I did? Even if I'd had a camera?"

"This time travel thing turned out to be less fun than you'd have thought, didn't it?" says Bob.

"Yes, it's a huge headache," says Keven. "We took pictures of the Snowball Room, but no one would recognize them."

"Or believe them, if they did," I add.

"Now, what do you want to do?" says Bob.

"Go back as soon as we can. If you hadn't showed up, my original idea was to get out of the cave and try to establish some sort of relationship with Archibald Miller, but I don't have any clothes, money, or anything except what's in my fanny pack. And if I started showing that stuff around, who knows what would have happened."

"Very complicated." says Bob.

"Yes, and I couldn't figure out how to make it work. Well, unless we surrounded a stagecoach and then left this part of the country."

"Well, I want to go up and look at the Rotunda before we leave," says Bob.

"Me, too," I say.

"I waited up there for hours while Stephen Bishop finished with his tour, but I was so overwhelmed trying to figure out what to say to him that I never paid much attention. Let's go see," says Keven.

The Wild Cavers say they will wait and eat a few more candy bars, so we climb the hill toward the big room.

"The trail's different. More so than I had imagined. The CCC moved an incredible amount of dirt," I say, bringing up the rear behind Bob and Keven striding abreast. Breakdown rocks litter the passage floor. The trail winds a bit and veers over to the wall on the left nearer the Rotunda. This room looms large and dark. I am used to seeing it with electric lights, not headlamps.

At the Rotunda, our lights appear to dim, but that's because they are failing to light the broad expanse of the big room. We are able to walk right up to the leaching vats. The wood doesn't seem any different. The locations of piles of leached cave dirt are different. The topography of the cave floor has been re-arranged. The peter-dirt miners and much later the CCC shifted a lot of dirt. The miners carried sacks of cave dirt on their backs and in ox carts. The one advantage the CCC crews possessed was wheelbarrows – that and they were paid. No mechanization. And they didn't have oxen.

Keven looks at his watch. "We have a long way to go back to Cathedral Domes. We better start."

"What about Stephen Bishop?" asks Bob. "I'm thinking we need to start, too, but can't we meet him, too?"

"We didn't set a time for when we would meet today, so I think I'll leave him a note. We better leave before anyone comes to check on us," says Keven. He rummages through his fanny pack and brings out a notepad — standard Park Service issue — and begins to write. I wonder what he's writing. At this time, could Stephen Bishop read and write?

"I'll leave this at the church where he can find it. He might miss it up here. I need to leave this coat, too." Keven fingers the worn garment realizing how valuable it is to its owner.

"Keven," says Bob.

"What?" says Keven.

"We sort of thought we might meet him, too."

"Oh. Well, I would sure want to if I were in your shoes," says Keven, but the expression on his face seems to say that he isn't all that enthusiastic about sharing. From the look on Bob's face, I see he notices Keven's hesitation, too.

I begin to see two pieces of Keven's reluctance. First, he has a unique relationship with the celebrated First Official Guide. Second, he worries about the additional stress on

Stephen Bishop with this continuous stream of cave guides from the future, who can travel into *his* cave at will. These future cave guides also know much more about *his* cave than he, the acknowledged expert. In effect, we could undermine his authority in the one place on earth where he has any at all.

"Bob, I understand Keven's reluctance," I say. "We don't want to cause any doubts for Stephen Bishop about his role and authority. Every one of us from the future knows parts of the cave he doesn't. Even me. I think if we can slip out, we have a good chance of minimizing our effect on what we know he does next month — and in the next few years."

"Cross Bottomless Pit, you mean," says Bob.

"I think so," I say. Keven nods in agreement. "If he doesn't receive the credit for crossing Bottomless Pit, it could affect the whole future of his career. We can't jeopardize that."

"Well, there is one question we need to ask. And answer," I say.

"What's that," says Bob.

"Should we take Stephen Bishop back to the twenty-first century?"

"What?" says Keven.

"First of all," says Bob. "Can we? What's the load limit on this thing?"

"I don't know, but I suspect it will transport whatever you can pack into the active area. I'm asking the question now so that when do get back to our time, the idea doesn't pop into someone's head, and we haven't even considered it."

"That's a tough question," says Keven.

"Yes, it is. Do you offer to rescue someone from slavery, and in doing that, deny him his place in history?" says Bob.

"We talked about his taking the Underground Railroad earlier. He's decided to stay with what he's got instead of risking all on the unknown. He believes his place is here in Mammoth Cave. I mean, it's his decision, but it's more than a little like playing god," says Keven.

"What effect would jumping into the twenty-first century have on him?" I say.

"What effect would even introducing the possibility that he could go with us have on him? Especially if he chooses to stay. How can we even consider it, much less bring it up?" says Bob.

I say, "Keven has Stephen's answer. If he's decided against the unknown of life across the Ohio River, how much more reluctant would he be to take a chance with us? If we can get away clean, just disappear, so much the better for him. We know he enjoys world-wide renown and success. We don't have any idea what could happen with these other moves. My guess, he is the critical person – together with Dr. Croghan – that has to remain in place for Stephen's own good and for the good of the cave."

"Glad you thought of that, Bob and Walt," says Keven. "I hope Stephen would agree. I think he would."

"Okay. Good. Let's round up the Wild Cavers and go to Cathedral Domes," says Bob. I see his disappointment at being this close and yet missing the famous guide. Even with my short time working in the cave, I am reluctant to forgo meeting Stephen Bishop. For Bob, it must be torture.

The Wild Cavers, Craig among them, seem eager to be on their way. The whole thing has been exciting, but somewhat less interesting for them than it has been for Keven. To my mind, and I'm sure to his, Keven has lived a dream. He might have some trouble dealing with the twenty-first century for a while after this is over. He explained how much trouble it was deciding how much to tell Stephen Bishop, and I think he will have the same trouble with what to tell the folks back in our time. Of course, we still have a trip ahead of us. And I am anxious to keep going. Faster seems safer. I refuse to consider the likelihood of being stuck here.

Keven leads the group in the climb to the entrance of the Corkscrew. Bob and I trail. Members of the tour offer to help with the packs and lanterns. Bob and I give ours up, but Craig hangs on to his pack. After I crawl off the ledge into the passage, I look back. Bob faces toward the Rotunda, and I see him silhouetted in a faint yellow glow swelling across the ceiling. The glow from Stephen Bishop's lantern coming into the Rotunda.

"Ah well," he says. We swing around and descend behind the group climbing down to River Hall.

Twenty-Three
Mr. Creighton Comes Calling

"Who's there?" Denise looked up with alarm.

"My name is Creighton, madam. And your name, my dear lady?" came the voice. She looked around, but found no speaker.

"I'm Denise Castleton. I'm with the National Park Service. May I ask how you got here? Where are you?"

"I am right here. I have been here for several minutes."

This time, Denise saw a pale figure of a man in a dark suit and hat carrying a lard-oil lantern. "You startled me. I mean I know that you came to visit Craig, that young man that was left here in the dark yesterday." *It was just yesterday in fact, wasn't it?* "But I didn't hear you approach."

"No. I try to be as quiet as I can. I offer you my most sincere apologies, madam."

"You're a ghost, then?" said Denise.

"I'm not sure, madam. For a while, I am here in the cave. When I go into my little room, I'm out with the stars. But I don't think it's Heaven. So I don't think I'm a ghost." Denise stared at the lantern. The flame flickered. She could smell bacon cooking. It lit the area of the cave around the lantern.

"You look — you know — real?"

"I must say, madam, I feel quite substantial."

"But, why start showing up in front of people now?" asked Denise.

"It's unusual for anyone to be alone in this part of the cave. That young man a little bit ago was the first in some time. And he was the first that didn't run away when he saw me. It's very off-putting, that is, running away," said Creighton.

"Why don't you come out for the tours?" asked Denise.

"I don't enjoy being in crowds. In fact, I abhor them. So I visit with the solitary figures. And solitude seems to suit me."

"What about food and — and — other things?"

"Oh, I see what you mean. Well, when I'm out in the stars, as it were, I'm in a comfortable bedroom and sitting room with an incredible glass ceiling and wall. None of the star patterns are familiar to me, so I don't know whose night sky I look at, but I assure you, it is quite spectacular."

"Amazing!" said Denise. "How did you find that room?"

"Oh, it was nothing. I was here with the guide, Stephen Bishop, and a few other people. This is a most delightful part of the cave. When I'm in the dome area, it's so light and airy. I feel free. All that space and no people. When Stephen led our small group on toward the domes, I lingered behind. I saw this shadow area where a small buttress jutted out from the cave wall. I toddled right up to it and noticed that the light from my lantern did not make it any less dark. It was pure blackness. I stuck my hand into the shadow. There was no rock. No wall."

"So you just sauntered right on in?" said Denise.

"Just so."

"And?"

"There was this room. It was neither too large; nor too small. It had a huge window with a great view of stars and curious celestial objects. It's very easy to spend a lot of time looking at the stars. I sleep very well. The food tastes quite good. Although, it did take some time to adjust to it. No meat, you know."

"But, you were never reported lost. What happened?"

"That's right. I left the cave with Stephen and the others after our tour. The next morning I said my goodbyes at the hotel and strolled along the way back toward Bell's Tavern. A little ways down the track, I hopped into the woods and circled back. I sat in some brush up above the mouth of the cave and spent a most relaxing afternoon. After dark, I slipped back into the cave and found my way back here."

"That's an amazing story. Who brings your food to you?" asked Denise.

"I don't ever see anyone on that side. There is a cold box that stays full of food, and I warm things up in another box. I have no idea how any of it works – or even why. Except for the chance visitor here in the cave, I don't see anyone."

"Don't you get bored?"

"Well, I suppose I might, but I haven't been here that long. I'm reading a new novel, *The History of Tom Jones*. Henry Fielding wrote it. I'm about to finish it. Have you read it?"

"Yes," said Denise. "I enjoyed his first book, *Joseph Andrews*, even more. Do you know that one?" *Haven't been here that long? Since 1848?*

"No, I don't. Could you bring it to me? It's very pleasant reading in my little room. But, back to your question. So. I guess about a month has passed. Why do you ask?" said Creighton.

"No particular reason," said Denise.

"Well, good-bye. I've enjoyed our little chat. I look forward to seeing you soon," said Creighton. He bowed to Denise and disappeared in the shadows.

"Wait, Mr. Creighton. Will you come back? How will I know where to leave the book?"

Denise started to follow Creighton when he waved over his shoulder and went around the curve of the passage. Denise paused to look at her watch. Over two hours past Bob's departure, and she was late to call Anne. How frustrating! What happened to her watch alarm? She shook her wrist.

Twenty-Four
Twist in the Corkscrew

Bob and I descend around and over from ledge to ledge. A much easier trip down than up. Plus, we know the route. The Corkscrew drops well over one hundred feet in vertical change with little horizontal movement. Being a direct route from Main Cave to River Hall, I am surprised that the Corkscrew wasn't discovered before 1870. And that was by accident. Surprising until you realize that there are almost as many options of ways to go as there are moves on a chessboard. The first person through was following one opening after another and lost his way. He was smoking his last cigar and writing his last will and testament on the wall of rock when someone smelled his cigar smoke. That Keven was able to find his way up through it without the ladders or the scuff marks of thousands of cave visitors and guides before him impresses me.

Bob stops on the edge of a drop. After a minute or two, I grow impatient.

"What's up?"

"Someone's been hurt. They're having to help him down." Bad news, indeed. A serious injury could stop us cold. We're over two miles from Cathedral Domes over rough, rocky terrain, in the dark. We do have first aid gear with us. And we do have a lot of bearers. This breakdown area may be the worst of it.

"I don't mind the rest," I say.

"Me either," says Bob. "I wish we weren't so wet."

"Well, we'll back in the river pretty soon."

"We're moving," Bob says over his shoulder.

"Any word on who and how they're injured?" I say.

"Josh. The kid with the glasses? It's his ankle. They think it may be just a sprain. He was close to the bottom.

"That's good news," I say. "You can't be too big if you're on the Wild Cave." That's a benefit of the Bear Hole, I never considered. If they can fit through that, they can be managed on a carry out. I was fortunate in my short cave career that all of the visitors on the tours I worked were able to exit under their own power.

We scramble down and around the last few ledges and emerge into Bandit Hall, past the future location of the old, smelly toilets, and emerge into River Hall. The group hovers around Josh lying on a pad on the cave floor beside a Coleman lantern.

Two members of the tour are standing in the group with our packs on. Bob and I retrieve the packs in case Keven needs some of the first aid gear they're carrying. Dan Ross joins Keven at work on Josh's ankle.

Rod is busy keeping the group from crowding too close. Doing something useful at last.

Bob approaches one of the other Wild Cavers.

"Do you know what happened," asks Bob.

"Hi, Bob. Josh was trying to go down that long drop back there? And when he, like, put his foot down, there was this rock? And it, like, rolled out from under his foot. Then he fell. And he hit his head, but he had his hardhat on, and that was way cool. But I think it still stunned him a little, like, you know?"

"Right. You're Dylan, aren't you?" says Bob.

"I am. You have a good memory. But. It's more Dylan Thomas than Bob Dylan, okay?"

"Right. The poet, not the troubadour. Thanks, Dylan."

"Sure thing."

"How are all of you doing?" asks Bob.

"We were, like, very worried until you guys showed up." Dylan smiled, encompassing both of us in his wide grin. "And we were very hungry. I mean Stephen Bishop and the guys brought us food, but they didn't have much, like, you know, food we're used to. A couple of the dudes were craving some burgers and fries. Know what I mean?" says Dylan.

"Yeah, I do. But everyone's okay now?" asks Bob.

"Well this ankle thing with Josh is not too good, but we're glad to be headed — are you ready for this? — *back to the twenty-first century!*"

Bob and I laugh. We are indeed going in that direction. But we are depending on some sort of system that we understand even less than the flux capacitor. And, like in the movie, there is just one shot at making it. Well, maybe more with the battery from the emergency light.

"That's good," I say to Dylan. "What are your impressions of Stephen Bishop and Mat and Nick?"

"Oh, they are cool. Stephen Bishop is like the coolest. I thought that if I were ever confronted with fourteen dudes from the future, I'd be freaking out so bad. But he took it all in, like we just rode in on the stage from Cincinnati or somewhere. I think Keven must have done a good job in cluing him in that first time. When we made it over from Little Bat to the Church, I was right behind him. He just sort of like glided over the trail. He was so smooth." Dylan smiled. "I think he and Keven totally bonded — you know? — like brother cave guides or something?"

"That's very interesting," I say. "Thanks for the information and insight. Glad you're okay." So the Wild Cavers are dealing with this trip in a post-post-modern we've-already-seen-it-in-the-movies sort of way. All except Craig. Still my main worry is how Keven is going to deal with life back in the twenty-first century. I look back on our departure from the Church, and I think there was more hesitation in his leaving than he meant to let on.

"Hey, Bob and Walt." It's Keven emerging from the huddle around the injured Wild Caver.

"How's Josh?" asks Bob.

"He'll be fine. It's just a sprain, but a pretty bad one. It's swelling. I've given him eight hundred milligrams of ibuprofen, a liter of Gatorade, and a couple of Hershey bars. Dan's a real whiz with an Ace bandage."

"It's a long way to Cathedral Domes on one foot," says Bob.

"Yeah, but we have thirteen reasonably fit cavers — experienced cavers now — and we can take it slow. They can work in shifts to help Josh along. No wood for a crutch down here."

"No," says Bob. "Walt and I can take our turns with the others."

"I want to hold you two in reserve. Ferrying him across the river will be tricky," says Keven.

"I have some MAST anti-shock trousers in my pack," says Bob. "How about if we use them to float Josh across the river?" Military Anti-Shock Trousers or MAST trousers, are a pair of vinyl trousers that can be placed over the legs of an injured person and inflated to maintain blood pressure after severe blood loss and stabilize a broken pelvis or other bones. They were invented during the Vietnam War.

"That's a great idea, Bob," says Keven. "How did you come up with those?"

"I found them in my pack back at the Church. But Denise supplied the packs. I didn't know the park had this kind of stuff, but when you think about it, it's perfect for someone injured way back in the cave."

"I wonder how Denise is doing," I say. "I haven't thought about her since we beamed back — or whatever we did."

"Where is she again?" says Keven.

"We left her at Hawkins Pass. If we weren't back in two hours, she was supposed to go for backup. I'm sure she's all right," says Bob.

"By herself?"

"Yes, by herself. It was her idea — sort of — and there was no way Craig was going to stay behind alone again. Maybe Creighton will visit with her," I say.

"Creighton who?" asks Keven.

"*The* Creighton. The one that left the footprints. Creighton's Dome," I say.

"That's right. You don't know about him," says Bob. "After you guys beamed back in time, Craig was left near the domes all alone in the dark. He said he banged a rock on the wall for a while. A man showed up carrying a lard-oil lantern, wearing old-timey clothes. He said his name was Creighton."

"I've never heard of anyone seeing or hearing anything back in that area. That's amazing," says Keven. "You're talking about the Creighton that carved his name on a rock near the footprints?"

"That's the one. The search team that found Craig said he was calling for Creighton to come back. And calling for you," I say.

"I want to talk about this some more, but we need to move. Bob, can you lead out? I'll go with Josh, and Walt, can you trail?"

We feel more secure with our packs in our hands, so Bob dons his pack. Keven belts on his fanny pack and advances to where Josh leans on Craig's shoulder. When I adjust my pack straps, Bob looks at me.

"At least the packs are a good deal lighter than they were coming in," I say.

"Are you okay at the back?"

"It's what I'm good at. It's not like any of these folks are going to try to stay behind," I say.

"It's not?" says Bob.

Twenty-Five
Calling for Backup

When Denise approached the spot in Martel, she was hoping that the lantern would not appear. It didn't. Creighton provided enough of that sort of thing. She should ask him about the ghost lantern. If he came back.

Denise sped along Boone's Avenue. At the first switch, she hit the green button for the lights. Even the cold, fluorescent light gave her some comfort and reassurance that she wasn't off in a different universe. Running the tour route in reverse was interesting. The guides didn't often see the cave from the reverse angle. Even so, the steps up out of Boone's Avenue were easy to spot.

Denise climbed the steps and trotted along the passage to the Snowball Dining Room. She hurried into the women's restroom. Emerging refreshed and with clean hands, she jogged along behind the serving line and up Marion's Avenue the short distance to the elevator. Compared to the elevator lobby in the basement of a twenty-seven-story building, it wasn't very fancy. There was one car-call button – it went up.

She was a lot more afraid of being trapped in the elevator than she ever was about being in the cave alone. The replacement, mineshaft elevator was used every day by concessions, maintenance and in emergencies. Even so, Denise lacked confidence in it.

She stepped out into the parking lot lit by the one security light and looked at her cell phone. The little screen showed four bars. She pushed the speed dial for Anne's cell phone.

"Hello, Denise. What's up?"

"You sound chipper for five in the morning. Can you meet me at the Snowball elevator building?"

"When?"

"Now. I need to show you something. You only. Understand?"

"I'll be there in thirty minutes."

"Thank you."

"Anne ... do you have a copy of *Joseph Andrews* by Henry Fielding?"

Twenty-Six
Cold Echo River

We strike out from River Hall down the passage toward Echo River. I have the advantage of the trailer position. I see the headlamps all strung out ahead of me. Bob in the lead sees no farther than the beam of his headlamp, but I have a hundred feet or more of cave illuminated. We straggle along, but still at a good pace, up to the Dead Sea – our first body of water. The early guides named this pool the Dead Sea because no visible inlet or outlet accounts for the water. Submerged cave passages connected to the main body of water control the water level in the Dead Sea.

Over the Natural Bridge, we cross the River Styx – the river inside the cave that issues through that spring into Green River where Barbara and I stood only the morning before. The morning before and one hundred seventy-five years in the future. The sky had been a brilliant blue against the green of the trees lining the ridges.

We hit the mud. Thick, brown mud. It sucks at your boots and absorbs most of the light. The walls and ceiling are coated with it. From here the mud deepens, and it slows our progress. Dan has wrapped Josh's ankle with an Ace bandage and secured it inside a nylon-fabric trekking boot. Even so, Josh can't put any weight on it. Keven takes his right shoulder, and Craig, his left. They slip and slide. In 1838, there are no guardrails.

After fifteen minutes, Keven calls a halt, and two Wild Cavers replace Craig and him. We wade Lake Lethe. There have been no storms in the last week or so, or else the level would be too deep to wade. In years to come, Lethe will be bridged and re-bridged. New bridges will replace bridges damaged by flooding so high that it got to the ceiling of River Hall in the nineteen twenties. The floods either demolished the bridges and boardwalks or filled them with sand and mud that had to be shoveled off before the next tour could go through.

On the other side we begin the *Great Walk*, a sandy passage that is also called the Sahara Desert, which leads to Echo River. After the group strings out, I count headlamps. Sixteen light the passage ahead of me. And checking to be sure, none shine behind me. The group travels with deliberate slowness over an easy path with no one lagging, but the mental stress must be pushing some of them toward the edge of their endurance. The ghost lantern accounts for some of it, but it is mostly being flung back to 1838 without a clue as to how they got there and no idea how to get back. Some of them may yet lack confidence in our ability to take them back to the twenty-first century. I share some of their doubt. Their chatter forms a low, constant hum.

At the ledge where we will embark upon our crossing of Echo River, the party stops. Bob unloads the MAST trousers from his pack, and Dan Ross takes them. He begins to inflate them from a small cartridge of carbon dioxide, going at it with the air of a professional. He smiles up at Keven.

"Air Force Pararescue." He tapes the ankles of the MAST trousers together and sets it in the water. It floats high. With Keven and Craig in the water to steady the small trouser raft, two other Wild Cavers help Josh onto the makeshift watercraft in a sitting position. Craig and Keven pull him along without ceremony. The next Wild Caver slips into the water.

"Damn! I forgot how cold this water is."

"Isn't it deeper than before?" comes a female voice.

"Deeper and colder," says a third voice.

Bob and I are the last ones left at the dock. The tour is strung out with Keven out of sight in the lead. The chamber echoes with exclamations and laughs. Laughs you emit when you jump into cold water. I look back along the dark path behind us. I see a light.

"Bob, look back here."

"What? Who is that?"

"Rod, is that you?"

"Relax, guys. It's just me. Not the boogeyman." Rod laughs, but seems nervous.

"How did you get behind us?" I say.

"Dan Ross is not the only one with fancy training. Army ranger, remember?"

"Right," I say. "Now off you go."

Rod slips on the mud at the edge of the water and with luck avoids a full-body immersion.

"Damn! That's cold!" says Rod.

"It's only fifty-four degrees," I say to his back.

Bob sits on the ledge and eases into the water. "I'm too old for this kind of thing," he says. "I think I'm too old for the cave."

"Are you doing okay? I mean, is it more than fatigue?"

"No, I think that's it. No problem with the heart. Not yet anyway."

"*But here, upon this bank and shoal of time, we'd jump the life to come.*" I say to the river and the cave. The splash and laughing of the Wild Cavers block any echo. "What do you think?"

"The Scottish play?" says Bob. "I guess we are trying to jump back to the next life, but to what was our own life to start with."

"Once we get out of the water, the hard part of the physical cave trip will be over," I say. "Then, it's just to worry about whether or not we can get home in the fourth dimension." If we fail, I'm not sure how many of us can make the trip back to the entrance again. We have some serious fatigue and exposure that could set in at any time – cold Echo River or not.

"They're right about it being cold. Woo!"

"We must have been running on adrenalin when we came through here before," I say grimacing and gasping at the same time. "We're going to have to break out some more hot liquids on the other side."

"If there are any left," says Bob. "We may have to run."

"Run?" I say, full of incredulity.

"I know. It's either a coronary or hypothermia."

"Well, maybe a trot," I say. "A short trot."

Up ahead we hear a sudden shout that grows into a cacophony of shouts and reverberation. Bob and I catch up to a cluster of Wild Cavers.

"Brian stepped in a hole," someone explains.

"Dale pulled him up on the other side," says another.

I see a Wild Caver shivering in the far group. His light still burns, and his eyes bug.

"Keep him moving. Get on either side," says Bob. "Walt, take the space blanket out of my side pouch on the right."

I pass the space blanket up to the three Wild Cavers. The two assistants wrap it around the shoulders of the wet and shaking caver.

"All right! Everyone, listen up. We have to get out of this water. Step it up. Be careful. Be fast!" says Bob.

Within ten minutes we are all on the sand of Silliman's Avenue. Josh alone stayed dry. Craig opens his pack and passes out candy. He announces his last Thermos of coffee. I pull out a baker's dozen space blankets and pass them around. Bob passes out Snickers bars, and serves coffee. From the bottom of my pack, I pull out the last Thermos of hot chocolate, a pair of socks, and a pair of coveralls.

"Brian, we need you to take off those wet coveralls," I say.

He looks at me like he's hearing voices. His head shakes, and his teeth chatter.

"Help him out of those," I say. I hold up the dry coveralls, and this speeds them along. "Take all his wet clothes off." With good speed they strip him and re-clothe him. I hand them the dry socks. They add these and lace on his boots.

"Good. Now, Brian, drink this. It's hot chocolate." His hands are shaking too much to hold the cup of precious hot liquid. A young woman in the group takes the cup in her right hand and puts her left behind his head to help him steady it.

She pours the first cup in. I refill the cup. Brian stays with it and drinks in gulps. The woman gives him a Snickers bar.

"Eat this, Brian," she says.

Brian takes the candy bar and devours it. "Thank you. You're Suzy, aren't you?" She nods her head, arm around his shoulder.

"How are you feeling?" she says.

"Cold, but not numb anymore," says Brian. His teeth are still chattering.

Keven asks, "Has everyone drunk something hot and eaten a candy bar?"

"Yay! Keven. Yay, Bob and Walt, Yay, Craig!" the group shouts in a broken, but enthusiastic series. While I was tending to Brian, Bob and Keven persuaded everyone to strip out of their coveralls and wring them out before putting them back on. They huddle together inside an outer wall of space blankets.

As I join Bob and Keven, I see that Brian and Suzy have joined the group, absorbed all the way to the center, an amoeba enveloping a bit of food. Josh sits dry and well satisfied on the MAST trousers.

"Walt, have you eaten anything?" asks Bob.

"Two Snickers bars and a sip of coffee. I'm good. How about you two?"

"I'm good," says Bob and looks at Keven.

"Not yet ..."

Bob and I both whip out Snickers bars and hand them to Keven with looks that say we're not going anywhere until you eat them.

"You were in the water a long time," I say. "Eat."

"Thank goodness for Denise," Bob says.

"Why Denise?" asks Keven.

"She loaded these packs. I don't know how she did it in the short time available, but thank goodness," says Bob.

"I second that," says Keven. "Let's move out. I'll keep Josh and Brian in the middle with me. Walt, are you still willing to trail?" Once Josh is up, Dan Ross deflates the MAST trousers and folds them under his arm.

I nod and pass along to the back of the group. I count heads filing past. Still fourteen visitors. Rod is accounted for. My earlier confidence in the load limit in this time machine feels more like bravado. Will it take three more and a twelve-volt battery?

Twenty-Seven
Revelations on the Elevator

In the time it took Anne to dress, find the novel, and drive from Park City to the Snowball elevator building, Denise drove over to the storage unit, packed another rescue pack, and grabbed a Stokes litter which she slid into the back of her mini-van.

She also brought Wild Cave gear for Anne, who wouldn't have guessed she was going in to Cathedral Domes.

Anne pulled in right behind Denise at the elevator building.

"What's going on?" asked the chief of visitor services.

"Good. You brought the book."

Denise launched into a description of events leading up to the present, all the while leading Anne along into the building where she coaxed her through a change of clothes and into the elevator.

About half way down, Anne exploded with, "They did what?"

"Bob and Walt and Craig followed Keven and the Wild Cavers to wherever they went. At least they disappeared. Is your cell phone charged up?"

"What's my phone got to ..." said Anne. "No way. We are not going there – wherever 'there' is – after them. No more cowboys and solo rescues. If they aren't back within an hour after we get to Cathedral Domes, I'm calling the rangers. If I could turn this piece of crap elevator around, I'd go call them right now. Denise!"

"I know, Anne. I know. But the rangers weren't paying any attention to Craig. Bob and I were worried about Keven. Whatever the rangers say, Keven did not lose a Wild Cave tour. They were going to leave him and the tour wherever they were while they searched around Frozen Niagara. They sure weren't entertaining any other explanation than that Keven was lost. He is not lost. Something else happened to them. I didn't have any choice. Wherever they went, they weren't equipped for a long stay. And Walt was worried, too."

"Walt! Who the hell is Walt? He hasn't worked here in forty years. All kinds of crap happens every time he comes to the cave. Craig is a civilian. Bob is semi-retired. The lawsuits will never end, Denise. Never end."

"Anne, if Bob and Walt bring them all back, maybe there won't be any lawsuits."

"Okay, Denise, but the publicity!"

"Anne, what would you rather have? Publicity about a lost cave tour that is never found – and there is little difference whether it's Keven and the Wild Cave tour or Keven, Bob, and Walt and the Wild Cave tour – or the publicity of this adventure, when it's successful?"

"How long have they been gone?"

"Six or seven hours. Thereabouts."

"Oh, God."

"Anne, if Bob hadn't gone in when he did, the DHS would have taken over, and Bob could never go after Keven. You know bureaucracy better than that. The DHS agents were never going to make the connection and follow Keven. They just weren't."

The ding of the elevator told them they were back in the cave. Denise helped Anne on with her pack and dragged the cut-down Stokes litter behind her.

As they stepped out into Marion's Avenue, Denise hit the switch for the lights. "We'll be faster with the lights on."

"Right. Let's move out," said Anne.

Twenty-Eight
Into Boone's Avenue, Dear Friends, Once more into Boone's Avenue

We cover Silliman's Avenue and hurry on through the Pass of El Ghor in about an hour and a half. About twice as long as a group of visitors would take. I consider that good time. And everyone but Bob and I has helped Josh hop along. And now we take our turn until Boone's Avenue narrows. Keven leads, and Craig trails.

"Josh, I'll help on the right side, you put your left hand out and use the wall," I say. Bob questions me with a look. "I'm good for now."

"I'll lead with Craig for a while and have Keven check on the rest of the group," says Bob.

"How's the ankle feel," I ask Josh after we've progressed along Boone's narrower section.

"It's hurting a little. But not too bad. I feel stupid."

"I know you do, but that's all wasted energy. It could have happened to any one of us. And with us older guys, it could have been a break, not just a sprain. Bad as that is. You're making pretty good time here."

"I think it's easier with just one helper. Swinging my left arm provides a little forward momentum."

"Good. When we get to the bend in the passage up ahead, we'll give you some more ibuprofen before we start climbing down."

"That'll be good. Thanks, Walt."

We hop along at a pretty good clip. The tour stays right behind, but they don't crowd us. We arrive at the fork with Rose's Pass. I help Josh settle onto a boulder; and, while we wait for the rest of the tour and the trailer to show up, I retrieve a canteen of water and four, two-hundred-milligram ibuprofen tablets. Josh swallows them down and drinks the rest of the water.

"Hungry?" I say.

"No, but I was thirsty. Thanks."

"What, ho?" says Keven, striding up.

"Walt just dosed me with some more pain killer," says Josh, smiling up at Keven.

"Are you hurting much?" says Keven.

"No, Walt suggested it before we start climbing down. It was hurting a little before we stopped."

"You guys were moving along pretty good," says Bob, joining the knot of cavers around Josh.

"He thinks he moves easier with just one on his right side. Climbing we may still want to use two," I say.

"Good. Everyone kept up," says Bob. "No one else seems to want to stay behind." The twinkle has returned to his eyes.

"Where's Rod?" I ask.

"Well up in the group. I think he has seen all the total darkness that he wants to see – by himself."

Keven checks out each Wild Caver one at a time. Even Brian is grinning and rearing to go. Ever the cave guide, Keven mounts the rock where Josh sits.

"We are, you remember, getting closer to Cathedral Domes. But we have some climbing to do still. It's not hard, but we need to take it nice and easy. You've done it before. We don't want to be reckless this close to our goal. Now then. Where are we going, gang?"

"*Back to the ...!*" comes the shout in one voice.

"Right. Let's go."

Keven starts the rotation with the first guy who helped Josh when we left River Hall. Bob leads out down Boone's Avenue, and I bring up the rear.

Before I get moving again, one of the Wild Cavers comes back to where I'm standing.

"Walt, I have a problem."

"I hope you didn't leave anything back there," I say pointing toward the Snowball Room.

"No, nothing like that. I've got the runs. Sorry."

"No problem." I shrug out of my pack and break out a roll of toilet paper, a pre-moistened wet wipe, and an orange, plastic trowel. I hand them to the caver. "Go back up Rose's Pass around the first bend."

"Okay. Then what?"

"What do you mean, 'Then what?'"

"I've never done anything like this," he says looking at his feet.

"Oh. Dig a six-inch hole, drop your pants, let her rip. Wipe, throw the TP in the hole, wipe your hands with the wet wipe, throw that in the hole, and cover up. Important part here. Wipe your hands with the wet wipe before you pick up the trowel again."

"What do I sit on?"

"Just squat. Remember, use the trowel for dirt. Not anything else."

"Oh. Right." I'm very glad I decided to mention that last piece of advice.

In less than ten minutes, the ailing caver returns. He holds the trowel and TP roll toward me. "First twist them around in my light," I say. They appear clean, so I take them from him. "Everything okay?"

"I think so. That was so weird ..."

"Yeah, I guess it must be. Here, take this. And this." I hand him an individual dose of non-bismuth, anti-diarrhea medicine and a sports drink in a plastic bottle.

"Thanks, Walt."

"Come on, let's catch up."

At the bottom of the first climb, there's another Wild Caver. Another one I haven't talked to yet.

"Let me guess. Diarrhea."

"He nods his head, "Sorry, but I'm cramping pretty bad."

I shrug out of the pack and send him with the tools of the trade into a corner.

"Walt?"

"Yeah?"

"It's all rock over here."

"Shove some rocks aside and cover back up with rocks. Don't forget to wipe your hands with the wet wipe." I ease a ways down the passage.

"Wait, don't leave me!"

"I'll be right here. Focus. Be careful. And clean." This must be someone, who, when his mother sent him out in the yard to play, stood in the shade, confused, playing his Game Boy. But he's in good physical shape, or he wouldn't have lasted on this excursion through time and inner space. I exchange the medicine and a sports drink for the toilet accessories, and we push on down the passage.

As I pick my way down into Martel, I see someone standing off to the left of the track we're following. When I see the carbide light, I know that it's Keven.

"Don't tell me you have diarrhea, too?" I say.

"No. Is that what y'all have been doing?" says Keven with a chuckle. "Cave crud strikes again."

"Two so far, that I know of. Two that have never done it off of white porcelain."

"You're kidding," says Keven.

"No, I'm not. I think that bothered them more than being back in 1838," I say.

"It never came up on the trip until now. Maybe time travel causes constipation."

"Could be, but the cave crud overcame it," I say.

"We'll be home before long now, I hope," says Keven. He's holding a lard-oil lantern in his hands.

"What's that?"

"This is one of the lanterns Stephen Bishop left us."

"And you're going to take it back to the twenty-first century?"

"No. I thought about it. I've scratched my name on the bottom, and I'm going to hide it under a rock over here." He crouches down and rolls a slab of limestone over the hole that hides the lantern.

"Interesting," I say. "You know what?"

"Yes, I do. It looks like the one that floated through here – when was it? Yesterday?"

"Day before, maybe. Yes, it does. So that's why the ghost lantern is here," I say.

"No, it wasn't here when I saw the spectral lantern yesterday," says Keven. "We hadn't gone back in time yet."

"I guess it depends on how you look at it," I say. "But I think so."

"No, it can't have been."

"Well, I think we're too tired and in the wrong place for a discussion of when we were where."

"You're right." He rolls the slab over the lantern and stands up. "There."

"Come on, let's go."

Twenty-Nine
He's not a Ghost

Denise dropped the litter at Nelson's Domes. She hoped that they wouldn't need it. It would be a close thing getting it out loaded if they did. Anne eased the pack straps off her shoulders. "I've never worn a full pack in narrow passages before. It's not easy."

"It's hard all right," Denise said. "Here we are. Craig said he was over there at the wall." Denise pointed to the spot where Craig banged a rock against the limestone wall. "Do you see this cutout in the cave floor over here?" Denise ran the beam of her light around the perimeter of the neat pattern cut out of the rock.

"Yes," said Anne.

"Bob figures that's where Keven and the rest of the Wild Cave tour were standing."

"Who marked out that pattern? What's it based on?"

"It's not marked, Anne. It's cut. Look at it."

Anne knelt down and took her right glove off. She ran her fingers along the glass-smooth edges of the cut. "This is incredible. The rangers didn't say anything about this."

"I don't think they saw it. And you can't blame them, what with Craig yelling about Creighton and so on. By the way, Creighton comes from over that way," said Denise pointing behind where their packs lay.

"Did Craig tell you that?"

"No, that's where he came from shortly after the three of them left."

"Is he going to come back, do you think?" said Anne, her eyes darting left and right.

"I don't know. He says he doesn't like crowds."

"You talked to him?"

"Yes, I did. No different than you and I are talking right here, right now. The book is for him."

"I don't believe in ghosts," said Anne. "Especially ghosts that read."

"He's not a ghost."

"But he would be very, very old. That can't be," said Anne.

"I think he spends most of his time in a place in the space/time continuum where he doesn't age with respect to what's going on here. In addition to this device that makes people – and rocks – disappear, there's some sort of gate that Creighton stumbled into."

"I don't believe in those either. You read too much science fiction."

"Well, you just wait right here, and you'll begin to think you don't read enough. Stay out of the cutout. I'm going to stroll back down the passage. We'll see if he comes out to talk to you. Give him the book."

"Denise, that won't be necessary," Anne looked at Denise with alarm and pulled her glove back on.

Denise smiled. "He's not frightening. Just talk to him. I'll be back in a few minutes."

"Denise! Denise!"

It was well over ten minutes later when Denise came back into the little alcove. Anne and Mr. Creighton were standing about four feet apart talking. He held the book open in his hands. Anne was smiling and waving her hands about.

"Miss Denise, how do you do?" asked Mr. Creighton.

"I am very well, thank you, Mr. Creighton. I see you have met my supervisor, Anne."

"Yes. We have been enjoying the most delightful conversation. I've been trying – with no success, I might add – to persuade her to step into my little room."

"Have you, just?" asked Denise, wondering why he invited Anne, but not her. Why wasn't she ever included? She would like to see interesting star patterns. Strange, new constellations.

Thirty
Energize!

Keven and I catch up with the Wild Cavers at Einbigler's Dome. How are we going to transport Josh along the narrow ledge?

"If we only had some rope," says Keven, "we could rig a modified Tyrolean traverse."

"Rope, we have," I say, shedding the pack and digging deep into the bottom. I emerge with a standard length of 10.6-millimeter Bluewater II caving rope, some slings, and carabiners.

"Thank you, Denise," says Keven.

In a short time, Craig and Keven on either end belay Josh sitting in a sling and being pulled along by two Wild Cavers. Craig coils the rope and slings it over his shoulder. His recovery appears complete. *How will he ever go back to the life of a college student?*

The rest of us cross over the thin ledge that looks a lot thinner now than when we were headed in the other direction. *Adrenalin.*

We negotiate through the domes into Hawkins Pass, and when I trail up, the group is bunched around the cutout, this time elevated above the cave floor. I count heads for the next to the last time. Fourteen Wild Cavers, two old guides, and me.

"All here, Keven," I announce.

"Good," says Keven and pitches into the beginning speech for a cave tour, but a Wild Caver distracts me, sidling up with his head down.

"Uh ..." he begins.

"I know," I say. Out of my pack, I hand him the now smaller roll of tissue, the orange trowel, and a wet wipe. "If there's no soil, cover with rock. And," I emphasize, "Wipe your hands before you handle anything else. Got it?"

"Right. Donnie told me about the rocks."

"Good." I dig out another sports drink and another dose of 'not-the-pink-stuff.'

"Okay, are we all ready?" asks Keven.

I raise my hand.

"Yes, Walt?"

"Can't time-travel with the runs. It shouldn't take long."

At the mention of the symptom, another Wild Caver breaks from the ranks.

"Bob, can we borrow your equipment? Mine's in use."

"Sure thing." Bob hands the stricken caver the necessaries, and off he goes back down Hawkins Pass. Bob joins me.

"I've been giving them some generic for diarrhea and a sports drink," I say.

"Good idea. Do you have enough?" asks Bob.

"I have a couple more, so I think we're okay."

The remainder of the Wild Cavers are restless. They're stomping their feet, except for Josh, and shuffling around. I notice that Suzy and Brian are huddling close together. No doubt Brian still feels the cold.

Keven brings the group to order. "Folks, before we head on home, we need to talk. You have been on an incredible adventure, and you have participated in something that no one else in our civilization has ever done – that we know of. You have traveled back in time and seen Mammoth Cave in its untouched and unmarred beauty. You fourteen people have a unique and special relationship with Mammoth Cave. You have met historic figures. We don't understand what made all of this possible, but it is something buried up in the very depths of Mammoth Cave. In one of the breathtaking and beautiful places in Mammoth Cave. A place no more than a few hundred people see per year." The stricken cavers wander back and exchange toilet implements for medicine and drinks while Keven talks.

"Bob and I have worked for decades showing the cave to interested visitors. We are dedicated to protecting the cave, and we have a special favor to ask of you. At the very least, for the next couple of months, or maybe the next year, we beg you to keep this adventure quiet." The Wild Cavers remain still.

"This whole trip is top secret. No one can talk to anyone about this until you get clearance to do so from the Department of Homeland Security," says Rod in what passes for his authoritative voice.

"Thank you, Rod. I know. I know I am asking a lot. But think about what will happen to Cathedral Domes if this gets out. There could be an outcry to dig this thing up, whatever it is. Cathedral Domes and a lot of the rest of Mammoth Cave will be destroyed. Please think long and hard before you tell anyone else about our adventure. Please," says Keven. Instead of the groans I have anticipated, the Wild Cavers agree with nodding heads and cheers.

"Keven, I would like to speak on behalf of this Wild Cave tour," says Josh, supported on his good ankle by Dot. "We already discussed this among ourselves." He looks around at all the Wild Cavers, except Rod. Heads nod. "We feel a special attachment to Mammoth Cave, and even though most of us have never seen Cathedral Domes, we feel a special attachment. Craig told us all about how majestic they are. You don't have to tell us what people will do to the cave. We saw the Snowball Room in all its glory before it was damaged by the presence and vandalism of human beings. We have seen the unspoiled Mammoth Cave. We have exchanged phone numbers, and we have each other if we need to talk about this trip. We respect your wishes, and we want to invite the three of you – and Denise – to our first annual 1838 re-union at this time next year at the Mammoth Cave Hotel."

"Thank you. Thank you all very much," says a much-relieved Keven. Bob smiles and claps.

"Yes, thank all of you, and on behalf of Anne, Denise, and Walt, we accept your re-union invitation," says Bob. "Now, to matters at hand. Each of you needs to stand as close as possible to where you were when you arrived here in 1838. The machine that brought you here took a circle of limestone about three feet in diameter for each of you. So at a minimum we need one person in each of the circles along the edges. Keven, I think you go in the circle at the head up there."

"Right. I'm so glad you guys figured all of this out. Where are you going to stand?" says Keven.

I troop around and pick up the six pieces of limestone we rode in on and put them in the circle around Keven. No need to leave that puzzle for Stephen Bishop when he makes it back here. Bob checks each Wild Caver around the edges to make sure they're in the right place. Craig sets the battery in a blank space that will be included in the field. He hands Zona's phone to Bob.

"The three of us will stand among those in the middle. There should be plenty of room for overlap."

"Bring all our gear. We're leaving only footprints and … uh … some organic matter. Bob, you brought a spare battery? Wow! Lead us back," says Keven.

"Everyone ready?" yells Bob.

"Ready!" comes the cry.

"Craig, send us back."

"Aye, Captain!" The loud buzzing starts and ends in a concussion of silence.

I look around. All our lights are on.

"Where's Denise?" yells Bob.

Thirty-One
Re-Past

"Walt, what? Where's Denise?" says Bob.

I step off my rock, and speed through the group to where we left Denise with a lantern and a pack. She's nowhere to be seen.

"Denise!" No answer. There are sounds of concern verging on panic coming from the group.

Bob and Keven join me.

"What's up?" says Keven.

"We're not back in the twenty-first century," I say. "Look at where Craig banged on the wall. No marks."

"What do you think?" says Keven.

"I suspect we've gone further into the past. Our footprints aren't here," says Bob. "Right?" He looks at me. I nod.

"Let's recharge Craig's phone," I say. As the group moves toward panic, Rod berates Keven.

"Keven, you better tell them what's going on," says Bob.

"Okay. Like I know," says Keven. "Listen up, everyone. Hey! Listen up!"

The group quiets down over several minutes. They face Keven.

"Look, we think we are now further in the past ..."

Shouts burst from the group, "What the hell?"

"Keven, that was not authorized," says Rod.

"Okay, I know, Rod. Thanks. This is worrisome and only temporary. But Bob and Walt, and wonderful Denise waiting for us back in our time, thought this thing through and brought along a twelve-volt battery. We're charging up the phone, and will be on our way in about fifteen or twenty minutes. So, everyone stand easy and comfortable, and thank you for your patience."

I think they calm down with little argument, given my own fears. "Good job, Keven," I say.

"But even with a charged phone, what do we do to keep from going further back than where — when we are. If we are moving backward in time at a standard jump of one hundred seventy-five years, we are in what year? 1663? Another trip further back would put us in 1488. Four years before Columbus went on his voyage to the edge of the world."

"Walt, check me on this. We entered the active area from the same direction when we went back to 1838 and did the same thing and got sent back even further. So, if it sent us further into the past, what would happen if we entered from the opposite direction?" says Bob.

"It's a great idea. I can't think of any other way to change direction. We have no other control." I shrug my shoulders. I just hope we can move forward again. 1838 would be a lot better than 1663. If nothing else, it gives us something to do before we all panic.

"It's worth a shot then," says Bob. "Okay, gang, about face. Forward march." We head toward Cathedral Domes, in the direction the tour was heading when they were caught up in this business. When we go as far down the passage as we can without having to climb, Bob calls a halt. "Walt, how long to reset?"

"Let's give it fifteen minutes." I hope that something this high tech can reset faster than that. Bob's theory, pretty shaky at best, gives us the one control on our way back. Keven explains the theory to the Wild Cavers.

"When we entered the cutout headed toward Cathedral Domes, we went back in time. Bob is hoping that when we approach the cutout going away from Cathedral Domes, the machine will sense we want to go forward in time. The delay may allow the circuitry to reset to send us in the other direction."

For fifteen minutes, we sit on the cold limestone floor. Rod grouses and makes threats, which increases everyone's confidence in Keven and Bob.

"I sure hope this works," says Bob. "I like Keven fine, but I'd much rather be in the twenty-first century with Zona than in 1838 – or worse – with Keven."

"I'm with you on that. And the sixteen hundreds really have no appeal. We may have lots of phone charges in that battery, but I think we'll run out of patience or sanity first."

"You're right there," says Bob.

"It's charged!" says Craig.

Without talking, we troop into the active area and re-form inside our circles. I check to make sure everyone has their extremities inside the boundaries of the energy field, but close enough to the edge to carry all of the rock, and assume my own position.

"Ready."

"Craig, are you ready?" says Bob.

"Aye, Captain."

I see the glow of his phone screen.

Bob says, "Keven, on your command."

"Keven smiles all around, "Energize!" The buzzing begins, becomes very loud. It stops.

Thirty-Two
Forward to 1838

"Are we there yet?" comes a tired voice from the group.

I scamper off my rock and check around. It all looks the same. An idea occurs to me.

"Who was the last one to relieve themselves before we left 1838?" I say.

A hand goes up in the middle. "Me, Hank."

"Great. Hank could you go take a quick check and see if your deposit is still there?"

"What?"

"That will tell us if we came forward in time or went further back. Go take a look."

"Okay." He shuffles through the group with his head down. Craig starts to go with him. "I got it, Craig. But thanks," says Hank.

"This whole trip, poop stains and all, is still classified," says Rod.

"Roger that," I say.

"Hey, Walt! It's still there. We're back to 1838!" says Hank, smiling now.

Loud cheers.

"Thank you, Hank, you are now the official, first time-navigator."

"Keven, we have spotted the poop." A voice from the anonymous middle. Laughter relieves a lot of tension.

"Bob, do we re-charge Craig's phone or go with Zona's?" I say.

"Let's try Zona's. She'll be proud," says Bob. If she and Barbara don't kill the two of us, I think. "All right gang, let's re-load from the rear one more time."

I make another perimeter check and count heads. "We're all present and accounted for, Bob."

"Ready?"

"Yes!" comes the cheer.
"Fire!"

Thirty-Three
Forward Into Time

"Oh, my god!"

"Holy smoke!"

"My word! I have to leave. Good-bye." A man in a black coat voices this last and zips into a shadow near the back of the alcove. I see nothing but his back before he disappears, but I think I know who he is.

There's no smoke, no blue electric sparks running all over everyone. Denise and Anne — and Creighton — appear in an instant. The dingier walls of the passage and the light from the Coleman lantern are the only differences.

"Well done, Zona's phone!" I say.

Whatever this thing is, it worked one more time. And in the right direction. I am weak with relief. I have been going along without giving too much thought about what was going to happen long term. Even on the long slogs through the cave, I focused on the excitement of seeing the cave unspoiled, and at the very least, making the next step. Now, the magnitude of what we've done hits me.

"Keven!" shouts Denise.

"Denise, I love you," says Keven, taking her in his arms and squeezing hard. It seems that my worrying about Keven adjusting to being back in the twenty-first century was unnecessary. He's elated. "Denise, the stuff you put in the packs was heaven-sent. You are an angel. You saved us. Thank you," says Keven, and he grabs her in another bear hug, and the Wild Cavers crowd around to shake her hand and thank her.

"Keven, welcome back," says Anne. "Are you okay?"

"Hi, Anne. Yes, I'm fine. We have one sprained ankle on Josh over there. With help, he's ambulatory. We have one who was close to hypothermia – a dunking in Echo River – but he seems to be coping."

Denise and Anne together say, "Where have you been?"

"We found them at Methodist Church, asleep. In the year 1838," says Bob.

"1838?" says Denise. "I knew I should have gone."

"Keven ate supper with Stephen Bishop, Mat and Nick Bransford," says Bob, wistful, but not bitter.

"Stephen Bishop is the coolest," says Josh.

"You all saw Stephen Bishop?" says Anne.

"Yes! Stephen Bishop!" the group says.

"What are we going to do?" asks Anne of no one in particular. "Keven! We need to talk."

"I'm with the Department of Homeland Security," says Rod. "Who are you?"

"Hi. I'm Anne. I'm the Chief of Visitor Services. How can I help you?"

"This entire mission is classified top secret."

"That's great," says Anne. "I am so glad. Thank you." Rod doesn't know what to say next.

"This is all too much," says Denise, huge tears running down her cheeks. Bob goes over and puts an arm around her shoulders. She leans into his shoulder, and sobs rack her body. The release of tension and fatigue and gratitude seem to have hit her all at once. "I didn't meet Stephen either. Neither did Walt. Maybe you can go on the next trip, Denise," he says.

She rears back from him and grips his upper arms. "You mean we can go back?"

"I don't know," says Bob. "But I don't see why not." With that, Denise buries her face in Bob's shoulder and hugs him.

I look at the edge of the cutout. The section of rock that traveled with Keven back into the past has come back with us to the present. I see a faint line in the cave floor. I want to ask Denise what she experienced when we re-appeared, but that can wait.

Looking around, I see Keven engrossed in conversation with Anne – no doubt talking about overtime pay – Bob talks with Denise, so I step up on the rock.

Thinking of Brian and Josh, I say "Listen up. We need to get a move on. One more time, we're heading over to Martel, up Boone's Avenue and over to the Snowball Dining Room. But this time, there will be cleared trails, handrails, and lights — for part of the way."

"Walt, will there be boats to take us across Echo River this time?" asks Brian from his embrace with Suzy.

"Even better, Brian. We're going up the elevator behind Snowball Dining room."

Loud cheers erupt. I wave my hand in the air.

"Craig, will you go ahead with Anne? I think it would be good if you ran on up to the surface ahead of us and call Myrna and arranged for some transport." Craig salutes with a big smile. I think he enjoys his role of rescuer, relieved of every bit of guilt for sending the tour into the past.

"I better go with the advance group to coordinate the recovery," says Rod. No one argues.

Bob pats Craig on the shoulder. "Myrna should know as soon as possible. Thank you, Craig. You were a great part of the rescue team." He shakes Craig's hand.

"I don't think we need an ambulance, eh, Keven? Dan?" I say. Keven looks to Dan, who looks at Josh and Brian and shakes his head. Keven gives me a thumbs-up. "Good. You three, Craig, Anne, and Rod, take off. We'll organize the exodus. Denise and Hank, why don't you lead once we're ready. We still need help for Josh, but it should be easier going all around."

"Thanks, Walt. Once a guide, always a guide, eh?" says Keven.

"Right you are, Keven. Thank you."

All the lanterns are lit and dispersed through the group. One of the Wild Cavers takes charge of the battery. Bob and I bring up the rear. It's a much cheerier group than the last time we passed this way, not knowing where or when we were.

"I'm damned glad that thing worked going back — or coming forward. Whatever." says Bob.

"Yeah. But, what if it kept sending us another one hundred seventy-five years further into the past?" I say.

"Beyond 1488?" says Bob. "Before the Vikings, you mean?"

"Yes, that's it. I don't know how we would tell which direction in time we were going or how far. I'm glad it knew when we reloaded that we wanted to go forward."

"I'm glad we thought of coming in from the other end," says Bob.

"I'm glad you thought of it," I say. "It worked. We're back. Thanks."

We pause in our conversation until everyone passes Einbigler's Domes and on into Martel. Keven steers everyone toward Boone's Avenue.

"Well, Keven, how does it feel to be back?" asks Bob. We walk at an easy pace well behind the group.

"You know ... back there when we were leaving Methodist Church, I had some hesitation about coming back. I wouldn't want to leave Myrna. If I had stayed for any length of time, it wouldn't be credit for Stephen Bishop and Mat and Nick. It would be me. It was too hard. So to answer your question, it feels great. Thank you both for coming after me."

"We're glad you're back," I say. "Is the lantern where you left it?"

Keven grins so wide I think his jaw might pop. "Yes, it is. And for now, that's where it stays.

"Did Denise and Anne see the ghost lantern when they came back the last time?" I say.

"I don't know. They may not even remember after all this. Poor Denise. I know how I would feel if you two went off to 1838, and left me behind."

"I could have stayed, I guess. But talking to Creighton counts for something," I say.

"Is that who that was?" says Keven.

"That's my guess," says Bob. "Craig talked to him before the rangers found him."

"It sure is great to be back in real time," says Keven. He heads up to Boone's and catches up with his Wild Cavers. Some of them drift back to talk to Bob. I trail, catching the light switches after we leave each section, enjoying the cave.

We stop at the Snowball Dining Room for a much-needed rest stop. Keven and Denise take the first group back down the passage to wait for Anne to send the elevator down. Bob and I will bring the second half up with us. We sit at the little round table after I retrieve my rock.

"For the archives," I say, stowing the sliced rock in my pack. I pull a Snickers bar from my pocket and pass it to Bob.

"The last one." He smiles.

The trips up the elevator take a while, but when we arrive at the surface, Keven is standing at the door to the outside thanking each Wild Caver for allowing him to lead them to 1838 and back. And he tells them what a great Wild Cave tour they are.

"Thank you, Bob and Walt," says Keven, pumping our hands with such force I think he's on another dose of adrenalin.

"Keven, I'm glad it all worked out for the better. But, I'm very glad to be back where we belong. How about you, Walt?" says Bob.

"Glad to be back. Very glad indeed."

All around the building, chaos reigns. Rod is yelling directions all over the place. I see the short man from our previous ranger meeting come over to him. They huddle. All to no good I expect. Rangers are all over the place, but they are outnumbered by men in DHS windbreakers. They have an ambulance, a bus, a couple of mini-vans, and several other Park Service vehicles.

I see Myrna and Daran drive up. Keven hurries over to them. Bob and I drift off to the side and wait for everyone else to be transported. All the rescue vehicles block Bob's Suburban.

"Hey, Sweetheart!" Barbara says over my cell phone.

"Hey. I missed you."

"Where are you?" says Barbara.

"We just came up the Snowball elevator. As soon as the traffic clears, we're headed out on to the sinkhole plain."

"Did you find Keven and the rest?"

"Yep. Sure did. Got everybody back with only one sprained ankle and one dunking in Echo River. We are tired and hungry. How are you?"

"Lonesome, but a lot less worried now that you've called. When do you think you will be here?" says Barbara.

"I'm not sure. They're herding the Wild Cavers onto a bus for the trip to the dormitory for their clothes and personal gear. We'll have to go over there, too, but it shouldn't take too long. Homeland Security is here, and who knows how much they'll slow the operation down. I'll call you back when we hit the road."

"Hurry home to me," she says.

"I will. Love you!"

Bob calls Zona at home using her cell phone. I look around. The mid-morning sky is a brilliant blue. Time for food. I dig out the cooler and retrieve wet wipes, bottled water, and two ham sandwiches. Denise and Anne stand nearby waiting for Bob to finish his call.

"Bob, you deserve a lot of thanks. You, too, Walt. I have to say, you really shouldn't have done that on your own," says Anne. "But, thank you for doing it all the same, and for doing it so well."

"I'm not sure what we did," says Bob. "And we wouldn't have been at all successful without Denise's amazing foresight and energy in preparing those packs. Except for Denise, we didn't think about what we were doing. We should have, but we didn't. We're very lucky the transporter worked the way it did. Walt and I were talking about what would have happened if we kept going further into the past. It's sort of hit me, but what the hell? It ended up all right."

"Thank you, Walt," says Denise.

"You're welcome, both of you. But I didn't do that much. I'm with Bob, I thought of it as going into the cave to find Keven. He seems happy to be back."

"He's happy. Myrna's ecstatic," says Anne. "I still don't know how we're going to handle the publicity and the research on this thing."

"Let the Flint Ridge Coalition handle it. They're pretty good at keeping cave stuff deep, dark secrets," I say, grinning.

"No pun intended?" says Denise.

"None whatsoever," I say, deadpan.

The chief ranger comes over and shakes hands all around. "Bob and Walt, you guys are incredible. Thank you for getting these folks back. I can't say I enjoyed the end run you pulled, but apparently it was the right thing to do. We can't thank you enough. Can you two come to the chief ranger's office to make statements and be debriefed later today?"

"We'll be in, but it will have to be much later," says Bob. "This trip has been hard on us old guys." I nod my head, glad to be included in this category of old and tired."

"We have the rehearsal dinner tonight," I say. "You'll need time to go over your photography gear."

"You're right. What if we come in at six this evening? We can give you an hour," says Bob.

"See you at six then. Thanks," says chief ranger, and he leaves us for another tirade from DHS.

After Denise and Anne head to their cars, Bob and I walk over to Myrna and Keven standing arm in arm. Daran stands close to Keven. We receive thanks anew, this time with a hug from Myrna. Keven looks like he might hug me, reconsiders, and offers his hand.

Once Bob and I are free, we take a moment to enjoy sitting in the soft seats of Bob's Suburban. Bob starts the engine, and we open the windows to the still, cool morning air. The continuing chaos outside the elevator building ruins my effort to enjoy a moment of quiet.

"The cavers seem more tired than we do," says Bob. "Why are these bureaucrats still roaming around the parking lot? No one wants to use the decon station here. We're all tired. Very tired. Changing coveralls here, and then changing into our own clothes again a half mile down the road at the dormitory is ridiculous."

"What do you think of the cave now?" I ask.

Bob says, "It's still a *dark, gloomy, and peculiar place*," he says, quoting Stephen Bishop. I think I'll go back on the historic tour and see the Rotunda."

I smile. He hasn't given up on the cave, or on himself. "Good."

While we wait for the rangers and the others to settle down and move out of our way, we see the banty rooster from Homeland Security strut around. Rod dogs his heals. They go over to the bus and climb aboard. A moment or two later, they bolt out in a bigger hurry than when they went in. The rooster's manner remains officious, but he and Rod seem to be leaving the cavers in a sprint while trying to save their delusional senses of dignity. When the bus driver makes a beeline for the bus, Sophy Ross climbs off, holds up her hand to the driver, and trots over to Bob's side of the car.

"I guess we aren't home *free* yet. Based on remarks made by that bureaucrat to the cavers on the bus, I think you might need this." She hands Bob two business cards, and he passes one to me. "My cell number is on the back. If anyone gives you trouble, please call me. Having faced the very real possibility of slavery in 1838, I'm in no mood to let these people push me around. Nor are they going to annoy my fellow cavers or heroes." I think she's including to us in that last term.

As Sophy speaks, I hear the bus start up. We're moving at last.

Bob and I thank Sophy, and she heads back to the bus. We scan the cards. *Sophia H.T. Ross, Human Rights, Counselor at Law,* with office and fax numbers and a web address.

Bob pulls out behind the bus.

By the time we go to the dormitory to change into our street clothes, the fatigue sets in. No one speaks while we change. Rod stops by.

"Bob and Walt, remember, you can't talk to anyone — no body — about all this. Don't be late for the debrief at 1800 hours." And he's gone.

Bob and I check on Josh's ankle and Brian's hypothermia. They are fine, and a nod from Dan assures us they are in good hands. Before we leave, the cavers say, "Thank you," but no one has energy to spare. Except Craig, who catches up with us on the way to Bob's car. While Craig and I exchange phone numbers, Bob checks out with Keven. We say goodbye and drive off along the Cave City road.

Thirty-Four
"Home Again, Home Again"

As Bob follows the driveway to the open door of the garage, Zona, Barbara, and Mary are standing outside the garage door waiting.

Barbara and I hug for what seems a short time, but when we pull a little ways apart, we realize that everyone else has gone inside. We hug some more.

"I want to hear all about it from you," she says.

"And I want to tell you all about it in excruciating detail. But I guess we have to pay attention to the others for a little bit."

"I'm glad you're back."

"Oh, I am so very glad to be back. I missed you a lot."

"This was more than just a trip into the cave, wasn't it?" Barbara says.

"Yes, it was. We went back to 1838 ..."

"1838? You're not kidding me? You better not be teasing me!"

"No. It's no joke. Keven really ate supper with Stephen Bishop," I say.

"But how did you go back in time? I thought time travel was impossible. How did you get back? How could you go so far away without me? How did you know you could come back?"

"We're not sure. Well, to be honest, we don't have any idea about much of it. I shouldn't have left you. It was stupid."

"It was that, but it was brave, too. I guess. And you brought Keven and the rest back safe and sound," says Barbara.

"Welcome back, Walt!" Zona gives me a pat on the shoulder when Barbara and I enter the kitchen.

"It's good to see you back, Walt," says Mary with a hug.

"Did Bob tell you we used Zona's smart phone to reverse course and come to the present?" Bob sits at the breakfast table with a cup of coffee. Zona's Newfoundland, Jessie, rouses up and nuzzles Bob's leg.

"No. Did my little phone do all of that?" says Zona. "We have scrambled eggs, bacon, biscuits, fruit, coffee, tea. And anything else you want, we'll fix or go get for you."

"Sounds great!" I say, rubbing my hands together. "Let me wash my hands and I'll be ready." After a good scrubbing at the sink in the powder room, I take a seat at the kitchen island. Barbara fixes a plate for me. Zona fixes me a cup of green tea. Bob and I dig into our breakfasts for a few minutes before he rests his fork and begins the tale.

"I don't know how it worked. I was there, and I still don't believe it. But I have these pictures of the Snowball Room before they made a restaurant out of it." Bob passes his point-and-shoot camera to Zona.

"Oh, Bob!" Zona pauses to look at the picture. "I recognize the snowballs, but this is too amazing. You really did it, didn't you?"

"My word," says Mary.

"We didn't see Stephen Bishop even though we were there at the right time. Keven shared supper with him and Mat and Nick in their cabin."

"That's incredible! What was their reaction to Keven and the Wild Cave tour?" asks Zona.

"Keven persuaded them that he was a real cave guide from the future. They brought food down to the Wild Cavers, but from what Keven said, it wasn't much," says Bob. "We were afraid that more cave guides might destroy Stephen Bishop's sense of the cave as his own mystery to explore. So we left before..." I could see that wistful look in Bob's eye.

"Didn't they go up to the hotel?" says Zona.

"No. There were fourteen of them," says Bob. "Remember, this was before Dr. Croghan bought the Cave, and the hotel was still small and kind of primitive. And Keven didn't have any money. Plus, Keven understood that they would have caused a major disruption even if they didn't wind up being hanged as devils or witches or whatever."

"And there remains the more important question of the black couple from Atlanta," I say.

"Oh my!" says Barbara.

"Keven says he talked with Stephen Bishop about getting them across the Ohio River, in case they were stuck back in time," I say.

"That never occurred to me at all," says Zona.

"That's the thing about time travel. It's all right in the movies, but Keven took the sensible approach. At least I think so. Walt, you may feel different."

"No, I think he was right," I say. "He told Stephen Bishop very little about the rest of the cave. It would have been stealing the glory from Stephen and Mat and Nick and all the rest. They had to do it on their own. He saw them and developed a very basic understanding of who they were; but, all in all, Keven recognized the great gulf of difference in common experiences that made communication of much significance too risky. We discussed bringing Stephen back with us – out of slavery. Keven had talked with Stephen about going north to freedom. Stephen believed that he was better off there where he was, plus he felt he had important things to do at Mammoth Cave. So, we dropped it. I hope we made the right decision," I say, realizing I was on the verge of climbing on the rock. No one spoke, considering the gravity of that decision.

"But if Keven was marooned there, he would have to do something or else starve to death," says Bob.

"You don't think of things like that, do you?" says Mary. "What do you feed fourteen, unexpected, drop-in guests when you're out in the middle of Kentucky in 1838?"

"What did they have to eat?" says Barbara.

"They said it was burgoo and corn bread. Not much," I say.

"I always imagined them having fried chicken, fresh vegetables, and I don't know — buttermilk," says Zona shaking her head.

"That would have been for guests at the hotel. Keven said that Stephen Bishop and Mat Bransford told him that they were treated pretty well. About as well as any slaves they knew anything about, but they were still slaves. They didn't eat fried chicken, that's for sure," says Bob. "It must have put a strain on the hotel's pantry for the slaves to provide one scanty meal for the Wild Cave tour. There couldn't have been much surplus for them to call on. But the cook promised Keven a 'possum if he was there the next day."

"That would have been interesting," says Mary.

"When did Stephen Bishop cross Bottomless Pit?" I ask Zona to check if the history of the cave has changed any.

"I guess it was October 1838, wasn't it?" says Zona.

"Well, at least we didn't upset that part of cave history," says Bob.

"No, he did that right before he found Keven's Corkscrew," adds Zona.

"Keven's Corkscrew?" Bob and I say in unison. We look at each other with mouths wide open.

"When he made it to River Hall, he must have seen our tracks," says Bob.

"I'll be," I say.

"What?" asks Barbara.

"Before Keven went back to 1838, it was always known by just 'The Corkscrew,'" I say. "And now, after we're back, the name Zona has always known it as, is *Keven's Corkscrew*. Because we are the time travelers, we know it by the name it had when we left, but now the past has been changed, and for those of you who stayed in the twenty-first century, you have always called it *Keven's Corkscrew*."

"You mean that it's named after Keven Neff?" says Barbara.

"That's exactly what it means," says Bob. "Holy Cripe!"

We go on talking about what we had seen — and not seen — until one o'clock.

"Come on," says Barbara, pulling on my arm. "You need to sleep."

"I can be persuaded," I say putting my arm around her waist.

"Sleep as long as you can," says Zona.

"I know I need to, but we have to get my camera gear ready for the rehearsal dinner and go talk to the rangers at six. I'll be up at four."

"See you at sixteen hundred hours," I wave and stumble toward the guest side of the house and a hot shower before bed.

There's nothing better than going for a long time without a shower to give you the proper appreciation for this major achievement of civilization. I climb into bed beside Barbara.

"You took a huge chance. You gave me no idea what you were going to do," she says. "I'm so glad you came back." We hug for a long time.

"You know, I didn't know either. But there I was. Bob was going in. I didn't feel like I could leave him with just Craig and Denise. If we had waited until the next morning, I wouldn't have gone. The rangers would have gone – or DHS – if they had tried the transporter idea at all. And the way they were headed, I don't think they would have. Not soon anyway. The idea was too far outside the box.

"Bob felt that following Keven was the right thing to do. He had to go in right away; time was critical. And the main advantage is that we went in with a low profile before any major disruption of history occurred. And the most that Stephen Bishop knows, Keven and the Wild Cavers disappeared the same way they came. I don't think the rangers or anyone else could have done that. It would have been an invasion."

"You're right, of course. I'm glad we didn't know what you were doing. We were worried about Keven. And Myrna. We didn't have any idea that we needed to be that worried about you and Bob."

"Thank you. It's very good to come back to you. I'm very lucky," I say.

"Yes, you are. How does it work?" says Barbara.

"I don't know."

"You have some idea. I know you better than that. What do you think?"

"It all started in a shallow, inland sea ..." I feel very tired and slow.

Thirty-Five
It's Just a Theory

We are up and dressed by four. Zona feeds us lunch. Barbara goes with Bob and me out to the studio to pack camera equipment.

"Are you doing portraits tonight?" I ask.

"No, only some hand-held shots. I'm taking two camera bodies. They're in the case here. I'll need the flash and a radio slave. Hmm. Based on where we've been, we might need to change that term. What do you think?"

"Radio remote?" I say.

"Better." He looks over the strobe and checks the charge. "I better take a tripod. Just in case."

Bob checks and re-checks for the better part of an hour.

Back at the house we all gather near the lovely goldfish pond behind the deck.

"One Scotch before we face the tribunal?" says Bob.

"One small one for me," I say.

When Bob shows up with two tumblers, the questions begin.

"Well, Bob, what's your theory on this time machine?" says Barbara.

"It all started in a shallow, inland sea …" he says.

"That's how Walt started. Did you guys plan this story?"

"No, Barb. That's the beginning of the origin of the cave story. The long version," says Zona.

"Coming from Walt, the geologist, it will be the very long version," Barbara adds, laughing.

"Well?" asks Zona, motioning with her hand for Bob to continue. Bob sips his Scotch.

"I didn't take it any further. It had to be something in the rock. Before the rock solidified."

"Walt?" says Zona. Barbara puts her hand on my shoulder.

"Well, I did take it a little further, but with no confidence that it's worth two cents."

"Let's hear it," says Bob. He leans back in his chair.

"I think it's an ancient technology. Advanced but very old. In this time scale, the Egyptians or the Babylonians are recent. Ancient, from the Mississippian Period. Maybe 323 million years ago or a little less. Give or take. After all, what's a couple of million years among friends?" I look at everyone and smile.

"Nothing at all. Proceed," says Bob, smiling back.

"Well. I don't want to go all science fiction on you, but I think it was something — a transporter, if you will — that was put in place back in the Mississippian Period when this part of Kentucky was much farther south, near the equator, and covered by that shallow, inland sea."

"But," says Bob. "It's sat there for hundreds of millions of years, and Craig comes along and activates it with his cell phone?"

"Craig must have been the first one to use one of the new smart phones on the correct frequency, and we're pretty sure he's the first to use that phone number, in that part of the cave. And there may have been astronomical parameters or something else unimaginable for us that factored into this awakening of such an ancient machine. And if that's the case, Bob, we were even more right to act when we did."

"But where does the power come from? Are there batteries that will last that long," says Mary.

"Keven explained the battery-powered lights to Stephen Bishop by calling it lightning in a bottle," I say. I sip from my tumbler. "Clarke's Third Law says, 'Any sufficiently advanced technology is indistinguishable from magic.'"

"Who is Clarke?" says Zona.

"Arthur C. Clarke, a science fiction writer. Walt likes him a lot," explains Barbara.

"He and Stanley Kubrick wrote the movie *2001: A Space Odyssey*. And this time/space transporter is magic to us in the way that Keven's light was magic to Stephen Bishop. Maybe even more so. We don't worry about it being the work of the devil. We are no less amazed, just less frightened."

Bob leans forward to ask, "So you're saying that some space travelers dropped a time machine in the middle of the Mississippian sea, that it settled into the muck on the bottom of the sea and was encased in solid rock?"

"Right. And when Craig punched in that phone number and hit send, it activated the thing's circuits, and sent Keven and the Wild Cave tour back to 1838," I say.

"But why did they put such a device in the middle of that shallow, inland sea? And why at that time? And how or why would they have used a time machine?"

I shrug and lift my hands, "Who knows. They were in the area? Accident? Random distribution? Things we could never think of."

"Well, Walt, that's an amazing theory," says Zona.

"That it is, Zona. That it is. But it covers the points the way we understand them."

"But, what about Creighton?" says Barbara.

"He must be associated with the transporter," says Bob.

"I think you're right. But why it lets him and no one else into that room, I don't know that either," I say. "And we don't know what would have happened if Anne had accompanied Creighton into his room."

"So, you don't think he's a ghost?" says Mary.

"No, I think he's very much alive."

Barbara says, "Well, what about that *ghost lantern* you've all seen?"

"Now, that may be a ghost," I say. "Keven and I argued over that lantern."

"Argued? What about?" says Barbara.

"Keven kept one of the lard-oil lanterns that Stephen Bishop loaned him."

"He brought it back to the present?"

"No, he left it in 1838 under a limestone slab at the place where we saw the ghost lantern."

"And it's still there?" asks Zona.

"It is. We checked this morning, and that's when we argued. I suggested that the lantern gets up and wanders. Keven disagrees."

"Strange," says Barbara.

"And don't forget the dark shadow that ran over Craig at that same spot," says Bob.

"And there's the Coleman lantern that someone turned off at the beginning of all this," I say.

"So, there is a ghost?" says Zona.

I go through the brief explanation of what happened to Craig when he tried to see the ghost lantern by himself. "I think maybe there is."

Bob looks at his watch and says, "Yes, I think there may be. But it's five-thirty and time to go talk to Anne, the rangers, and who knows who else."

"Yes, speaking of spooks ..." I say.

Thirty-Six
Back to the Park

On the way back to the park, I power up my cell phone and see a message. Craig's voice mail. He wants to talk to Bob and me before we talk to the rangers. I punch the missed call and put the phone on speaker while it rings. After a brief hello and status check, Craig's enthusiastic spirit takes over.

"You guys should have seen Sophy Ross in action. Josh and Brian told me about Keven's concern over Sophy and Dan back there in the time of slavery. That would have been awful. But this morning? Last night? When that government guy got on the bus and started telling us about what to do and to answer to him, none of us liked it, but no one did anything. Then he started criticizing Keven. That was too much. Sophy almost levitated out of her seat. She started speaking in a, 'You-have-pushed-the-wrong-button-now' voice. I don't remember everything she said, but she put that guy in his place in no time. She told us to draw up a phone notification tree while she went to talk to you guys. By the time she jumped back on the bus, the driver had already shifted into gear. Well, you saw that." Craig pauses for a breath. His adrenaline reserve must be empty. We hear a deep intake of air, and he takes off in another verbal sprint.

"I had to call Maggie and tell her not to give her phone number out to anyone until I could talk to her in private. I know it isn't fair to use this time-travel thing to get a date, but I have to do something to convince her to go out with me. Telling her that her number opens the portal to time has to impress her. Anyway, after I talked to Maggie, I collapsed. I'm surprised the phone woke me, but thank goodness it did.

"Some guys in suits were going around to all of the Wild Cavers, Josh, Ryan, David, Dot, and them. Bullying and making threats." He pauses. "I wonder why they never contacted me. Anyway, Josh activated the phone tree, and Sophy had us all come to meet with her in the lounge at the hotel. Dan checked on Josh and Brian; they're in good shape, except Josh still limps pretty bad.

"Sophy told us not to worry. We all signed papers saying that she speaks for us in any dealings with the officials at Mammoth Cave National Park or any other government agency. She kept a copy and gave each of us two copies of it. She made an appointment for three-thirty and wanted all of us to go together.

"You could see by the way their faces fell when we marched in to the rangers' conference room all right behind her, those guys were on the ropes. Sophy did her thing." Craig paused. "Maybe Sophy would put in a good word for me with Maggie. Maggie will love her."

"Maybe she will, but Craig, what did Sophy tell them?" I ask, hoping to give him time to breathe and focus on the matter at hand.

"I don't remember it all. *How* she said it made the difference. I know she called them Philistines. She also said that while she doubted that they could ever appreciate much beyond the end of their noses, she hoped they appreciated the wonder of Mammoth Cave. That Keven's little finger contained more appreciation for the cave than all of them combined. Sophy picked out the little guy in a suit who must be the one in charge. I didn't think he was important, but once she focused in on him, it was clear from the way the others acted, she was right. She stood over him and told him that those of us on the Wild Cave tour experienced the cave in a way he could not believe.

"Then she told him that his arrogance in disturbing us after our ordeal was a matter for further discussion and possible litigation. We were exhausted in body and mind and were traumatized by an experience thrust on us by a federal agency, and he couldn't even provide a chair for those of us who had been injured on federal property."

As Craig takes another deep breath, Bob says "I think he remembers a lot of what she said. I wish I had seen this."

"Next, she said that they sure collected a lot of officials for this meeting, when they couldn't get anyone to find us last night. I guess we were all still pretty tired because that started the giggling. Dot covered for us. While Sophy was talking, she pulled out one of the copies of the paper Sophy gave us to sign, strode up to the table in front of Sophy, slapped it down on the table, whipped out a pen, and signed it in front of them. She whipped around and stomped out.

"The rest of us caught on and started going up one at a time. David and I helped Josh. You would have thought he was in agony the show he put on. Before I left, I saw Brian go up all shaking and shivering. Dan was the last one to sign the form. He and Sophy came out together. Dan said that Sophy kept on ranting until he finished signing his paper; she added her business cards on top of the pile of papers, snatched up Dot's pen, and they marched out together.

"Those guys didn't know what hit them. Sophy didn't tell them anything. She said that we didn't know what happened or where we were. And that we couldn't get back there without a guide. I think that's what they're going to try to get out of y'all. Those are the guys we have to protect the cave from." At last, Craig runs out of steam.

Bob and I have been trying to control our laughter so that we don't miss anything. Now we let it out. I manage to say, "Thank you, Craig. That's great, and I imagine it will be most useful to know when we go in."

"Sophy is talking to Keven. I told her that I needed to talk to you about something anyway, so I would call to let you and Bob know."

"We appreciate it." After a long moment of silence I ask, "Craig, did you have something else?"

"Yeah." The timid Craig returns. "I wondered … well would you please … see, I'm not sure that Maggie will believe my story. When you get back to Atlanta, could I take you to lunch to help me? There's a country buffet near campus, we could …"

"Sure, Craig, I know it well and would love to have lunch with you and Maggie. Listen Craig, if you go home as the guy who went back in the cave to rescue the others, not the guy who wants a date so much, I bet she'll believe every word you say."

"Uh-mm, I don't know. You think?"

"Yes, I do think. I will see you in Atlanta next week or the week after."

Thirty-Seven
Debriefing the Bureaucrats

I hang up with Craig as we pass the Wayfarer Inn on the right and re-enter the park.

"Funny as that is," I say, "It gives us an option, we could just traipse in, drop Sophy's card, and leave. After seeing that twit at the elevator, I'm not in the mood for any nonsense."

"Tempting, but we can't do that. Anne and Denise's careers and Keven's job could be jeopardized. Also, I want to find out who is up to what in the cave. I never doubted that the Wild Cavers were going to keep the trip a secret, but all these bureaucrats pushing the Wild Cavers around seems to have carved their commitment in stone – so to speak. I don't think they're going to talk to anyone, least of all Homeland Security or the Park Service. Nobody. Not that I think that is what DHS intended, but they have done a great job of keeping a lid on the Wild Cavers' experience through their strong-arm tactics."

Here at the end of the day, few cars occupy the parking lot, but Bob passes up parking places until he finds one with cars on either side and no empty spaces across the lane. A Park Service Jeep idles a few spaces behind us.

Over Bob's shoulder I see two burly men in suit coats too tight for their arms and shoulders lumbering over in our direction. When we leave the Suburban, they fall in behind us.

When we reach the sidewalk, I see Keven approaching with his own guard. We wait for him with our two escorts bouncing around, trying to keep us apart. We exchange greetings and walk into the building.

In the waiting area outside the conference room, we see two groups of people. Anne and Denise are talking with two men, one of whom I recognize to be a member of the Flint Ridge Coalition that I met last fall. Anne and Denise look exhausted and miserable. The park management makes up the second group.

Denise looks up and gives us a weak smile.

"How are you two doing?" says Anne.

"Better than you two look. What's wrong?" says Bob.

Anne shakes her head and says, "This is Alan and Doug with the Flint Ridge Coalition."

Bob and I shake hands with the men, but before we can say much, the short man from Homeland Security appears in the doorway, "We have waited on you people long enough. You need to come in here, take a seat, and be quiet." I look at Bob and Keven. This would be funny if it did not seem to bother Denise so much. Anne leads us into the conference room.

As we enter, I see three tables set up in an isosceles triangle. One long table holds stacks of folders and papers and name tents. Anne and Denise go to the other long table. The other park employees and the FRC members sit with them. I see that the name tents say National Park Service, but list no names. The other table has few name tents. Three empty chairs occupy the shorter, base of the triangle. Bob, Keven, and I sit in the three chairs in front of our minders from the parking lot. Their chairs are invisible under them. The track lighting seems to be brighter on our table.

At the bureaucrat table sits a woman with a tent saying Department of Energy. Other tents in front of the seats being taken by two men read DHS. At the middle position, sits another small man who could be the twin of the little guy we've already seen. This new person has more of a pinched face and sits with his nose in the air as if trying to identify an unpleasant odor. The man we'd seen harassing the Wild Cavers on the bus earlier this morning, and who appears to have transformed into a room monitor, goes to sit behind and to the left of pinched face. Red Hat Rod sits to the right. He doesn't look in our direction. Pinched face's name tent reads, *J. Randall Sourwood, Department of Homeland Security*. Another man, without an identifying name tent, sits at the apex of the triangle. He begins.

"This is an informal meeting to establish the actions and results of those actions taken by these three gentlemen.

Lawyers will not be necessary because these individuals are not being charged with anything at this time."

The people from DHS are insane. They are posturing over turf and ego, not security. How far will they take this? They seem to have no bounds. Could they dynamite the cave just to prove their personal power?

Bob eases out of his chair. This theater director knows how to focus attention. The men behind us jump up and stand behind him. Bob pivots part way towards them.

The man in charge speaks to the minders, "Gentlemen, please leave. We have no need of you, and your presence detracts from the proceedings."

"Absolutely not! These people called the press!" Sourwood yells while pointing at us, "They are a threat."

"You three! Go deal with that chaos I hear outside; I suspect members of the fourth estate have arrived. Or, go guard the vehicles in which these gentlemen arrived. But leave this room now," says the man at the apex.

Thirty-Eight
Listening

Without looking at Sourwood, the three men leave the room. Once they are out of the room, the man in charge addresses himself to Sourwood while pointing at us. "If these men wanted to talk to the press, they would have met with them – as their constitutional rights allow. Instead, the press followed them here and were set to ambush them in the parking lot. The leak lies not with these men, and I'm quite certain not with the Park Service or DOE." Sourwood does not reply, but pushes his chair back, petulant and sulking. Rod crosses his arms and scowls.

The man in charge says, "My name is Paul Worland. I'm with the National Security Agency, which I believe Bob and Walt were familiar with in their youths?" Bob and I look at each other. NSA? What the hell are they doing here? Worland focuses his attention on Bob. "I believe you have the floor, Mr. Cetera."

Bob faces Sourwood full on, his baritone voice filling the room as it does in even the largest rooms of the cave. "You are out of line." He focuses back on Worland, in effect dismissing Sourwood. Keven and I chuckle.

"Mr. Worland, we're happy to give you our report. Maybe someone left something out, but I think you know everything we do."

"Nevertheless, Bob, for the benefit of those of us here, we want to hear your stories. If you please?" Bob shrugs and sits down.

Bob tells ours. Keven goes through his story.

After they go through the whole thing in excruciating detail, the chief ranger says, "Keven, would it surprise you that a team went in today and failed to reproduce your trip?"

"It is clear to me that you are hiding something," begins Sourwood. "If this event took place, and this is not some sort of mass hysteria you have concocted to further your misguided sense of being some sort of heroes." I look at Keven and Bob, mystified by these remarks.

"Yes, I know about your grandstanding last year. Denise there, and her supervisor, may think you are clever, but I see right through you." He jabs his finger in the direction of Denise and Anne while he speaks. "You should have been arrested for your outrageous interference last year. You will not escape with impunity this time." I notice Bob reading a text message from someone. He pulls a business card from his wallet, punches in some numbers, and sets his phone on the table.

"Our team is composed of a seismologist, an energy wave specialist, and an electronics engineer to replicate your experience. They found nothing where you told us to look. Did you make this up and bribe those people to help you, or have you drugged them with a powerful hallucinogen? If this preposterous story is at all true, then you are refusing to report everything you know. The Department of Homeland Security can stop you from profiting from your lies and your secrets. And we will. You are playing with much greater forces than you know. You are a national security threat. This nonsense is terrorism plain and simple," says Sourwood. Rod beams behind him.

I have a hard time keeping my face neutral. Fools in positions of power are the real threat. I realize I have tensed every muscle. I look at Keven, and he seems tense. I look at Bob, but he seems calm, almost amused. He must have something up his sleeve. I relax a bit.

Ignoring Sourwood's diatribe, Keven says, "Yes, it would surprise me. What happened?" at last getting to answer the chief ranger's question.

"Nothing. No buzzing, nothing left the cutout area on the floor," says the chief ranger.

"Are you saying we're lying — or that we're crazy?" says Keven.

"No. We have no reason to doubt the same story from the three of you. And we have statements from Denise and Anne for corroboration. Everything is in agreement."

"Nice to know you trust us," says Keven.

"This is all highly irregular," says the woman from DOE. "You should not have gone off in such a way," she says looking at Keven.

"I assure you, given a choice in the matter, I would never have taken a group of cave visitors on such a dangerous, indefinite trip," says Keven.

"You should have been more careful," she continues, staring at Keven.

"Prior to this morning, was the Department of Energy aware that there was a time machine in Mammoth Cave? Are you aware of any other time machines in this area?" asks Keven.

"Well, no, we did not."

"Have you been in the cave, down to Cathedral Domes?"

"I have. We all have."

"Did you see any evidence of a time machine? Or any other type of machine?" asks Keven.

"No, I didn't. No one did," says the woman from DOE.

"But you expect me to have known to take care not to activate one?"

"Well ..."

The Park Service regional representative says, "Keven, no one blames you ..."

"She does. She's blaming me right now," says Keven with a cold smile for the woman from DOE. "She not only blames me, she calls me an absolute fool. On the one hand, she's saying I carelessly took my tour into the past, and on the other hand, Mr. Sourwood is accusing me of not having done anything but play a trick on everyone. You all appear to be confused, and I've entertained all the unsupported, spurious accusations I can handle for one day. Only a fool would take a tour group into such a dangerous situation. And only a fool would have thought I was lost enough to have to stay overnight in the cave with thirteen visitors.

"While you're telling me I'm irresponsible, you'll have to explain to me why the DHS didn't come after us and one of their own agents." Keven simmers. I have never seen him this upset.

Bob says, "I think you are wasting the time of everyone in this room. Why have you been bullying the Wild Cave tour? What are you after?"

"This is a matter of national security ..." begins Sourwood, the man from Homeland Security, gesticulating in what appears to be an uncontrolled manner. "You people have bumbled into the biggest internal security threat ever found in the history of this country." Little flecks of spittle collect in the corners of his mouth. "You don't have any idea what you are dealing with here." He stands and points at the three of us. "You are bunglers. You, yourselves, are threats to the security of the homeland. You ..."

"Bob – if I may interrupt," says Alan from the Flint Ridge Coalition. "I think you are asking the right questions. Here's how we see it. We have requested that the Park Service route the Wild Cave tour away from the Cathedral Domes area for the time being. We're prepared to station observers in there around the clock with a wide-spectrum, electromagnetic field analyzer."

"This is all out of the question, and ..." continues the man from Homeland Security.

"Observers?" I ask.

"One person in the immediate area of Cathedral Domes. There will be a one-person back up stationed in Martel Avenue with audio and video feed from the observer station. We're hoping that Mr. Creighton will come out to talk," says Alan.

"Mr. Creighton is under the protective custody of ..."

"So you believe that part?" I say. No one pays attention to Sourwood.

"Yes, we do. We believe three credible witnesses on three separate occasions with such consistent stories would be hard to arrange in advance in such a short time span. We know you guys. Did you actually see Creighton?" says Todd.

"I did. His back, as he left."

"And you believe he is alive?" asks the FRC representative.

"I do."

"Do you understand what happened?" he says, focusing on me.

"No one understands this incident. It is way beyond your clearance level. Way beyond ..."

"I do not. The physical evidence suggests a device that can be activated by a signal from a remote control at the frequency of the newer cell phones, maybe using that phone number ..." Worland and the woman from DOE look at each other. It appears that the phone number may be the key to the time machine, and they didn't use the right number. Or the peculiar conditions that opened the gateway to the past no longer exist, and it is now closed. "Once activated, it generates a large, electromagnetic pulse. And it transports people and objects through the space-time continuum to the exact location on this planet, but one hundred seventy-five years in the past. That explanation fits our experience," I say.

I don't bring up my theory about an alien invasion during the geologic past. But I think I have figured out why NSA and DOE are here. NSA monitors signals, and that pulse could have been a powerful transmission to deep space. DOE showed up because nuclear weapons emit huge EMPs. No reason to go into all that now. Bob watches me out of the corner of his eye. The look in his eye matches the grin on his face. I resist the temptation to expand on my theory.

The FRC representative swivels to face Bob, "And you, Bob?"

Bob's smile fades. "What Walt said."

"Keven?"

"Me, too."

Sourwood jumps up and begins charging about like the roosters used to do in my dad's chicken houses. I can see that the room/bus monitor gets his rooster characteristics from his boss.

"The Department of Homeland Security has declared this entire park a national security incident, and everyone concerned will be held as a person of interest until we resolve what this device is, who put it here, and how it can be used to serve my department," says Sourwood. No one talks while he pauses to wipe his mouth with a powder blue handkerchief.

"The Flint Ridge Coalition is herewith restricted from entry onto the property of Mammoth Cave National Park, and you will not be allowed to discuss or participate in any so-called research regarding this national security incident."

"You think you can close the park and hold all of us hostage while you *try* to sort this thing out? Is that what you're saying?" Bob asks.

"No, he cannot close the park. I don't know about taking prisoners, but the park will not be closed," says the southeast region person.

"Who are you? You are nobody!" retorts Sourwood.

"Your departments," Bob says, gesturing toward the nameless paper tents, "may not have anything better to do than this, but we do. It has been a hard couple of days, and we have an important wedding rehearsal dinner to attend. We have been through an ordeal that you cannot imagine. Keven, even more so. Walt and I at least expected something to happen. If your people could not activate the machine, our experience says that they are lucky. 1838 is no place for twenty-first century bureaucrats, and who knows what sort of disruption you will cause in history if you go barging back to 1838 with the force of a small invasion.

"Now, you have threatened and insulted us. We have told you everything we know. Perhaps you didn't pay enough attention to what Denise told you, and you screwed up, or maybe your people are not as skilled as you think they are, or the peculiar conditions that opened the door to the past are no longer met, and the door has closed.

"If you think you can swallow up the three of us with no outcry, you are mistaken. Your threats did nothing to further your cause with the Wild Cavers, and you have exhausted my patience. Now it is time for you to answer some questions. What are you intending to do to Mammoth Cave? You have shown no respect for the cave, the public, the National Park Service or its employees. I am a concerned citizen, and I want to know what you are up to."

Rooster number two is one strut from exploding. His master steams and rocks side to side. Red Hat Rod is redder than his hard hat.

"Bob," says Worland, "We understand your concern, and I agree, we have not shown any care for the condition of the cave or of history, for that matter. Let me assure you, despite some appearances to the contrary, we are not going to blast into the rock or into the past until we know a lot more than we do now."

"Mr. Sourwood, you cannot shut down a national park," says the man from the Southeastern Region.

There begins a protracted argument that ends with a statement from Alan, the FRC representative.

"We will file for an injunction against this lunacy in the 11th Circuit before the end of the day. And that's when your worry about the press really begins." Alan leaves the room, with every appearance of starting that process. Doug stays put.

"In addition, we happen to have," says Mr. Worland, "a statement from an active FBI agent who was on the tour. Keven, you will be interested to know that he praises your cool handling of such an unforeseeable crisis. Based on his statement alone, I would suggest that the Park Service reward you in the manner that best besets your status. Well done."

"Thank you, Mr. Worland," says Keven. Bob, Anne, Denise, Doug from the FRC, and I applaud with gusto.

The Southeastern Region Park Service person says, "Thank you Mr. Worland. We will take your suggestion seriously. Shall we bring in the colonel now?" Worland nods his head.

"Oh no," I say to Bob.

"What?"

"This is not going to be good," I say, shaking my head.

Thirty-Nine
Zack to the Rescue

Anne escorts in a middle-aged man in fatigues wearing the insignia of the army, including that of a lieutenant colonel. No one stands at attention. When I was in the Air Force, we weren't allowed to wear fatigues off base. Anymore I seldom see military personnel in anything but fatigues. Even when traveling on commercial airplanes. It strikes me as irregular. And the insignia on these new fatigues are very hard to decipher at a distance. Back in the seventies, you could spot an officer a mile away — even when they were wearing jungle fatigues. Now it's not so easy.

The Southeastern Region representative says, "Let me introduce Lieutenant Colonel Arnden from Fort Campbell." He points to the lieutenant colonel — in case we missed him — smiles, and says, "Colonel, they're all yours." Bob and I look at each other.

The lieutenant colonel takes a seat and lays his leather portfolio on the table. He smiles at Bob and says, "You must be Bob. I'm with what you would have known as G-2 in your days in the army. I understand you fellows took an amazing trip. The Wild Cave tour visitors have taken legal counsel, and they are beyond reach. Although I think two of them are in the reserves, and we can take care of them, NSA sort of thinks you and Walt are ... well, loose ends.

"Between you and me, I think Mr. Sourwood wants to reactivate the color code alert system." The lieutenant colonel laughs. "From what they told me, I thought we were going to DEFCON 5 or something. But now that I'm here and see you guys and talk to Mr. Worland, I see we have no real problem. However, you are within Mr. Sourwood's reach."

Bob and I look at each other and shake our heads.

The lieutenant colonel clears his throat, "You're Walt, right?" I nod. "You were Air Force?" I nod. Well, our associates here have put, at least on a temporary basis, a cap on any further, out-of-school discussions of these events." He nods to Mr. Worland. "Keven's in the Park Service, as are Anne and Denise. So they pulled us in to be proxies for the people you used to work for."

"I'm not following you, Colonel," says Bob.

"This may seem unusual to you both, but it goes on more than you would think. I'm here to help you out. Hard though you may find that to believe."

"What does?" asks Bob.

"We are re-calling you to the active reserve. Just for the duration, understand."

"What?" says Bob.

"I told you this wasn't going to be good," I say to Bob. To the lieutenant colonel, I say, "Bob and I have as much dedication to Mammoth Cave as anyone here. We don't even want you folks here. We are the last people you need to be worried about. Why recall us?"

"Now, don't get all excited. It's mostly a formality and gives the upper level folks something of a feeling of control. To be honest, they think you two know more about this than you're letting on. I mean, you two guys made that contraption work. Two or three times. They can't make it do anything. So they think you will cooperate more if you have a formal relationship — and you get paid something. And, I think you should give careful consideration to this aspect of it. You will be well beyond the reach of DHS and their Mr. Sourwood."

"This is absurd!" says Bob.

"I have all the necessary paperwork right here. And, if you will sign on the line at the bottom, we can get you sworn in."

"Sworn in?"

"Are you kidding?" I say.

"Can't we just go back to the Park Service?" asks Bob.

"Colonel, these people are being held in custody by the Department of Homeland Security. They are not available for recall for any reason," says Sourwood.

The door bursts open. Through it explodes Colonel Zack from USAMRID, or the United States Army Medical Research for Infectious Diseases, based out of Fort Dietrich, Maryland. Lieutenant Colonel Arnden stands to attention at the entrance of a full-bird colonel. Silver eagles to his silver oak leaves.

"Good evening, Colonel. Thank you. Good evening everyone." He looks around the room. "Keven, Walt, Bob, good to see you." We nod back. He trains his twin lasers disguised as eyes on Mr. Sourwood. "Randy, what kind of mess have you made now?" Use of his first name, and a diminutive at that, has the little man's pinched countenance flushed and his lips purple with rage. Rod and rooster number two stand.

"Captain, you have no authority here. These are confidential proceedings," says Sourwood.

"Randy, my friends and colleagues call me captain. You can address me as Colonel Zack. Someone on your staff has half the press in Kentucky following this story. You are officially a laughing stock. You have insulted these good men who saved these civilians and the Park Service's bacon. Whatever was in the cave isn't going to work for you.

"Not that you would ever respect something truly great like *The Mammoth Cave of Kentucky*, but plenty of people in positions of power do. You need to pack up your buddies here and clear out right now. And you better hope that your careless, ham-fisted actions haven't caused harm to one of this country's great treasures."

Showing the bad grace and lack of attention to detail that we have come to expect, Sourwood stands and looks ready to deliver another diatribe. Zack stops him by handing him a satellite phone the size of a brick. "This is for you."

"Sourwood. Who am I speaking to? Yes, sir, Mr. Secretary. I shall do as you say. Apologize, sir? To whom? Yes, sir, I do like my job. I understand you, sir. Yes, sir. At once, sir." He continues to hold the phone and faces the three of us. "I have been informed that I have been outside the boundaries of my authority, and that the Department of Homeland Security will no longer be directing this project, but we are ready to offer whatever resources at our disposal to support you."

From the tiny speaker on the phone, we hear, "Sourwood!"

"Yes, sir. I'm getting to that. I apologize most profusely for my actions here today, and I can assure you all that I was not speaking on behalf of the Department of Homeland Security, and above all, I was not representing Secretary Wellings." He hands the phone back to Zack.

"Okay, Randy," says Zack, who looks at the little angry man who once thought he was in charge, "You take Timmy here and the Rod Man," he points at the puffed out chest of the former room monitor and Red Hat Rod, "and the rest of these," he stops and looks at the blank name tents, "these folks outside. Mr. Chief Ranger, can you go along and make sure that they don't start chipping away at the cave themselves. I want to discuss things with Bob, Keven, and Walt."

Sourwood grabs his briefcase and storms out of the conference room with his entourage at his coattails. Bob and I wave at Rod. The chief ranger follows, talking into his walkie-talkie.

Zack holds the phone to his head, "Thanks Ron. We're all square now. Great. See you soon."

He looks up and smiles, "Hi. I'm Colonel Zack from USAMRID. I've met Anne and Denise before, but I don't think I know anyone else. Colonel, please be seated. What kind of op have you three been running?" He shifts his gaze back to Keven, Bob, and me.

"Look, guys, it comes down to this. DHS is handled, and I don't think Randy can do anything that will cost Anne, Denise, or you, Keven, in the long run. Am I right?" Zack looks at the Park Service regional management. They shake their heads, stop shaking in confusion, and begin nodding their heads. "But the paperwork for your recall is already in the works. If I stop that process, it will set off alarms rather than letting the turmoil die out. However, I think we can keep Bob out of the army."

He addresses the Park Service regional management, "You can re-hire Bob, can't you?"

"Well, there's a lot of paperwork involved since Bob already retired, and ..."

"But it is no more than paperwork, so you can take care of that. Walt, your reactivation seems to be the most onerous. What do you say?"

"Well let's see. If it's like the reserve meetings in Atlanta that I've heard about, I give up eight hours a month, get paid for it, and have access to intel. Provided it keeps me away from Homeland Security, I can live with it."

"Great. Bob, Keven, what do you say?" Zack asks.

"I hate giving anyone the satisfaction of thinking that they can push us around, but it is the lesser of the evils and the best for the cave, and I do want this to die down as soon as possible," replies Bob. "It won't inconvenience me that much."

"It doesn't make much difference to me so long as I can keep working here," says Keven. "I appreciate your ridding us of Sourwood and his people before they do any more damage."

"I think I can back up the colonel on this," says Mr. Worland, who remained quiet throughout Zack's delivery. But, the strong point of NSA is *listening*. "Mr. Sourwood wasn't going to be long on this operation anyway. We've been keeping tabs on him and his crew for some time – off the books of course – and we knew he was the one who tipped off the press. His ego requires a lot of reinforcement. So, we'll work with the army, and you can forget all about Sourwood."

"Thank you, Mr. Worland," says Zack. "Now. What's all this about anyway?"

Chaos ensues.

Forty
Recalled to Service

Bob drives us over behind the visitor center parking lot to the pavilion where the rehearsal dinner is being held. He seems satisfied. The southeastern region guy agreed to bring him back into the Park Service even though it created a lot of paperwork to re-hire someone who already retired some time ago. Too bad about the paperwork. *Who were they kidding?*

"Sorry it didn't work out so well for you," says Bob. He pulls into a parking space in the picnic grounds.

"They pay me something under five hundred dollars a month for going to a one-day meeting in town. Plus, I'm now a tech sergeant with commissary privileges. So I don't guess it will be too bad. Barbara's not going to like it. Hell, I don't like it, but it might be interesting."

"No, it's nuts," says Bob. "You're not in the security service, are you?"

"It's not called that anymore. 'Air Intelligence.' But, yes. I'm assigned to a regular unit until they complete the security clearance. Or, until I complete the paperwork for my security clearance. What a pain that's going to be. It was hard enough when I was nineteen and never been anywhere west of Dallas or east of Chattanooga," I say. "That may take a while."

We go around to the back of the truck to start unloading camera gear.

"I thought Keven enjoyed this whole thing rather a lot, don't you?" says Bob.

"Yeah," I say. "Small price to pay for his getting to eat supper with Stephen Bishop."

"The Park Service is uncomfortable when someone on staff does something outstanding. They'll take Keven off the Wild Cave tour for sure."

"Maybe not," I say, thinking of the kind of power Colonel Zack swings.

Once we are clear of the Suburban, we see Zona, Mary, and Barbara beside our station wagon. They cross the road to where we're standing.

"Well, hello," says Zona. "How did it go?"

"May I present to you the latest Park Ranger assigned to assist the Chief of Visitor Services," I say with a sweep of my hand toward Bob.

"You're back working?" asks Zona.

"Yes, sort of. No big thing. I can set my own schedule. And may I now present the newest Technical Sergeant in the U.S. Air Farce!"

"What?" This comes from Barbara.

"Also not a big thing. It's the feds' way of having the appearance of control over us. They insist that we are the problem when it comes to blabbing about time travel to the unwashed and uninitiated. Let's go inside. Bob needs a Scotch," I say.

"But what about the people on the Wild Cave tour?" says Barbara.

"They can't touch them because Sophy Ross has them all as clients. I think the cave is in less danger from them than from the government," I say.

But the much-anticipated libation is delayed, because we run into the groom's, Bill Soonscen's, psuedofamily, his old unit at USAMRID that came with Colonel Zack. The first is Major X-ray who rushes up to hug Mary. Members of the active unit do not use their real names, but alphanumeric designations instead.

"Mary! Did you bring us any brownies?"

Mary is surprised, but holds her own, "X-ray, those were Barbara's brownies!" She points to Barbara. X-ray takes up Barbara in his arms.

"Barbara, did you bring us any brownies?"

"X-ray, it's nice to see you. I did. Emphasis on the past tense. We've been in high-stress operations mode, and we ate them last night."

"Well, I am here to testify to their steadying effect during operations. Yes, I am," says X-ray, the disappointment shows in his eyes.

"Send Walt an e-mail with a mailing address, and I will send you a double batch," says Barbara. I nod at him. He seems mollified. The rest of the elite unit file in behind X-ray, and they greet each of us like long lost pals. Last year, on our visit to Mammoth Cave Country, we became involved in keeping a valuable, and potentially dangerous, rapidly mutating bacteria from being sold to the North Koreans. Zack and his team came to the rescue.

I stand next to Barbara and speak to all of them. After a while, when the noise and milling about subside a little, Bill and his bride-to-be, Courtney, come over to our corner of the pavilion, and we go through more greetings and updates.

At last, Bob, Zona, Mary, Keven, Myrna, Barbara, and I maneuver Zack to a corner. "Now, Zack, what part of the sky did you drop out of?" I say.

"That's a good question, Walt. Whiskey picked up some chatter on the circuits coming into the park, that there was some sort of flap in progress, and he heard Keven's name a lot, and yours and Bob's. I called their home number," he nods at Zona. "But you guys run a tight ship. Zona told me it was on a need-to-know basis. She said she would contact Bob and let him decide if he could tell me what was going on."

"And that was it?" I say.

"No, not at all. Zona texted Bob. And Bob dialed my number and let me listen in."

"I remember him receiving a text message," I say. "So that was what you were doing," Bob nods.

"I heard Randy Sourwood give his speech. It came in kind of squeaky over your cell phone, Bob. That was all I needed. I got onto the secretary and set this up on the way over to the chief ranger's office.

"Set what up, says Zona. "We haven't heard."

"Zack came into the ranger's conference room and put this idiot Sourwood from Homeland Security on the phone with the Secretary of DHS. Secretary Wellings set Sourwood straight, made him apologize, and leave the meeting. It was great!" says Bob.

"Zack, you know cabinet secretaries?" says Zona.

"Zona, I know lots of people. And, except for you folks, they all owe me favors."

"Well, Zack, in addition to us here, the entire Mammoth Cave National Park, the staff, and millions of visitors owe you a favor now," says Bob.

"Why, what happened?" says Myrna.

"Mr. Sourwood from Homeland Security was going to shut down the park and hold everyone involved in custody as material witnesses. Zack stopped all of that," says Keven.

"Thank you, Zack," say Barbara, Zona, Mary, and Myrna in unison.

"Ladies, you are most welcome."

"What happens now?" says Zona.

"FRC will monitor the area. We will provide backup through our FRC liaison, and the DOE will be involved. But all low key."

"You guys have a liaison with FRC?" asks Keven.

"Yeah. Don't you know? There are all kinds of bugs in caves." He laughs hard. We laugh along. "Hey, I have to see to my duties. I'm the host, remember? Great to see you guys."

"What do you think will happen to this thing?" asks Keven.

"You know, except for Denise's hurt feelings about not getting to go back to 1838, I kind of hope that it never starts up again. If it does, you know they're going to try to dig it up and move it out of the cave," I say.

"I agree," says Bob. "But they might do that even if it doesn't work."

"I hope it winds up like the Arc of the Covenant did at the end of that movie. Stored away in a warehouse and forgotten," says Barbara.

"With DHS and Sourwood out of the picture, maybe they'll be content to just leave it where it sits and add it to the Park Service inventory of historic artifacts. Like the stuff left behind on the moon," I say.

"What Teddy Roosevelt said about the Grand Canyon applies here," says Bob, "'Leave it as it is. The ages have been at work on it, and man can only mar it.'"

Epilogue

"Do you have tickets for the Cathedral Domes Cave?"

"The Cathedral Domes Cave?" asked the woman behind the ticket counter in the Mammoth Cave National Park visitor center. She was wearing the gray and green uniform of the National Park Service, and for years, she had dealt with visitors who wanted to be here, but didn't quite understand why. She had never heard this question. "Oh, Keven!" She called to the passing guide who had been guiding tours at the cave since the nineteen sixties.

"Yes, Maylene?" said Keven in his characteristic good humor.

"This gentleman wants tickets for the Cathedral Domes Cave." She smiled with relief when Keven took care to guide the visitor away from the ticket counter.

"Hi. I'm Keven Neff. So, you want to go to Cathedral Domes, right?"

"Ah. The cave guide Keven Neff. We have heard of you. Very acceptable. Yes. That is correct. We wish to see the Cathedral Domes. They have been described to us as the most wonderful part of the cave. Can you take us there?"

Keven thought the man was a little strange. The tone of his voice was flat. No real inflection. His eyes were a transluminous gray. His use of English was unusual. And, he wanted to know where this visitor had heard his name.

"The only tour we have that goes to Cathedral Domes is the Wild Cave, and it's only recently been re-opened. That's a six-hour trip with crawling and climbing. It gives the cave visitor another way of seeing the cave. We have two of those tours every day, but they are usually sold out months in advance. Did you make an on-line reservation?" says Keven.

"An online reservation? By computer?" asked the visitor.

"Yes, through the internet."

The visitor paused. He stared into the distance. The corners of his mouth turned up, but it wasn't a real smile. "Yes. We will have reservations for today."

"I'm leading the ten o'clock tour. Are you on that one?" asked Keven.

The visitor paused. Keven resisted the urge to look over his shoulder in the direction of the visitor's gaze. He noticed a patch on the left breast of the visitor's shiny jacket. The symbol resembled a spiral galaxy. *Oh, no. Not another graduate of the Star Fleet Academy!* Keven couldn't translate the text. He thought maybe it was Klingon. But, when he looked back, he could read it, "Galactic Transport – Service Department." Keven's eyes widened a bit, and he smiled.

"Let's step over to this computer terminal," said Keven. At the information desk, Keven brought up the roster for his ten o'clock tour. "There are only twelve on there right now, so there is room. You know, there's been some pretty intense interest in that part of the cave."

"Yes, we are on the tour in the tenth hour. We have been aware of this interest."

Keven looked back down at the screen. There were thirteen on the list. "And your name is?"

"Wemberley Twelves," said the visitor.

Keven looked back at the screen. *Wemberley Twelves* was the thirteenth name on the list. He looked up at the man.

"You're on the list, Wemberley."

"This is most acceptable to be going into the Cathedral Domes with the guide Keven Neff."

"You know, there was some concern that they were going to dig up that part of the cave to retrieve an artifact."

"Yes, we are aware of that, too. But that is an action that no one on this world — or on any other world — should want to happen. It would not be ... sustainable." The corners of his mouth turned up again in his not-quite-a-smile. Keven heard these words, and he felt that Mammoth Cave would be safe from that particular threat.

"Cave Guide Keven Neff, we need to speak with you in private," said Mr. Twelves.

"Yes, sir?"

"When we arrive at the Cathedral Domes, we wish to leave the tour."

"You know, we have rules about having to stay with the tour?"

"Yes, we understand. But I have work to do with the artifact, as you call it. Do you understand?"

"Yes, Wemberley, I think I do. Will you be leaving with us?"

"No. If we are successful, it will not be necessary."

"It will start working?" asked Keven.

"It will work for you and for the cave photographer Bob Cetera on a limited basis. After we install the upgrade, it will function in a much less disruptive mode. We may broaden the use — later. But we do not think your inhabitants are quite ready for such a device at this point in the development of your civilization." He handed Keven a thin, shiny disk, 175 millimeters in diameter. "Keep this secret, Keven Neff."

"I understand, Wemberley," said Keven. "I'll see you out by the buses in a few minutes."

THE END